ALICE IN WINTERLAND

A FANGIRL NOVEL

D.K.S. Dhara

Taylor Tsuruye

Thalia Books

The Muses of Mercury

ALICE IN WINTERLAND: A FANGIRL NOVEL

Published by The Muses of Mercury

Copyright © 2018 D.K.S. Dhara

Printed in the United States of America

First Printing, 2018

Thalia Books is an imprint of The Muses of Mercury.

ISBN: 978-0-9998343-0-5

"Who in the world am I?
Ah, that's the great puzzle."
—Alice in Wonderland

FOR FANGIRLS AND FANBOYS

Contents

ALICE IN

WINTERLAND

CHAPTER 1

Winterland

With a wave of a hand, regions of Winterland faded in and out of the orb's vaporous depths. Slowly, the cloudiness lifted. A kemonomimi bobbed into sight, the half-girl scuttling through the permafrost. Her long, white rabbit ears perked up, listening for any hint of danger. With a furtive glance behind, Usagi broke into a run.

Eyes flickering with suspicion, the Snow Queen raised a finger to her viewing glass. Before the snow under Usagi's feet could glaciate her, the scene blurred. A sharp gasp cracked the wind. The queen jolted from her throne. A new figure was emerging within her crystal globe.

The queen's eyes blazed cold fire at the face A43C2 4E3R111111

My books dropped on my laptop, keying a string of gibberish into my fanfiction file. I quickly hid my

Winterland manga back inside my Chemistry textbook and hit backspace.

I blew my black bangs out of my face. My gaze wandered from my desk, where I had spent the last half hour of lunch secretly working on my winterfic, to the girl who had just flounced past my shoulder.

Flipping her long, ombre locks behind her, Olivia separated from her girl squad and waltzed across the library. I eyed her lacy-tunic, Coach bag, form-fitting jeans, and Louboutins, then took in my own ensemble: striped tights, a sweatshirt much too big for me, a home-made Ravenclaw scarf, and worn-out sneakers with faintly drawn chibis. Even though I liked my nerdy style, Olivia had the uncanny ability of making me feel like a frump next to her.

To be perfectly honest, a small part of me wished I could dress more bravely. Maybe not in Louboutins, exactly, but I'd consider a badass cloak or a frilly Hara-juku dress. Something that was still me, but slightly out of my comfort zone. The stuff of comic-cons.

Unfortunately, I knew myself. As much as I liked the idea of dressing up, I wouldn't be able to handle the attention that came with it. My goal was to hide. Be invisible. Let girls like Olivia dress up. *They* could handle the spotlight.

I fiddled with my hair as the slender blonde sidled next to Andrew Lewis. Her free hand dropped to his arm.

"You'll come early, right?" Two manicured fingers dangled a glittery card in front of him.

Ugh. Olivia's annual ice skating party. Every year, snow or no snow, December rolled around—and everyone who's anyone in Charles Dodgson High received a personalized invitation to the party of the year.

Not that I knew any of that first hand, of course. Olivia never invited…my type. The day I receive a snazzy invite with the name *Alice Leira* calligraphed on it will be the day my fictional characters came to life.

Andrew's smile faltered. He stepped away from the desk where he had been printing swim try-out forms. He retracted his hand from Olivia's hold and ran his fingers through his hair, like he was trying hard to make the gesture look natural.

Or maybe it was my wishful thinking again. Sighing, I bit my lip behind my laptop. I could watch him stroke that mussed, flaxen hair all day. It was no mystery why Olivia—and half of the high school—were so interested in having the head of the swim team around. Tall, toned, and trim, Andrew Lewis was like a 90-degree angle. Like the corners on the un-punctured edge of my A+ physics paper…

Right in every way.

Andrew's face had been chiseled out in conformance to the golden ratio. The Vitruvian man had nothing on him. Of course, I wasn't superficial enough to ogle over a boy just because of his perfect arrangement of atoms. No. Andrew Lewis was much more than that.

For starters, Andrew made the Honor Roll almost every semester, volunteered at the local aquarium in the summers, shared my zodiac sign of Gemini, and—according to my dubiously innocent Google searches—even identified as an INFJ, my favorite of all the Myers-Briggs types. His only tragic flaw was hanging with the likes of Olivia.

The pair had known each other forever. They even went out briefly freshman year before deciding to stay just friends. I should have been used to it by now, but seeing them together still nauseated me.

I clicked my tongue. Why was I getting worked up over them? As if Andrew and I would ever become canon. Even getting noticed by an out-of-reach senpai stood more of a chance. Still, my heart did a wicked little victory dance as I watched them interact. Something about their usual casual chemistry was off today.

"Wish I could, Olivia, but I can't this year." Andrew lowered his gaze to the papers he held. "Swim team is holding try-outs."

Olivia narrowed her eyes. "On a Saturday *night?*"

"No, but I'm meeting up with some friends afterward." Andrew shifted his feet, not meeting her stare. "We already made plans to go to this event together."

A frown marred her pretty face. "But my Christmas party only comes once a year. Plus, I'm putting a two-page spread about it in the yearbook—perk of being the yearbook photographer." She peered at him through her mascaraed lashes. "You should have at least half a page to yourself."

"Tempting, but I can't bail on them last minute."

"But—"

Andrew shook his head, but this time he held her gaze. "Sorry, Olivia. I just can't."

For a second, I could've sworn Olivia's winter blue eyes turned glossy. Before I could tell for sure though, one of the librarians shushed the pair, then disappeared into the office across the hall. Wordlessly, Olivia tucked the invite into her purse, letting her long, ombre locks conceal her face. She took a breath, collected herself, and sauntered back to her squad.

I frowned. A part of me almost felt bad for her. *Almost.* I found it hard to have sympathy for a girl who had dropped me as a friend in fifth grade...

Shaking off my thoughts, I returned my attention to my laptop screen and cracked my knuckles. I had more important things to do than fret over some silly, only slightly amazing Christmas party. Like uploading my fanfiction by midnight. After months of working on it, I had gathered a slew of Winterlanders on Tumblr who followed my fanfic updates regularly. I knew they'd be waiting for the newest chapter to go live tonight as promised. My lips curved into a small smile. One wouldn't want to disappoint fangirls.

If only my internet popularity translated to the outernet.

With a wistful sigh, I adjusted my thick-rimmed glasses and resumed typing my rough draft. Head bent, fingers furiously clicking away, I was so absorbed in my winterfic that I hardly noticed the shadow looming over me until—

"Hey there, Hogwarts. What do we have here?"

My head snapped up.

Shimatta.

I didn't know how long Olivia had stood there, but it'd been long enough for her to find the *Winterland* manga hidden in my textbook. Her slender hand curled around its crisp, white pages, holding them captive. Distaste clung to her angular features, making her face look sharper than usual. She eyed me like I was that weird kid in class who liked anime—which self-admittedly, I was.

With two fingers, Olivia dangled my manga upside down as if to avoid nerd cooties. Her girl squad swarmed her. Claire, her best friend, and a pair of brunette twins named Isabella and Anastasia watched the scene in glee. Outnumbered, I mustered some bravado in my voice. "Forgot you don't know how to read?"

"Oh, very funny, Alice." Olivia flipped through the manga and scrunched her face. "You've got to be kidding me. Aren't you a little old for Pokémon?" Her girl squad broke into an infuriating whisper-giggle, cupping hands around each others' ears.

My cheeks burned. "It's not Pokémon. It's called Winterland."

"Whatever." Olivia crinkled her nose and flipped through more pages.

"Why do they all look bug-eyed?" asked Claire.

"Because it's manga." I tried to contain my indignation. Olivia and her lackeys were worse than internet trolls. "It's a Japanese drawing style."

"Spare us the explanation, Professor Wapanese," Olivia drawled.

I stared at the Chemistry textbook on my desk and whispered under my breath, *"Bismuth-technetium-hydrogen."*

Olivia raised a flawless eyebrow. "What did you say?"

"Nothing," I murmured. If only the girl knew her chemical symbols.

Olivia narrowed her eyes. Tilting my *Winterland* manga, she displayed it to her friends. They took in the image of the kemonomimi—a half-human, half-rabbit character—named Usagi.

"Honestly, Alice, I don't understand the appeal of this unless you're a ten-year-old boy." Olivia tossed the manga onto my desk in boredom. Her gaze drifted to my laptop screen. A shadow of a smile touched her lips.

"Well, well. What's this now?"

"None of your business." I protectively covered my laptop screen with my hunched form, glaring at Olivia over my shoulder. A shrill yip blared in my ear. I jumped out of my seat, only to realize that the twins had snuck up from my other side. Seizing her chance, Claire snatched the laptop and brought it to Olivia.

"Give that back!"

"I don't think so." Olivia scrolled the trackpad up. Her eyes flashed. "*Usagi's Flight—Draft #3.*"

My palms went damp. *She wouldn't.*

Olivia cleared her throat.

Shimatta. *She would.*

Hushed whispers traversed the library. A circle of students flocked around us. I could feel their eyes on me, watching, burning into me. I dug my fingers into my scarf.

Taking in the growing crowd, Olivia curled her lips into a twisted smile. She began to read aloud—making a spectacle of my fanfiction. She butchered the Japanese names, making every inch of me cringe. Her girl squad laughed to the flow of her cruel, satirical tone. I slunk down in my seat, wanting to melt.

Olivia's glossed lips moved in slow motion, but the words no longer registered. Every laugh, every whisper, every nuance of sound magnified, then blended together. My senses grew distorted. Like watching a movie, I stared at the scene, aware of my surroundings, but disconnected from it.

Overwhelmed from it.

My heart thudded; my palms grew sweaty. Struggling not to spiral into oblivion, I scanned the sea of blurry faces in desperation, trying to find something to anchor myself on. It was then I noticed Andrew in the crowd.

He stared at my laptop screen, his brows slanting into two hard lines. Slowly, he eyed me with a disturbed expression.

That did it.

Face aflame, I veered away from his scrutiny. Not caring if I looked like an overgrown inchworm, I leaped awkwardly across the desk. I yanked the laptop from Olivia's grip, breathing hard.

"Let. It. Go."

"As you wish." She released it lightly, sending me reeling on the floor. A burst of laughter hit my eardrums. I winced.

Face glowing, the girl towered before me. "Word of advice, Alice. If you're going to spend all day writing like a little nerd, it could at least be something *worth writing*."

I staggered to my feet, clutching the laptop to my chest. My mind struggled for a comeback, but the cat got my tongue.

A ringing pierced the air.

I heaved a deep sigh. Saved by the bell.

The librarian emerged into the room and paused. She lowered her glasses at our little crowd. Everyone began to disperse.

Olivia was about to join the murmuring crowd when she stopped. Her lips inched upward, her cheekbones sharp as glass. She whispered a single word to me. A word that made me choke back a gasp.

"*Weaboo.*"

Waterworks obscured my vision. This was a new low. The girl had called me many things before, but this insult felt so personal…even worse, accurate. As much as I hated to admit it, maybe she had a point.

I rubbed my stinging eyes. Olivia was still watching me. Her brows tensed. Then, without another glance, she whirled around and made for the exit.

Andrew waited for her, leaning against the door. Without meaning to, we made eye contact. I held my breath. An uncomfortable silence hung in the air. Casually, he looked away and reached for his phone. He slipped into the hallway of students, texting as he walked alongside Olivia.

A hand squeezed my slumped shoulder. "There you are. I've been looking for you."

A familiar red-head stood beside me — Deanna Kitlyn, a gap-toothed booktuber who happened to be my best friend. Concern tinged her features as she took in my expression. "Did something just happen?"

"Olivia happened." I let my black tresses cover my face in angst. "She just read my fanfiction. Out loud."

Sighing, Deanna brushed my hair back without missing a beat. I suppose that's one of the duties that befalls a bestie.

"You know…high school pecking orders aren't the end of the world, Alice."

"Is this another one of your pick-me-up speeches?"

"Yes, it is. Your stories are wonderful. You know that, I know that…all your Tumblr followers know that. Don't let a *Spitzbub* get to you."

I blinked. "A what?"

"Spitzbub. It comes from the German word, 'Spitzbuben'—Christmas cookies with evil little smiles."

That's an understatement.

"Trust me, Alice, one day that girl will find herself... and really, really wish she hadn't."

I forced a half-laugh. This time, my friend's pep talk fell flat. I appreciated the effort, but as I crammed my belongings into my Totoro backpack, I couldn't help but snap back.

"You're right. Olivia might risk looking into a mirror one day and realize how pretty and popular and socially perfect she is. Thanks, Dee. You've really turned my opinion of this day around."

"Don't be ridiculous," she chided. "You speak almost as if Olivia is never not looking into a mirror."

"Ha, ha, ha."

"C'mon, cheer up." My friend's gaze fell on my *Probability & Statistics* textbook in my bag. An elfin gleam touched her eyes. "Did you know you have a better chance of marrying your favorite K-pop idol than winning the lottery? If that doesn't brighten your mood, I don't know what will, Alice."

This time, I laughed for real. Deanna grinned.

Ever since we had first met, back when we were just two little eighth-graders hiding out between bookshelves on rainy days, she made me believe that the best friendships are made in libraries. With her obscure words and amusing factoids, she always managed to pick up my mood when Olivia kicked it to the curb like a mangy puppy.

Deanna looped her arm around my shoulders, and I stood a little straighter as we weaved through the bustling hallway. As we stopped to part to our respective classes, I glimpsed a glittery card sticking out of her satchel. My insides turned hollow and cold.

"Is that…?"

Deanna's face bloomed pink. "One of Olivia's she-wolves gave it to me this morning. Obviously, I'm not going. Her Christmas parties are *way* overrated." A pang of disappointment twisted my stomach. Her dismissive tone sounded so…feigned.

I squinted at the florid, calligraphed initials, D.K., on her invite. Why was she even carrying it around in her bag? Betrayal seeped under my skin.

"Maybe you should go. I know how *badly* you've been wanting to try ice skating."

"What?" Deanna whispered. Hurt flashed in her eyes.

My insides pinged with guilt. "Sorry, it's just…you skip Olivia's party every year because of me. Why not go and see what the hype is all about for once? Live the fancy life for a day." I shuffled my sneakers. "My weekend is booked anyway."

"Rigght. Booked as in playing DDR by yourself and re-watching the dub of *Winterland?*"

Heat swiped my cheeks. "Of course not." *Sub.*

"Alice ..."

"My weekend is booked. Literally. I have a stash of manga I borrowed from the library—it's due Saturday." Next Saturday, technically, but she didn't need to know that.

Deanna cast me a skeptical glance. "You're really okay with me going to this thing?"

All I had to say was no, and she wouldn't go. My lips parted. Shimatta. I couldn't say it.

I knew she could see through my web of white lies, but I couldn't let her boycott the biggest party of the year again because of me. A real friend wouldn't let misery have company.

"Get your skates ready because you're going for once," I said. "And that's that."

"I don't want to go if you're missing out on the fun, Alice."

"…Having fun isn't hard when you got a library card."

Rolling her eyes, Deanna stuck her hand into her satchel and rummaged through her belongings. She pulled out two tickets—each with the shape of a crystal heart on the stub. A frisson of anticipation rushed through me.

That symbol.

"A weekend pass for Winter-Con." She handed me my convention ticket with a smile. "Because your weekend needs to trump Olivia's."

"Get the flake out. I thought they were all sold out."

She winked. "My brother knows a guy. He pulled a few strings for us. Consider it an early Christmas gift from me."

"Deanna, my appreciation for you is like a limit approaching infinity."

"You dork."

"But I'm your dork." I glomped her right then and there, paying no mind to the onlookers in the hallway.

Deanna grinned until she glanced at her watch. "Shoot, almost noon. I have Lit." She broke my choke-hold and hastily zipped her satchel. "Maybe you can stop by my place later this week and help me with my costume."

"Sounds fetch." I curled my hands and raised them catlike, imitating my favorite Winterland character. "I've been updating my old Shiroi Neko cosplay anyway. You know, the white, stretchy cat-suit with the neko ears and—"

But Deanna didn't hear the rest. She had run off to class, leaving me alone in a hallway echoing with snickers.

~~~~~~~~~~~

The rest of the day went by at a glacial place. When the final bell rang, I rushed to my locker. The hallways bristled with noise. I couldn't make it from one corridor to another without overhearing someone speculate about the number of ice sculptures Olivia would have this year. As I skirted around some junior girls from homeroom fawning over the silvery monograms on their invites, I was reminded why books are better than people.

I fought a sigh as I collected my belongings from my locker. I didn't understand what spell Olivia had cast for everyone to obsess over her like this. Nor did I want to understand. I just wanted to get away from it all.

As I made a beeline for the entrance, a glitz of silver made me stop in my tracks. An empty envelope with beautiful calligraphy lay strewn on the floor. I picked it up.

Olivia's.

My fingers dented into it. Just as I was about to dispose the crumpled envelope into a nearby trash can, I caught the initials A.L. on it. My hand froze.

Hesitantly, I stole a glance around me. I reeled my arm in. With an unsteady finger, I traced the sleek, cursive lettering and bit my lip. Before I knew what I was doing, I had pocketed Andrew Lewis's envelope and bolted through the exit.

~~~~~~~~~~~~

"Holmes, sweet Holmes."

At the sound of my voice, a white cat with a long, bushy tail sauntered into the living room. I kneeled down, letting him nuzzle against me, and stroked his fur.

"At least I have you, Catpernicus…"

He purred and rested his head atop my lap, as if sensing my despondent mood. I could always count on Catpernicus to be there for me.

I ruffled his white fur. "Want a treat?"

He meowed.

After feeding him, I grabbed some comfort food— Pocky and a steaming mocha—and dragged myself to my bedroom. I slammed the door, and a zig-zaggy "D" fluttered down from my favorite decal. Now, it just read "UMBLE." As I stretched up a hand to re-tape it, I read the phrase above the door frame.

"Don't let the muggles get you down."

I drew in a deep breath and repeated the quote to myself like a mantra. I needed the reminder now more than ever.

Slowly, I turned around. My fangirl safe haven welcomed me like a warm, tight hug. Three full shelves of YA novels lined my bookcase, each decorated with Sailor Moon dolls, empty beakers, and the occasional plastic Tardis. Fanart of my OTPs coated the walls: Jelsa, Sebaciel, Johnlock, Dalix, and my favorite ship of all— *Winterland's* Sanbou. Well, second favorite ship.

I walked up to a holographic print featuring my fictional crush. Akihiko the Winter Prince. Since junior high, I had shipped him with me, and now, five years later, the ship was still sailing strong. His eyes glimmered at me as he rested a hand on his Vorpal sword. I trailed my finger along his elfish ears. If only he'd stop being the square root of -1 and become real. Sighing, I backed away from my husbando.

Once more, my fandom world invited me with open arms when the rest of the world cast me aside. It was the place I found my feet again, the place I always found my inspiration.

The place where I could escape reality.

At the same time, fandoms have always been my gateway to understanding reality. With anime and manga, I could enter a world free from judgement, form new friendships, embark on fantastical journeys. Fanfiction let me delve into a character's head, explore relationships and different identities—all while giving me a place to release my daily stresses and anxiety. My fandom world was a balm to my psyche. As an Aspie, I took refuge in that.

I flung my backpack onto a mountain of Winterland plushies on my bed. I maneuvered to my closet, stumbling on fabric pieces of my Shiroi Neko cosplay. After changing into my cozy FANGIRL sweatshirt, I cleared the Japanese stationery and art pens cluttering my desk to make space for my laptop.

"I...am...Sherlocked," I murmured, keying in my password. Obvious, maybe, but a safe enough choice at my school. No one there besides Deanna and me could pick a non-Turing Cumberbatch out of a lineup.

The thought of school sent an unpleasant shudder through me. No. *Repress it.*

I turned on my fanfic playlist, trying to set the perfect mood to delve into my fanfiction. The buoyant, upbeat tune of *Not Literally's* "I Ship It" blared. Loud as it sounded, it still didn't drown out the laughter echoing in my head.

Distraction. I needed distraction. I opened my Tumblr. There, I found a message from Winterpuff.

Perfect timing. A fellow fanfic writer (who specialized in crackfics) and always the first to review my chapters, Winterpuff never failed to leave me with a toothy smile. I clicked the notification.

11:56 AM Winterpuff:

Hey. Just wanted to tell u how psyched I am for the new ch. I know it'll be totally awesome—just like it always is.

Below the message, an anime gif of the Winter Prince winked at me. With his lips quirked, eyes lit with mirth, long, sculpted fingers on the hilt of his sword... I blushed at my computer screen. But then my face fell. I closed the tab. Winterpuff was right. My fanfic *was* good, and I felt proud of it. Just one teeny issue remained.

I had no chapter.

At least, not a good one. I slumped over my desk and bit into a Pocky stick. I'd already written three different drafts. But they just weren't *right*. I couldn't let Winterpuff and my other readers down like that. They deserved better.

Exhaling, I opened my fanfiction profile. My eyes skimmed the various fandom groups I had written for.

SnowBaby23's Works:

Adventure Hour (1)

Blitz on Titans (1)

Cadet Moon (5)

Daphne Holmes (6)

Grey Butler (5)

Kiss Me, Not Him (1)

Light Note (3)

Lore of Lora (1)

Mariyaholic (2)

Narudo (1)

Our Host Club (3)

Phan-fics (2)

Revolutionary Maiden Umena (1)

S.H & J.W (5)

Stevie Galaxy (1)

Totally Spy (3)

Umaru - kun (1)

Victuri on Ice (7)

Winterland (12)

I hovered the mouse over the last entry and clicked. I opened the unfinished draft of *Usagi's Flight*. The cursor blinked at me. I blinked in return. An unsuccessful staring contest ensued. Tch. Nothing was coming to mind. Not even the usual plot bunnies.

In an attempt to overcome my writer's block, I donned my NaNoWriMo Viking helmet. Elbows propped on my desk, Pocky stick balanced along my cupid's bow, I meditated on my story so far.

Long ago, the kemonomimis of Winterland lived together in harmony. Then, everything changed when the Snow Queen attacked. She froze over their world, condemning it to eternal winter. Nobody could break her curse. I frowned. But where was Usagi running off to? And what did the queen see in her globe that made her so upset—

My door swung open. I jerked up, hitting backspace. The Pocky stick dropped to the floor with a sad little crack.

Lori barged into my room. Catpernicus and Earl Grey in hand, my older sister took in my crooked Viking helmet with a look that said, *'I'm not even going to ask.'*

With her sophisticated pixie cut and priggish manner, Lori was my polar opposite. If I was, as Olivia kindly put it, a 'weaboo,' then my sister was a 'teaboo.' She preferred British classics, adopted British spelling whenever she could—and had once roasted her teacher in iambic pentameter when her poem got a B. For two sisters, we couldn't be more different.

"Easy on the ears, Alice. *Pianissimo.* I can't concentrate on my SAT prep with your K-pop boy bands blaring through my wall."

"It's not K-pop," I murmured, turning down the volume. *"This time."*

Lori didn't look the least bit impressed. "Can't you wear headphones? Fur Elise is sensitive to your loud music."

"Funny you mention that as *Catpernicus* loves watching me write to this song." On cue, the cat meowed and jumped from my sister's grasp.

Glaring, Lori folded her arms across her tartan dress— another outfit she had probably copied off her beauty muse, Kate Middleton. Her gaze drifted to my laptop screen. "Let me guess. More fanfiction?"

My sister leaned over my shoulder. Her eyes twitched at the screen as though she had stumbled across the weird part of the Internet again. She read the tags on my fanfiction homepage. "One Shot, Coffee Shop AU, Crackfic, NSFW, OOC, Fujoshi, Drabble, Lemon... Honestly, Alice, all of your fandom things sound like a foreign language to me."

I almost giggled, but then Lori turned to me.

"What's...yah-oy?"

"Nothing," I blurted before scrolling down the page. I didn't dare correct her mispronunciation. Some things are better left unsaid—especially *yaoi*.

Rolling her eyes, Lori straightened back to her full height and took a sip of her tea.

"I don't understand why you waste so much time on fanfiction—it hardly qualifies as literature if you ask me." Great, she was doing that Lori thing again. "Why you can't you read something real and write something that has…substance?"

"Fanfiction does have substance," I replied indignantly. "You would know since you read it all the time."

"I most certainly do not."

I smothered a snort. Lori turned pink, which was comforting. It was nice to see that she was a *little* self-aware when she crossed into unbearable pomposity.

"You do read it, Lori. In your AP English class."

"You know that's not true."

"Do I?"

Catpernicus purred at our feet. At least someone was entertained by our squabble.

"Take your textbook," I said. "Dante's *Divine Comedy* is a self-insert fanfic where he hangs out with his dream-girl, an OC named Beatrice, and befriends his senpai—aka his favorite poet, Virgil. And Virgil wrote fanfics for the Homer fandom. *The Aeneid* is a fanfic sequel to *The Iliad*. It was all in this Tumblr meta I read in clas—"

"Right, because Tumblr is so academic."

She'd be surprised.

Ignoring my sister's scowl, I picked the larger half of the Pocky stick up off the floor and balanced it back on my cupid's bow. "The post was saying how all the greats got inspiration from the works of others. It's just that fanfic writers are more honest about their inspiration."

Mic drop.

My sister's eyes flashed. "Don't drag the greats into this, Alice. They wrote works that actually had *worth*—literature with artistic and intellectual value. Fanfiction doesn't have that. It's subliterature."

"Lori."

"Poorly written, lacking depth."

"Lori."

"Unoriginal, no plot, full of slash—"

"*Lori.*"

"What?!"

"Peel back that poster behind you."

Her eyes narrowed at my 3x4 periodic table. She turned up an untaped corner and coughed on her tea. Her eyes went wide as saucers. I wish I could've photographed her. Like a mannequin in shock, she stared, unblinking, at my poster-sized fanart.

Two bishounens greeted her. One, with amused green eyes and alabaster skin, the other with coy amber eyes and a rich, bronzed hue, the young men complemented each other like the sun and the moon. Eyes heavy-lidded, arms entangled, waist to waist, *Winterland's* Sanbou ship stood before her in full, unabashed glory.

Lori flushed. "W-what is—"

"Yaoi," I replied. "You did ask."

"*Son of a biscuit.* Come here, Fur Elise." My sister scooped the mewling cat into her arms and stormed out of my room. A moment later, her bedroom door slammed shut.

Well, that settles that.

Satisfied with my petty victory, I returned to my fanfiction. The familiar sound of muffled violins told me Lori was playing Tchaikovsky next door. I exhaled. Still nothing. Even after that impassioned fanfic speech. Nibbling on Pocky sticks, I turned off my own music and listened to Lori's classical soundtrack instead. I hoped it might help me focus—but again, zilch. My shoulders sagged. A bad case of writer's block felt worse than any book hangover.

My hands hovered over my keyboard, but the only thing that came out was a Google search for baby penguins. Well, this was going nowhere. I flicked the empty Pocky box and rose from my desk.

I grabbed my *Winterland* manga for inspiration. I plopped onto my bed and nestled myself in a blanket burrito. Lori's classical music drifted into my room. Its whimsical tunes cast a soothing spell on my senses. Languidly, I flipped page after page.

My eyes grew heavy-lidded as I stared at the manga panels. Fairy-lights from my bed frame bathed the page in a soft, ethereal glow. Winterland's snowflakes shimmered with invitation. My Usagi bookmark seemed to leap off the page and bound soundlessly around my room.

A stream of silver light trailed behind the kemonomimi as she circled my bed. The streaks of silver blurred together, forming the walls of an ice tunnel. Usagi slid through it. I found myself sliding behind her —at a terrifying speed.

In seconds, flurries of white swallowed Usagi from sight. A small circle of light emerged overhead. It grew larger and larger and larger—until I shot out of the tunnel like a human cannonball. A scream froze in my throat. The world below me glistened as I tumbled toward it.

Everything went black. And then, my alarm clock rang.

I panted with relief. The fall… It had been some Pocky-induced lucid dream.

Rubbing my eyes, I sat up. Cold air slid through my fingers as I reached for my duvet. Whiteness flooded my vision. When my eyes adjusted, I sucked in a sharp breath.

N-no way.

Instead of a warm duvet, my hand clutched a fistful of snow. I staggered to my feet. A blanket of snow surrounded me, stretching over the endless white expanse of… I swallowed hard.

Winterland.

CHAPTER 2

Iced Tea

Did my eyes betray me? I rubbed them again and took in the swirling white Narnia-like landscape. Okay. This *had* to be a hallucination.

I had always thought of books as magical little portals to other dimensions, but this…this looked like an actual AU. I grabbed my spinning head. No. Of course not. There had to be a rational, logical explanation for this. Alternative Universes only existed in fanfiction. They couldn't possibly exist in real life unless…

Oh my gawd.

Maybe the multiverse theory in quantum physics wasn't just a theory after all. What if an infinite number of parallel universes really did exist, and I had somehow fallen down a wormhole? Or did string theory explain tha—

"Wha—oof!" My frantic thoughts curtailed as I skidded on a sheet of ice. Someone had prodded me from behind. I whirled around and found myself face to face with a teenage girl with…rabbit ears.

A *kemonomimi*.

And not just any kemonomimi, but the character Usagi—from *Winterland*. I gawked at her long, white ears and the silver plaits cascading below them. As I stared at her prominent front teeth, I realized she bore an uncanny resemblance to Deanna.

The kemonomimi bent down to pick up a small ringing clock. She must have dropped it in an attempt to wake me when I had blacked out. Usagi silenced the brass clock and shoved it into her satchel.

"Dee?" I said shakily. No response. "U-Usagi?"

The rabbit kemonomimi gave an unsteady nod. Every animal nerve in her human body seemed to quiver with caution and dread. Quickly, she ran an eye over me, taking in my FANGIRL sweatshirt. "You are an outsider?" she whispered.

"Um, I guess you could say that."

Her ears twitched. She neared closer, scrutinizing my face. At last, she expelled a disappointed sigh.

"*What?*" I asked.

"For a moment, I thought… never mind." She stepped away, her interest in me fading. "Well, don't just stand there. Hurry up or we'll be late." She stole a frantic glance over her shoulder.

"Late?"

"Shh." Usagi crossed a finger over her mouth. Her eyes darted around us as if Bigfoot would pop up from the snow. "We must hurry—unless you want *her* to find us here."

"Her? You mean the Sno—"

"Just follow me," she hissed over her shoulder.

Not having much of a choice, I hastened behind her trail. She bounded through the thick falling snowflakes, hurdling roots and icier stretches with little effort. Meanwhile, I zigzagged through the path less gracefully. My long, black tresses whipped my face as I rammed into snow-glazed shrubbery every five seconds. I exhaled a white puff of air. Given that my usual workout consisted of reading in bed until my arms hurt, I struggled to match her pace.

A thick, white branch smacked my wrist. I winced. Shaking the snow off my hand, I spied a faint mark underneath. I rubbed the patch of skin, but the weird ink smudge remained.

Probably from the chibis I had drawn on my shoes earlier.

Dismissing it, I returned my gaze to Usagi who showed no sign of slowing down. The distance between us stretched. I pursed my lips, about to request a break from the lightning-speed marathon when a small clearing emerged. Usagi halted.

I doubled over and panted for breath. Before I could catch it, Usagi prodded me again, her voice impatient. "No time for a rest, we're here."

She swiped aside some shrubbery. I blinked.

All around us, garlands of stars draped over the snow covered boughs. Usagi didn't give them a second glance. She passed the whimsical decor and squinted at a blizzard of winter jasmine and pansies in the distance. I followed her gaze.

Peeking behind the frosted flowers, two young men sat huddled over a starry tablecloth. Their backs to us, they conversed in murmurs. Shoulders brushing, heads leaning toward one another, the duo appeared to be enjoying a private tea for two.

Just when I thought the scene couldn't look more sickeningly romantic, the fellow in the top hat whispered something into his paramour's ear. I cupped a palm over my mouth.

I was so drawing this for my next fanart.

We stepped deeper into the alcove, and the dandies turned. The shift was slight, but I caught their side profiles. My eyes flared.

"Great flowers of moe," I whispered. *The ship is afoot.*

Usagi arched a brow. "What?"

"It's—it's them." With an unsteady finger, I pointed to my OTP: Boushiya, a tall, dapper hatter, and Sangatsu, a hare kemonomimi. Together, they formed *Sanbou*, one of the most popular—and ambiguous—ships in the Winterland fandom. Though the relationship was never confirmed in canon, I refused to believe it was a case of queer-baiting. Sanbou belonged together, like books and tea.

Unaware of our presence, the hatter stroked the green carnation in his buttonhole and sipped his tea. "How curious. The tea is unpleasant as ever yet the company sweetens it."

"My sentiments as well." Sangatsu touched the matching carnation on his coat and smiled. His teeth gleamed white against his bronze skin. "More tea please, Boushiya."

As the hatter poured, Sangatsu fumbled with the china. The teacup tipped toward the hare kemonomimi, but something was amiss. The tea should have spilled over the table, but I didn't see a single drop. Still, the kemonomimi fussed as though he'd been splashed.

"Not again." Sangatsu raised his sleeves and shook them as if they were sodden.

"Thrice in one sitting."

Tsking, the hatter reached for a napkin and dabbed the supposed tea off Sangatsu. As a fangirl with a sixth sense for subtext, this simple gesture confirmed my head-canon.

The hatter was the seme in this ship.

Slowly, his hand migrated lower and lower until I lost sight of it under the table. My inner fangirl felt a nose-bleed coming on. Doujinshi didn't compare to the real thing.

Usagi pressed her lips into a taut line and cleared her throat. The two fellows jerked their heads in our direction.

"My, it looks like we have company, Sangatsu." Inching away from his paramour, the hatter chuckled. He placed his top hat back over his dark, disheveled hair, then reached for his gloves, which lay strewn among the silverware on the table.

Usagi sniffed and seated herself. "Hope we're not interrupting."

"Not at all," said the hatter. His eyes flickered to a cup and saucer. "We were merely enjoying some tea, weren't we, Sangatsu?"

"Tea and treats." The handsome hare kemonomimi exchanged a dim smile with the hatter. The glorious double meaning hardly escaped me. I fanned myself, despite the cold.

Sangatsu smoothed the golden locks around his long, dark ears, then gestured to a teapot. "Some tea, Usagi?" He passed a cup to her.

Usagi's nose twitched. "As if that's why I came here. We need to—"

Before she could finish, Sangatsu turned to me. "Tea, Chibi?" And before I could answer—or retort at being called such a diminutive name—Sangatsu handed me a heavy cup. "Hope you fancy iced tea."

I looked to Usagi for direction. Seeing her take a forced sip out of hers, I followed suit. A tiny trickle of tea reached my mouth, then stopped. I stared at the frozen solid wedged in the cup.

"Of course," I murmured to Usagi. "He meant it literally."

"Speak up, Chibi." Boushiya intertwined his long gloved fingers and fixed me with an irate stare. "Are our paltry tea party provisions not up to your standards?"

My lips went taut. While I loved reading about Boushiya's and Sangatsu's escapades in the Winterland manga, I couldn't help but find myself liking their flamboyant personalities a smidgen less in person. My voice rose in mild indignation. "My name isn't Chibi."

"Then why do we keep calling you that?" asked Sangatsu.

"I don't know *why*. But my name is Alice."

"Well, I don't know why your name is Alice either. What does it mean?"

"I don't know, but—"

Boushiya tsked. "You don't know Why or But, yet you still insist we know your name? Seems rather cavalier to declare yourself so bumptiously when you can't even conduct yourself properly at our simple tea party."

Frustrated at this illogical chatter, I heaved a sigh. This whole exchange was starting to resemble a crackfic Winterpuff had once written. "I just don't understand how anyone could enjoy drinking frozen tea ...you'd have to be, well, mad to do so."

"I suppose we are a tad mad, but the best people often are." The hatter laced his fingers under his chin and cocked his head. "Genius cannot exist without a touch of madness, Chibi."

"A genius still knows you can't drink a block of ice," I muttered.

"We know that." The whisper was icier than the tea. I turned to Sangatsu. His long ears stood straight up as though I had struck a nerve. "You think we wouldn't prefer a nice, piping hot pot to this? If we had the bloody mirror, we could have tea so hot it'd scald your tongue." He slammed his fist on the table. The silverware clattered.

Mirror?

"Calm yourself, Sangatsu. She isn't worth your ire." Boushiya took Sangatsu's hand in his and discretely lowered it. Once again, I discerned subtle movement under their table, but I forced my eyes away from the distracting duo.

"What mirror?"

"The Looking Glass," Usagi said darkly. "At least, that's how I know of it. It goes by many names. The Magic Mirror, the Mirror of Truth, Mira Mira... Regardless of its polyonymy, its purpose is the same." Her features sharpened. "It can imprison the Snow Queen and end this eternal winter."

Usagi studied my wide eyes. With a sigh, she dropped her attention to her tea.

"According to legend, the Mirror Princess is the only one who can use it unfortunately," said the hatter.

"Why unfortunately?" I asked.

"Because no one knows where she is."

"Or who she is," Sangatsu added.

A shadow clouded Usagi's face. "I do."

Sanbou gaped at her, but Usagi ignored them. "Her name is Ariel Ecila and she lives in the outskirts of Winterland. The legend describes her as a lotus-eyed maiden who radiates beauty and power. A maiden who appears spawned from the fairy realm itself."

An unbidden image of a pretty blonde dancing in a flowing Christmas dress invaded my thoughts. Great, my mind was roasting me with Olivia even here.

Sangatsu frowned. "How exactly do you—"

"That's not important," said Usagi. "We need to find the Looking Glass and bring it to her if we want to break the queen's spell."

My fingers tightened like a coil. "*We?*"

She nodded. "Winterland's inhabitants refuse to take a stance against the queen. Some fear her retaliation." Her voice grew quiet. "The others...well, they've already succumbed to the darkness in their hearts."

I blinked. "Come again?"

The hatter stared at his gloved hand, face tensed. "Ever since the Snow Queen cursed our world with eternal winter, it affected more than just the land. All those who reside in Winterland are becoming darker versions of themselves. Colder. Harder. With each passing day, the light within them dims." His eyes darkened. "Even...in us."

"That's terrible," I whispered.

"I'll say." His eyes swept over me with a strange expression. Something akin to pity. "Chibi ..."

His foreboding voice sent a chill down my spine. My heart thumped. *What*, it pounded. *What, what, what?*

Hesitantly, Sangatsu pursed his lips. "You're included in this too."

"*Me?*"

"Darkness consumes all those who inhabit Winterland. Outsider or not." Sangatsu fixated on the hatter. "So far we've managed to stave off the curse by clinging onto…other emotions, but it's only a matter of time until the darkness takes over us completely." The kemono-mimi turned to his side, revealing a faint heart peeking out behind his long ear.

A shaky breath escaped me. "That's…"

"Once this materializes, we'll become cold shells of ourselves. Unfeeling monsters. Just like the Snow Queen herself."

My mind reeling, I touched the odd smudge mark on my wrist. "You can't be serious."

"Now do you see why we must take it upon ourselves to break her spell of winter?" Usagi yanked her sleeve. Following her cue, the hatter bit down on his glove and tugged it off, revealing his bare hand. My eyes widened at their heart-shaped marks.

"Our markings are faint for now," said Usagi, "so the Snow Queen does not hold control over us. Yet." She tried to maintain a calm and matter-of-fact tone, but her forced composure didn't prevent me from wigging out.

I felt like I had found myself in the plot of one of my YA novels: embark on harrowing quest; find magical object of great importance to stop Supreme Evil Baddy.

I took a steadying breath, my mind grappling with this info-dump. "So…if you find this mirror, everything returns to normal?"

"It's not that simple, Alice. The Looking Glass is broken. Its shards are scattered all across Winterland—and at the most precarious locations, too. We'll need to find all the shards if we ever hope to end the queen's reign."

"Sort of like hunting down Horcruxes to stop You-Know-Who …"

"Who?"

"Er, nothing. So you complete the Looking Glass and take it back to this Mirror Princess?"

Usagi nodded. "Bringing it to her will be simple enough." She yanked a parchment out of her satchel and began to draw a map. "The outskirts are here. And the shards are in the four quadrants of Winterland." She scrawled four x's.

I arched a brow. "How do you know all this?" Sanbou's narrowed eyes echoed my query.

"I just do." Usagi shifted her gaze, avoiding mine and the duo's. "We'll start at the North end: inside the queen's chamber. She's holding an event at the palace today, which provides an opportune moment to steal the first shard right under her nose."

Stealing? I swallowed hard. The only thing I ever stole was second base—and *that* was in a weird sports RPG I tried out one time, since I lacked athletic graces in real life. "Er, then what?"

"Then, we'll only have three more shards to collect." Usagi's fingers darted around the map. "We'll check the frozen lake—in the East quadrant, here—and the Chrysali's garden—here."

"We'll *check?*" Boushiya clicked his tongue at the word. "This isn't a game, Usagi. We're playing with our lives here!"

She ignored him.

"Is this a goose chase," said Sangatsu, "or do you somehow know more that you possibly could?"

"Just trust me," she said quietly. "I have my sources." She pinned her gaze on the map again, drawing a convoluted maze. "For the last shard, we'll need to navigate through the ice labyrinth by answering a series of riddles—"

"Usagi," I began, "what happens if we can't find the shards and the princess?"

"Then we risked our lives trying." Her sharp words cut like a sword.

"Those are pretty high stakes," I said shakily.

"That tends to be the case when you're dealing with pure evil."

I opened my mouth, but the words didn't come out. Her brows creased. "You will assist us, won't you?"

I nervously twirled my hair. Apprehension unfurled in my stomach, its smoky tendrils wrapping around me. Why couldn't I have fallen into an otome game or a nice, fluffy rom-com? Like a coffee shop AU or reverse harem. Even one of Lori's bookscapes would have been far preferable to this.

As though she sensed my hesitance, Usagi gave me a beseeching gaze. A part of me wanted to refuse her, but I couldn't bring myself to say it. Sure, I had my own stakes. Becoming a cold, empty shell of myself didn't sound appealing, but Usagi had always been there for me when I needed her the most. She may have not known it, but she had provided me a shelter on stormy days. Now, I needed to return the favor.

I took a deep breath. "Count me in."

Seeing Usagi's lips lift, I wanted a cliché storyline. The less plot twists, the better. I only hoped Usagi wasn't misplacing her confidence in me.

"I think I could help with the riddles." I fidgeted with my striped navy scarf and murmured, "It'd be a bad mark on me as a Ravenclaw if I couldn't…"

"A Raven?" Sangatsu squinted at me. "But you haven't a single quill."

"Not a Raven. *Ravenclaw*. They're good at solving riddl—"

"Pity, not one single quill." The hatter interrupted me before I could explain the complexities of my Pottermore versus self-assignment dilemma. He sniffed. "What a sad little writing desk you'd make, Chibi."

Usagi rose from her seat, her voice a harsh whisper. "Enough, you blatherskites."

My head spun. "Blah...what?"

"Blatherskites. Those who speak at great lengths without making any sense. You'll soon see these two are the very definition of the word." She shot the duo a cold glare. Her anger was mirrored in the hatter's twisted face. They stared at each other, their eyes like chips of ice. I swallowed hard. I had never seen them like this. Were they turning into their darker versions right before me?

On cue, Sangatsu barked with derisive laughter. "Boushiya and I are the most sensible of the lot. We *blatherskites* are only trying to dance in the storm."

Dance in the storm?

Like a flash of thunder, his meaning struck me. Hadn't I always done that? Hadn't I always dealt with the harsher parts of life by immersing myself in the things I loved? Spending hours in the library's manga section, seeking solace in my fanfiction when I was treated like a social misfit at school, sketching fanart of the strong, magical girls I aspired to be like... Sanbou's banter wasn't that different from my own coping habits.

"Usagi," I said quietly, "I think they have a point."

She stared at me hard, then reluctantly closed her mouth. Sangatsu flashed an appreciative glance in my direction. He dragged his eyes to the hatter who was cradling his tea.

"Boushiya."

The hatter glanced up. The duo held each other's gazes with a quiet intensity. Once more, they were in their own private bubble, communicating with each other without a single word. A part of me felt jealous that I couldn't be part of that—but it was a very, very small part. The rest of me, despite the bad timing, was fangirling hard.

Pinching her nose bridge, Usagi faced me. "I should warn you, Alice. No one has answered the riddles to date."

Fantastic.

"But *if* we can answer the riddles correctly," she added, noticing my dispirited expression, "we can collect the final shard."

She sketched an ominous looking terrain, filling it with rough, towering, snowy mountains. "Once we exit the maze, we'll find ourselves in the coldest, most desolate place of all—the outskirts of Winterland."

Of course, the princess we needed would live there.

"Once we bring the princess the mirror fragments, not only will she put a stop to the Snow Queen," said Usagi, "but she may also be able to return you home, Alice."

Home. A pang of wistfulness pricked me. The thought of home hadn't struck me until now. Everything flooded back to me. Deanna, Lori, Catpernicus, my fanfiction, my readers…and then a certain flaxen-haired someone. Of its own accord, my hand touched the crumpled envelope in my pocket.

How cute, whispered a treacherous voice in my head. *You think you stand a chance with a boy oblivious to your existence.*

I shook Dark Kermit's voice away and inhaled a deep breath. "When do we start, Usagi?"

"Now." Flashing me a tight smile, she gave my arm a squeeze and turned to her right. "And you two?"

Boushiya and Sangatsu exchanged a glance as if checking in with each other before committing to the quest. The hatter rubbed a finger along his jaw. "Let's see. Pilfering from an evil Snow Queen, crossing a treacherous lake, solving impossible puzzles …" My resolve dwindled. "I suppose it could be more cumbersome."

"Quite so," Sangatsu deadpanned. "Though you forgot the menacing insect creatures."

Okay, definitely not helping.

"You're coming with Usagi and me, right?"

I didn't know why, but I desperately wanted them to say yes. Something about their ridiculous banter comforted me. Between reading and writing about them, they had become more than words on a page. My fictional characters had turned into my rainy day friends. I'd need that sort of familiar comfort if this journey proved half as perilous as they made it sound.

"I don't think we will come with you, Chibi." Boushiya lifted his chin as he tucked a few pieces of silverware into his tailcoat.

My face collapsed like a pin-pricked balloon. "But why?"

"Because I don't like to tag along, you see. Terrible for my ego. Sangatsu and I shall embark on this little quest, but we refuse to come with you. However, if you and Usagi wish to tag along with us, you are most welcome to." A wily smile crept his mouth.

Before I knew what I was doing, I jolted from my seat and smothered him in a hug. His eyes widened.

"Sorry," I squeaked, loosening my grip. "I didn't mean to—"

"No… it's fine."

Reluctantly, the hatter patted my head, then straightened the lapels on his suit. He flashed a conspiratorial glance over his shoulder. The hare kemonomimi joined our little bubble.

I swooned. Never in my wildest dreams did I think I'd be sandwiched between my OTP. The group hug was everything a fangirl could have hoped for. Was that a gloved hand grazing Sangatsu's hip? Before I could tell, the duo let go. Breathless, I sat back down.

"Don't sit," Usagi chided. "We don't have time. The banquet will begin any moment."

Sangatsu and Boushiya nodded in tandem. They stood up with force and toppled over each other in perfect synchronization. I suppressed a giggle at their adorkable antics. The ship was certainly sailing full steam ahead.

The duo disengaged their entwined forms and flanked me, standing ramrod straight like bobbies on guard. We all looked to Usagi for instruction.

"Well, whatever are you standing around for?" Her ears twitched with nervous energy, but I caught the unmistakable glimmer of adventure in her eyes. "Let's start this heist."

A rakish smile tugged my lips.

"*Let's*."

Chapter 3

Alice on Ice

"This way." Usagi darted past a line of frosted birch trees. "When we reach the fork in the road, turn left."

Well, someone certainly knew her way around.

I followed close behind her and made a sharp turn, wincing as the white branches scraped my arms and legs. Sangatsu and Boushiya crashed into the tree behind us, holding hands to keep from falling. With great difficulty, the four of us trudged through the snowy woodlands until a patch of ice-glazed shrubbery emerged in front of our faces.

Usagi stopped dead in her tracks. She gave us a sharp look and placed a finger over her lips.

"What's going on?" I whispered.

"See for yourself." She stepped into the bushes, carefully parting the branches that obscured our view. When I joined her, my breath stilled.

A crystalline structure towered before us. Decked with ice roses and ghostly blue archways, it glinted like a thousand diamonds.

The Snow Queen's ice palace.

Needle-shaped leaves pricked my cold fingertips. The bush we were crouching behind wasn't just shrubbery, but part of the frosty juniper hedging that lined two sides of the palace's courtyard.

I stared in awe. The space reminded me of a square snow globe—minus the glass. Beside the juniper shrubs, a section of the palace and a tall wall of ice marked the other two edges of the courtyard. Inside the perfect square, a flurry of snowflakes sprinkled down without ever touching the ground. I guessed that the Snow Queen had enchanted the sky. It vaguely reminded me of the ceiling in Hogwart's Great Hall. Though I hated to admit it, the queen had good taste.

Banquet tables made of ice pressed into the snow-blanketed ground. They seemed to sink under the weight of silver platters, crystal goblets, and a slew of white desserts. Chiffon cakes, towering baumkuchens, dangos, white chocolate mousse, cream puffs, vanilla macarons, and munchkins coated in powdered sugar... My mouth watered.

Then, my eyes watered as well. Steam wafted up from the tall crystal decanters and an overwhelming aroma perfumed the air.

"Mmm," breathed Sanbou together. "Peppermint tea."

If the food was impressive, the aesthetics were out of this world. Elegant kemonomimis swept about in silky winter dresses and warm, fashionable coats. Rainbows danced between the snowflakes, and azure banners fluttered past a line of Grecian ice sculptures. The banquet was truly a fit for a queen.

An ice queen anyway.

Usagi's nose wriggled as she directed my gaze toward a procession of tiny creatures. Clad in Lolita-styled garb with a sea of azure ruffles, they floated above the banquet tables. Doll-like smiles surfaced their angelic faces. Their graceful, gentle movements transfixed me. I couldn't tear my eyes away from their gossamer wings.

"What are those?"

"Jabberwocks." Usagi's frosty accents jarred the picturesque scene.

"They're so kawaii—"

Usagi silenced my squeal by clamping her hand over my mouth. I couldn't help it. With their cherub cheeks and coy glances, they evoked a romantic aura. One-by-one they fluttered past us, their powder blue wings show-casing heart patterns.

"Thank goodness. She's not with them." Usagi released her hand and sighed. "The Jabberwocks aren't anything to ogle at, Alice. They're wolves in sheep's clothing. Except worse."

I skeptically eyed the dainty little things. "They don't *look* dangerous."

"Don't be fooled." Usagi's pupils darkened. "The hearts on their wings show their loyalty to the Snow Queen. Look how dark their marks are. They're completely under her control...whether they like it or not." Her voice grew strangely pensive.

"Usagi?"

"The creatures serve as her surveillance," she said, fixating on their wings. "They're her eyes and ears in Winterland. We must avoid them at all costs."

"Point made." Sangatsu and Boushiya mumbled their confirmations as well.

Usagi returned her attention to the scene in front us. "Looks clear. Is everyone ready?"

Pulse skittering, I nodded.

Time to crash this party.

We alighted onto the snowy courtyard where a large crowd stood, their backs to us. Every single one of them looked distracted. I followed their entranced gazes to an empty ice arena and raised a brow.

"Don't just stand there, Chibi." Sangatsu and Boushiya nudged me into the huddle of mesmerized guests. With the packed crowd as our coverage, we crept closer to the ice palace. But that was easier said than done.

"Watch it, you blundering fool." A dormouse kemonomimi snapped at me as I trod on her foot. I squeaked an apology, but a reindeer kemonomimi, clad in what I hoped were faux ermine furs, harrumphed at me for backing into him. I thought he was going to reprimand me, but he shook his antlers and stared off in the same direction as the rest of crowd. What on earth was going on there?

"Come on, Chibi."

Brows pinched, Sangatsu reached for my hand. His other hand threaded with the hatter's. The four of us weaved through the banquet's eclectic crowd. The reindeer kemonomimi followed us, taking advantage of our human chain to gain a better spot in the crowd.

Sangatsu shivered. Furtively, Boushiya stole two knitted gloves from the reindeer's fur coat and slipped them to his uke. Sangatsu tugged them on before rejoining hands with the hatter. I sighed wistfully. Talk about living the thug life for *amour.*

I returned my attention to Usagi, who hadn't noticed their high-jinxes. An aura of intense concentration surrounded her. I could see the cogs in her mind clicking away, trying to form a strategy. Despite her small stature, she stood tall like a bawse, determination rolling off her in waves. I wished I could exude confidence like that.

A wave of appreciation flooded through me. The motley duo and I would be lost without her leadership. Between the power of her venturesome spirit and her tunnel vision, maybe we stood a chance of bringing this ice queen down.

My shoulders relaxed. Perhaps I was worked up over nothing.

We navigated to the edge of the crowd when a trumpet blared. *"Welcome,"* a voice boomed, *"to the annual performance of the frostmaidens!"*

Frostmaidens? Unable to contain my curiosity, I craned my neck and stood on the tips of my toes. A considerable force rammed into me. I staggered backward, arms flapping like a penguin.

That blasted reindeer kemonomimi.

Hoping for an even better view, he had sidled beside me and knocked me off my feet. I crashed sideways into a pair of the silky, azure banners. They tore and draped around me like wings. I glared at the reindeer, but before

I could regain my bearings, a brusque voice filled my ear.

"Stop thumb-twiddling."

"Wha—?"

A royal guard yanked me with unrelenting force and shoved me, banners and all, into a marching line of petite, azure-winged girls wearing circlets. It was all I could do not to get trampled.

"Hurry up," ordered a sharp, familiar voice.

I glanced up and gawked.

Lori?

"Where is your headpiece?" Arms crossed, the leader of the frostmaidens scrunched her face. Distaste clung to her elegant features. If not for her fairy wings and cerulean pixie cut, she would've made a convincing doppelgänger of my sister. Well, in that anime sort of way.

She took me in, disapproval gleaming in her eyes. Great, I got Lori's attitude in this AU too. Before I could say anything, she shoved a pair of ice skates into my hands.

I blinked. Did she seriously take me for a frost-maiden? Well, maybe my height and banner-like wings might've given her that impression, but...

"There's been a mistake. I can't skate. I'm not—"

"Silence," she barked. "You will not jeopardize our performance in front of Her Majesty."

"But I'm not a frostmaiden—ask her!" I pointed to Usagi.

Mirror-Lori squinted in her direction. "You there, does she speak the truth?"

A cool gleam in her eyes, Usagi sauntered near us. She tilted her head, scanning me from head to toe.

"Well?" said Mirror-Lori.

"Never seen her. Though if I had to wager, she looks like a frostmaiden to me." Usagi crinkled her nose. "Only a peculiarly dressed one."

"I thought as much." Mirror-Lori curled her lips and gestured to a pair of nymphets.

My gaze flicked to Usagi, who watched the scene with indifference. I glared daggers at her. "What are you—"

"Just go with it," she hissed.

Before I could protest, the leader shoved a circlet made of blue narcissus and dark azurite onto my head.

"I do not tolerate lies."

"I didn't—"

"Nor do I tolerate failures," she whispered. "Our performance is a rendition of masterpieces by the greats. Our art provides salve for the ache." She put her lips against my ear. "Do not muck this up."

With a snap of her fingers, two frostmaidens grasped my wrists while a third forced the skates onto my feet. Seconds later, I found myself skating awkwardly alongside the elegant nymph creatures. How, oh how, had I let this happen?

"And now," said the resounding voice, *"the frostmaidens shall grace us with Vivaldi's Winter."*

An instrumental reminiscent of Lori's Fantasia soundtrack wrapped around me. I turned. An orchestra of kemonomimis played on glittering cellos and frosted violins. Smooth, brisk strains filled the air, evoking the fall of snowflakes and icy rain. Despite the frosty notes, the melody sounded...enchanting, like the instruments themselves were magic.

The unearthly opus enveloped my senses, filling the courtyard with its rich, breathless tempo. The frostmaidens glided across the ice like graceful swans while I struggled to find my balance.

Arms flapping, knees knocking together, I must've looked like an inebriated penguin. I winced. How did the characters from *Yuri on Ice* make skating look so easy?

The frostmaidens performed a series of pirouettes, but the audience barely noticed. An ocean of faces focused on me, making my pulse speed. So much for blending in.

I sucked in a breath as I crashed into the rink wall. The crowd broke out in murmurs.

Okay, I was totally getting pwned out here.

I needed to find Usagi, not draw attention to myself. But I couldn't jeopardize our thieving operation by joining them now...

Ignoring the dozens of eyeballs, I gripped the rink wall and gave myself a mental pep talk. Deep breaths, Alice. It's just DDR on ice. You can do this. *Fighting.*

Working up some courage, I pushed off the wall. But when I glanced past the scrutinizing crowd, I recoiled. Flanked by her female guards and peering down from the stand was...*Olivia.*

And yet, it wasn't her. Just a matching face, icy blonde locks, and a mirrored sneer. The rest of her looked entirely different. Clad in a diaphanous robe which shone like crushed diamonds, she sparkled more than Edward Cullen. The silvery tendrils of her crown secured her chignon in their snare. Below it, a blue heart-shaped mark—the same insignia as on the Jabberwocks's wings—shimmered in the center of her forehead.

The Snow Queen.

She pressed forward in her seat. I took in her perfectly symmetrical face, carnelian lips, and eyes which gleamed like blue zircons. I couldn't deny she was beautiful—but less in that pretty girl way and more in a mathematical way. She had a beauty that was cold and austere.

The queen narrowed her eyes. Her colorless finger stroked a crystal globe in her grip. My insides churned. I could have sworn she saw no one but me. Averting her penetrating stare, I rejoined the lineup of frostmaidens.

The rhapsody quickened. The biting strings grew louder. And along with them: the slicing noises from the skating blades. The frostmaidens lifted one leg up and skated in a fast, furious circle. Round and round they went like spinning tops. My head spun at the dizzying azure blurs. The frostmaidens glided to the left. I toppled to the right. They danced; I fell. They twirled; I tumbled. If figure skating was poetry of the feet, then my blades just composed an abysmal haiku.

The Jabberwocks began hurling cream puffs from the banquet table, tipping off my balance even more. I cringed. Lovely. I was getting creamed—*literally*. Filling splattered across my glasses, I carried on with my abysmal performance. Gasps spread rampantly through the crowd. When a butchered salchow landed my shin on the ice, the queen rose from her seat. Her shrill voice reverberated through the rink.

"What sort of entertainment is this?"

Her Jabberwocks swarmed me, their buzzing growing louder. Like day into night, their innocent expressions morphed. Into something horrifying and fiendish. Their doll-like faces contorted to reveal sharp teeth, the delicate wings on their backs turned rough and leathery, and their fingers grew claw-like. Now they reminded me of harpies. I gulped. Nothing kawaii about them anymore.

The Jabberwocks lifted me up, nipping at my attire and clawing at me. Somewhere in the fracas, I made out Mirror-Lori's acrid whisper. "One worthless frostmaiden brings down the lot."

Worthless?

The murmurs of agreement didn't help. My insides shrank as the Jabberwocks dropped me in front of their queen. They dusted their hands as if to dispel the filth they'd acquired from touching me.

The Snow Queen flicked her gaze from her snow globe to me. She scrutinized my face, her expression contemplative. "State your name."

My mind went into a tailspin. Should I lie? I couldn't blow our cover.

The queen rapped a finger against the crystal globe. I anxiously fidgeted with my hair as her unnerving eyes bore into mine.

"Well?"

"Chibi," I blurted without thinking.

"Your name is Chibi?" Her voice dripped with skepticism. I knew she could read my poker face. Looked like I would have to come clean. My knees trembled. I never thought it would require this much courage to say my name.

"Alice." My voice shook like violin strings. "My name is Alice."

"Alice..." The Snow Queen lingered over the syllables as if testing the name. She stared at me in silence until a shadow of relief touched her features. She resumed her seat and stroked the globe.

"Well then, Alice, it would be most unwise to make a mockery of my banquet." I discerned a threat veiled behind her honeyed voice. "But I am a merciful queen. I shall give you one more chance to redeem yourself." She waved a dismissive hand at me.

The Jabberwocks thrust me forward. The tempo grew faster, rife with sharps and flats. I careened toward the frostmaidens who, during my trial, had arranged themselves in a semi-circle. I skated haphazardly across the rink, trying my best to mimic the moves from my favorite ice skating anime.

Like a burst of wind, the music swelled with fortissimos. I winced, the sounds bombarding my ear. As the piece reached its crescendo, my feet tripped over each other. My glasses skid off my face. I rammed—or rather head-butted—into a quartet of frostmaidens. Like bowling pins, they spun blurrily in place before hitting the ice.

Shimatta. Shimatta. Shimatta.

I shoved my glasses back on and bit the hollows of my cheeks. Mirror-Lori looked like she wanted to wield a saber at me. Out of the corner of my eye, I glimpsed Usagi, Boushiya, and Sangatsu in the crowd. Their faces turned white as snow. My gaze darted to the stand. The queen's eyes had narrowed to slits.

Taking in their faces, my vision disfigured. I felt like I was viewing the scene through a fish-lens. Like the crowd was swallowing me up. My breathing grew shallow.

It's over, I thought as I fell on my derriere. *I friggin blew it—* A soft chirrup broke me out of my panic. I raised my head.

The queen was laughing.

I held my breath. Slowly but surely, the rest of the crowd joined in. Before I knew it, laughter erupted in every direction. Everyone shouted, clapped, and hollered over my unintentionally comedic act.

With the queen and her guards diverted, I caught Usagi, Boushiya, and Sangatsu slipping into the Ice Palace. I sighed in relief and fell backward into a slapstick crash—this time, intentionally. The audience roared with more laughter.

Yes...just like that. I needed to distract everyone as long as possible.

Gathering momentum, I collided into another frost-maiden who then toppled over another, then another in a domino effect. Everyone clapped, except Mirror-Lori. I grinned at her.

Oh, I'll show you worthless.

My ridiculous charades continued. I tumbled. I tripped. I even twerked.

"Stop it this instant!" The leader of the frostmaidens skated behind me, her blades carving slices in the ice. "You're ruining everything."

"Am I?" I replied innocently as I skated further from her.

"Come back here!"

Feeling surprisingly daring, I readied myself for a botched up double axel when a royal attendant stormed out of the ice palace.

"Stop this performance."

Vivaldi's *Winter* stopped mid-finale. Echoes of a discordant fourth hung in the air. A huddle of kemonomimis parted to allow the royal attendant through.

"Out of my way, move, move."

An attendant, who resembled Claire, needled through the stands. She whispered something into the queen's ear. Everyone went pin-drop silent. The queen rose from her seat. Her face turned a mottled shade of purple. For a moment, I thought she might explode. It was an optimistic thought.

"Guards, secure the premises." Her voice dropped to an icy whisper. "We have a thief in our midst."

And the plot thickens.

The guards barreled through the screaming crowd. I rid myself of the banners draped around my back and scavenged the chaotic muddle. My body shuddered against the high pitched noises and turbulent movement of spectators. In my sensory overload, I found more than I could have hoped for. Four dorsal-fin rabbit ears—two brown, two twitching and white—swam along the edge of the frenzied crowd, followed by an eccentric top hat, a trailing scarf, and a strange flicker of light.

They had found it.

My heart raced. Now I just needed to get to them without running into those pesky Jabberwocks. My eyes darted about the rink and courtyard, surveying my surroundings. Palace, stand, crowd, tables, wall, hedge… angry Jabberwocks, angry guards, more angry Jabberwocks…

Shimatta. Where was an escape path when you needed one?

As hard as I searched, the only path I could find was ahead—through a cluster of buzzing Jabberwocks. I had no other choice but to dodge them. As I readied myself to hurdle through them, I glanced up for the briefest moment. Bad idea. Every nerve in my body rattled on edge.

Like a red flag to a bull, the queen's piercing gaze latched onto me.

Crapola. I skated backward toward the tumultuous crowd whose cries of pandemonium engulfed the arena. A blast of arctic air missed my ear. I yelped and jerked around.

Globe in hand, the queen hastened behind my trail. She glided across the ice like a terrible phantom, her silvery voile dress billowing behind her. She skated fluidly as though the ice underneath her glass heels was a part of her. My stomach did a somersault. At this rate, I'd turn into a popsicle in no time.

In one swift move, I yanked off my left skate and flung it behind my shoulder. A loud shriek pierced the air. Seizing my chance, I threw myself into the crowd. The mounting chaos worked to my advantage. Shielded by the commotion, I yanked off my other skate and made a mad dash until—"*Chibi!*"—I ran into the hatter head-first.

"Thank goodness we've found you."

Usagi tossed me my sneakers. I caught them and crammed my feet in. I hadn't even finished lacing them when a vise-like grip claimed my sweatshirt. Usagi dragged me through the chaotic crowd. Through the screams and pointed fingers, we dodged flying desserts and hurtling snowballs. If the real Lori was here, she'd deem the whole situation a horrific Shakespearean comedy.

"Jabberwock incoming!" Sangatsu shouted. We narrowly avoided the hellion and jumped onto a tilted table.

"What do we do?" I panted as we bolted past a line of Grecian ice sculptures.

Usagi breathed hard, gesturing us ahead. "Back to the hedges... This way... Sangatsu, do you see any more Jabberwocks?"

"We're fine for now, but Usagi ..."

"*What?*"

"I don't think we can use the hedges. The circumference the Jabberwocks formed is airtight." His face tensed. "We'll never escape unless we scale the wall."

My eyes widened. "How on earth do we do that? It's made of *ice*." I stared at the wall. Its dizzying height made my head swim.

"I don't know *how*, but we're going to have to try, Chibi." Boushiya spoke with an urgency I'd never heard in his voice. If the hatter and hare kemonomimi were making sense, the situation must've have been more dire than I had imagined.

I searched the scene in desperation. The Snow Queen had disappeared, but a small comfort that was. A barricade of guards blocked our path to the hedges. I glanced to the right, only to see a horde of Jabberwocks rushing toward us. Shimatta. Everything around us was snowballing out of control. We had to change course. *Fast.*

"The Jabberwocks are multiplying faster than plot bunnies," I said breathlessly. "Sangatsu and the hatter are right, Usagi. The ice wall is our only ch—"

"Ch-Chibi." All the color in Sangatsu's face drained. The hatter mirrored his expression. And then, curiously, so did Usagi.

My brows pinched. "What's wrong—?"

A cold hand tightened on my shoulder. I froze. The chill spread over me, stirring the hair on the nape of my neck.

A silken voice whispered into my ear. "Going some-where?"

With a sinking feeling, I turned my head.

The Snow Queen smiled.

CHAPTER 4

The Treacherous Lake

Panic frosted my skin.

The queen had emerged from behind an ice sculpture. A line of crimson trickled down her cheek where the blade of my skate had cut her. Her face flickered between shades of darkling wrath and radiant triumph. I inched backward—but only to find myself pressed against an ice sculpture. My breath hitched.

She had me cornered.

A serpentine smile slithered across her lips. She raised a slender finger at me. I squeezed my eyes, bracing myself for the worst. Curiously, nothing happened.

I cracked open a lid. An arc of colors danced between us. The queen froze, shielding her face against the spectral rainbow. Her blindness lasted for only a moment, but it was enough. Her gaze swept over me and landed on Usagi—and the glimmering shard in her hand.

"*You*," the queen whispered. With a blurring speed, she lunged at Usagi.

"Look out!"

I dove toward my friend, racing the jet of ice heading for her. Somehow, between my intuitive impulse and my two-foot head start, I won. Usagi and I toppled headfirst into the snow. The arctic blast missed us by a hair's breadth and hit one of the guards instead. Frost crawled over his body. His pupils shook, horror-struck, until he was completely encapsulated, matching the row of ice sculptures behind him.

The queen drew in a sharp breath, taking in the statuesque body of her fallen soldier. A hair-raising scream ripped from her throat.

We all made a break for it.

Enraged with her miss, the queen raised both arms into the sky. The chignon of her hair came loose, the strands flying in a conjured wind. Thick, white clouds overhead transformed into a snowstorm.

A wraith-like mist swirled around us; biting winds buffeted our faces. We barreled through the raging blizzard. Past the sculptures, past the desserts, past the muddled banquet tables.

The Snow Queen shot another jet of ice my way. Thinking fast, I reached for a platter of dangos and flung them in between us. They froze mid-air before raining down on her like a hailstorm. A sharp gasp left her. The queen jerked to her left, then her right, protecting her crystal globe from the assuage of snowball desserts.

Bangs and shrieks erupted all around us, but we continued forging our way through the chaos. Usagi ducked and rolled under a table, confusing a Jabberwock on her tail. Boushiya dodged an attacking guard by shielding himself with a twelve-tiered frosted baumkuchen.

I increased my pace, and a glimmer of hope flickered through me. We had almost reached the ice wall. All too quickly, a yelp extinguished that optimism. Usagi and I wheeled around. Boushiya had frozen in his tracks.

"What's wrong?" Usagi breathed.

"Sangatsu. Where's Sangatsu?" The hatter's eyes darted around the thick, swirling frost until he brought his hand to his face. A stolen glove lay in his trembling grip. His voice cracked. "Sangatsu ..."

Shimatta.

My gaze scavenged through the thick, ubiquitous flurries. No longer aesthetically pleasing, the courtyard resembled the aftermath of a food fight and battleground. Sculptures of pastries frozen mid flight cast murky shadows onto the overturned tables. Silk banners flapped in the brumal wind, tattered and tangled. As hard as I looked through the bedlam, I could see no sign of the hare kemonomimi.

"Sangatsu!" The hatter's desperate voice carried in the whistling wind, until a weak cry met it. We spun around.

A pack of guards circled Sangatsu. The Snow Queen's magic had imprisoned him in an ice cage created from the snow under his feet. Without hesitation, Boushiya turned in the direction of the guards.

Usagi gripped his cuff links. "Boushiya, we can't."

"We have to. Usagi, I have to."

Lips trembling, Usagi shook her head. A choking sound escaped the hatter. My chest tightened. It felt as though someone had sucker punched me right in the feels. But as I took in the guards fast on our trail, I knew what we had to do.

"We'll come back for Sangatsu." I squeezed his hand. "We'll rescue him, but now we need to—"

A jet of ice whizzed past me, grazing the nape of my neck. I yelped. The guards and the Snow Queen had almost closed the distance between us. We had no time to lose.

"Please, Boushiya."

The hatter blinked hard, as though he realized he couldn't fight the queen on his own. But his will was stronger than his logic. Ignoring our frantic pleas, he lunged at the guards.

Usagi and I exchanged panicked looks. After missing the first beat, we sprinted after him.

I knew Usagi's initial instinct to retreat had not been born of cowardice. It had been last-ditch, utilitarian logic. We simply couldn't take them on. If we wanted to complete the mirror and save *anyone*—including Sangatsu—we had to flee.

A jet of ice raced toward the hatter.

"Look out!"

Though she remained some distance away, the queen hit Boushiya square in the top hat. He yelped, lifting his hands to his head. The hat was glued to him.

The queen smiled at the scene. A shiver ran through me. She hadn't missed. She was merely proving her power.

Sangatsu's shout broke though the howling wind. "Boushiya, go! *Please.*" He gripped the bars of his confines, his pained eyes locking with the hatter's. His lips parted again, teetering on speech, but when he spoke at last, the storm swallowed up the lost words.

Reluctantly, the hatter staggered backward. Before he could do something impulsive, Usagi and I gripped his cuff links and steered him to the towering wall. We needed to climb it—fast.

Usagi's eyes darted back and forth in a wild frenzy. I could see the cogs in her mind racing. She had to have a plan. Usagi *always* had a plan. She would get us out of this.

Her eyes landed on a banquet table. "Alice, take that."

And she delivers.

I sprinted to the upturned table and wrestled a frayed banner poking underneath it. "Now what?"

"Follow my lead." She grasped the fabric from my outstretched hand and faced the hatter. "Boushiya, toss me the highest you can."

The hatter asked no questions. He hoisted Usagi onto his shoulder and launched her into the air. Like a cheer-leader, she sprang high, the banner in her hand flut-tering in the wind. With her free hand, she managed to grab the slippery ice wall. I watched in horror as she dangled from it.

"Usagi!"

"It's okay." Nimbly, she propelled herself up. I sighed in relief, though I guess I shouldn't have worried. What else could be expected of a rabbit kemonomimi?

"One of you take that," she ordered from above. In my panic I hadn't noticed the banner in front of me. Usagi had made us a rope ladder.

Raising a foot, I grasped the banner. So did Boushiya.

"I'll go first, Chibi. I'll lift you afterward, unless you prefer to ro-sham-bo for it."

As much as I appreciated the hatter's deference for democracy, a game of rock-paper-scissors lost its appeal at the moment. *"Hurry up,* Boushiya."

The hatter gripped the torn banner and climbed, his tailcoat fluttering in the icy wind. With Usagi's help, he scrambled atop the wall and peered down. "Hold on tight. I'll pull you up."

I held fast to the banner-rope as the two hauled me up. A quarter of the way through, a barrage of snowballs bombarded the wall. I stifled a shriek, ducking in time. In the reflection of the ice, I could see a storm of guards behind me. And then in the far distance, I glimpsed Sangatsu—captive in his cage.

He gripped the icy bars and mouthed something over and over. A silent, but fraught litany. I read his trembling lips.

Bou—shi—ya.

Fury ignited in my chest, chasing out the fear. I clenched my fist. That did it.

No one messes with my OTP.

Throwing caution to the wind, I abandoned the banner and landed in the snow ninja-style.

Usagi's voice rose in terror. "What is she doing?"

Ignoring her, I darted to a muddled banquet table. Maybe I couldn't rescue him, but I could get a little revenge.

"Are you mad, Chibi?"

"The best people are, aren't they?" I stood on the table and hurled a heavy chiffon cake at the hatter. "Catch!"

He caught it in one hand. Confusion marred his features, but slowly, it faded. Usagi stared ahead, her lips lifting.

"We'll need to be quick about it," she said.

The hatter cracked his knuckles. "Then let's get down to business."

And defeat those guards, my inner fangirl cheered from the shadows.

Without another word, the hatter and Usagi pulled the banner up and set to work: they stretched the banner taut, positioned the massive cake inside it, and launched the dessert at the guards. It made contact with two of the guards and deflected a snowball that looked destined to hit my face.

"Boushiya, Usagi—incoming." I sent platter after platter flying like Frisbees. "Get the Jabberwocks," I shouted. "They have wings. I don't want to climb this wall for nothing."

The duo nodded. They caught the platters and chucked them in tandem. The Jabberwocks proved easy enough to take out—their delicate wings couldn't take a hit—but the guards still had to be dealt with. The projectiles only temporarily slowed them down. We needed something more substantial—fast.

I scavenged the table. White chocolate mousse? No. Vanilla macarons? Meh. Cream puffs? Hail no. My tenacity dwindled. There had to be something I could use. Then, it struck me. I snapped my finger. Of course...*that*.

"Boushiya, lower the banner!"

He followed my order. I tied a massive glass pitcher to the end of the fabric, and he reeled it up. The contents sloshed inside. He untied it, held it up, and cocked his head.

"*This*, Chibi?"

"Trust me."

Askance, the hatter glimpsed inside it. His fingers tightened around the handle, and his eyes locked with mine. I knew he had read my mind.

He placed the vessel inside the banner and stretched it with all his might. His face twisted, and his pupils darkened to black. I stiffened. For a moment, I hardly recognized him.

His voice dropped to a cold whisper. "This one's for Sangatsu."

He released the banner. The pitcher hurtled through the air like a missile and smashed into smithereens. The guards fell back, glass shards in their hair, their eyes burning—with strong peppermint tea.

Boushiya dropped the banner again, and I quickly grabbed hold. Usagi and Boushiya hauled me up, but whatever small respite I had fleeted me. The sound of ripping fabric filled my ear. The banner was tearing. I sucked in a sharp breath.

"Alice!"

"Usagi, Boushiya, do something!"

"Keep calm," Usagi shouted.

"I'm a fangirl, we don't do calm!"

My legs dangled like noodles. I tried to hang on but only slipped further. When I thought things couldn't get worse, a reflection flashed on the ice wall. The Snow Queen's face grew clearer and clearer. My adrenaline levels spiked. She was close. Too close.

A violin shrieked. Three more joined in. My ears went numb with the noise. Vivaldi's *Winter* blared across the courtyard. Each note pulsed with an undercurrent of anger. Louder than a howler, the music blasted at impossible decibels. The queen shielded her ears from the deafening sound. Her face contorted with rage.

Behind the ice rink, the orchestra played their hearts out...conducted by the leader of the frostmaidens. My heart stilled. *Were they helping us?*

Questions swirled through my mind, but I was in no position to grapple with them. I had seconds to save myself. Thinking fast, I yanked off my Ravenclaw scarf, balled it up, and hurled it up with all my might.

"*Boushiya!*"

The hatter grabbed the scarf. I released the ripping banner as he hoisted me atop the ice wall. I glanced backward. An army of frostmaidens and jilted musicians had pinned dark gazes on their queen.

"Come on!"

Schwoop. The three of us slid down the other side of the wall. Instantly, the music stopped. Like the snowfall, the song was enchanted to fill only the courtyard. Usagi, Boushiya, and I plopped into the deep, powdery snow.

"We did it," I said, panting. "Somehow."

A puckered brow marred Usagi's face as she took in my feeble smile. "We only retrieved the first shard, Alice —probably the easiest task of them all."

"Positive as a proton, aren't you?"

Usagi crinkled her nose. "Well, I'm sorry I can't be more of a *micaber.*"

"A what?"

"Micaber—an eternal optimist. Which is a foolish thing to be in a world like this." Usagi clipped the words tight.

She shook off the snow from her ears and stood. I followed suit, throwing my scarf around me. Boushiya, however, didn't stir. He remained slumped against the wall, staring vacantly at Sangatsu's glove in his hand.

"Boushiya." Usagi placed a placating hand on his shoulder, her face softening. "I know it's hard for you, but we didn't have a choice." The hatter said nothing. Usagi darted her eyes at me, then at Boushiya. I understood her cue.

I crouched down, extending my pinky to the hatter. "We'll rescue him," I told him fiercely.

"Do you promise?"

"Promise." I extended my pinky.

With a strained smile, Boushiya curled his own pinky around mine. I didn't know how exactly I'd reunite my OTP, but I'd find a way, even if I went down with the ship.

Usagi jumped. A sharp thud resounded against the wall. Then came another. And another. Fissures formed on the ice wall. Behind it, a frustrated scream pierced the air. Though I couldn't see the other side, I imagined the queen expressing her displeasure by hurtling her guards against the barrier. And how long would it be before the Jabberwocks recovered and flew over the wall like it was nothing? And couldn't the queen just use her ice powers and make a staircase out of snow?

I chewed my lip. Why wasn't she doing that? Unless something was stopping her... The dark, steady gazes of the frostmaidens flashed in my mind. I wondered if I had witnessed the start of a uprising. I shook myself. No, this wasn't the time to think. This was the time to *move*.

I looked to the hatter, torn between empathy and anxiety. "Boushiya…"

"I know. We need to leave." Dropping Sangatsu's glove, he sobered up. He stood and dragged his feet through the carpet of snow. Looking at the tracks he left, you would've thought he wore skis. I winced.

Right in the feels.

I hooked my arm with his. Usagi followed suit in an attempt to bolster his spirits. Arm-in-arm, the three of us trundled through the thick, endless flurries. Once we had trekked a safe distance from the palace, Usagi reached for the map in her satchel.

"The lake is closest. We should stop there first."

We ventured along a narrow, winding path that led into the woodlands. Despite the sound of the whistling wind and blowing snow, a heavy silence lingered between us. If only I could do something to break it.

Make a drabble, my inner fangirl whispered.

I thought back to the old fanfiction drabbles I had written. Light and fluffy, those one shots always took my mind off things, even in the most melancholy of moods. Maybe I could recreate one of them.

"Ever played Truth or Dare before?"

Usagi blinked at me. "Sorry?"

"It's a game where you either answer a question truthfully or do a dare. I figured we could use the distraction."

Usagi considered it, then shook her head.

I grinned. "Truth or Dare?"

"Truth."

I considered what I knew about Usagi in the manga. Her strengths, her weaknesses, heck, even her blood type. Still...there was one thing that was never mentioned. "Do you have anyone you like?"

A flush crept across her face. "I'm not interested in anybody. At least...not like that." She fiddled with her hands. "Do characters in books count?"

"A booktuber I know would say yes." My smile faded a bit as I thought of Deanna's quirky book reviews on YouTube. Usagi might've resembled my friend a bit, but she could never replace the real thing. No one could.

"Typical," murmured the hatter. "She likes reading about romances, yet refuses to experience one herself."

Usagi lowered her eyes. "Ask me something else."

"Fine." I contemplated what else I wanted to know about her. Her favorite book, her worst habit, whether she kept a secret diary. Before it even reached my mind, the question left my lips. "How do you know so much?"

She blinked. "I read?"

"No. I mean, how do you know about the Looking Glass and where the shards are and… just everything?"

"I read."

The hatter rolled his eyes. Knowing I wasn't going to get anything more out of her, I turned to him. "Why don't you go next, Boushiya?"

"Ask away."

"Truth or Dare?" I asked.

"Truth."

My inner fangirl spouted a string of steamy questions at me. I waved them away, settling for the most appropriate of the lot.

"How did you and Sangatsu meet?"

"*Alice*," Usagi whispered.

I bit my tongue. Okay, maybe not the best way to distract him from his beau. "On second thought, maybe we should just settle for a game of ro-sham-bo—"

"Stargazing."

"What?" I asked.

"It's how we met." A tinge of wistfulness colored his voice. "I set out one night to find the Teapot asterism. It turned out I wasn't the only one searching for the constellation." A languid, far off look came over the hatter. "Lying under the stars, gazing at the steam of celestial clouds, talking about our dreams, hopes, and wishes…I knew I had met a kindred spirit that night."

"A nefelibata," Usagi whispered to me.

"Sangatsu and I met again and again," he continued. "Every moonless night. To find that asterism together. With every encounter, we drifted closer, until we found ourselves closer than two pages of an unopened book."

"I confess, that's rather romantic," said Usagi.

The hatter slowed his pace and stared into the leaden skies as if he didn't hear her. "From then on, we existed within ourselves. Spiraling through the stars in a free fall. Amusing ourselves with teas and frivolity. Losing ourselves in our madness..." His fingers grazed his green carnation. "It was all so wonderful."

"That. Was. Beautiful," I gushed.

"Agreed." Usagi sighed. "A poetic monologue if I do say."

The hatter gave her a tiny grin. "Not a blatherskite now, am I?"

"Hardly." She fought a sheepish smile and faced me. "Your turn, Alice."

I walked backward, facing the duo and smirked. "*Dare.*"

"Who would've thought the Chibi had moxie." The hatter rubbed a finger along his cupid's bow. "Let me see. I dare you to...to ..." He stopped in his tracks.

I spun around, but only to find myself gazing at a stretch of frozen water. "What?"

"The Treacherous Lake." The hatter's whisper sent a shiver down my spine.

"Come again?"

"It's the name of the lake," said Usagi, surveying the thick trees at the opposite side of the lake.

"Sounds like the title of a Lemony Snicket book." I let out a nervous laugh. "Do I want to know why it's called that?"

"I haven't the foggiest idea. No one who journeyed to the lake ever came back to tell me...or Sangatsu."

"Awesome sauce." So we would just have to find out firsthand if the lake lived up to its name.

"Alright, who's going first?" I asked.

"You are," said Boushiya.

"And why would I do that?"

The hatter leaned against my ear. "Because you've just been dared.

I chewed my lip. "Can't we just rock-paper-scissors for it?"

Boushiya shook his head.

For the love of ships.

Swallowing hard, I gazed at the frozen surface. The lake glinted coldly, as if challenging me to a duel. Mustering all my courage, I stepped forward. I pinned my eyes on the murky waters below, my insides tingling with unease. I took a step, then another.

"See guys, nothing to it."

The hatter eyed my fake smile, then the ice below. Warily, he stepped onto the hardened surface and grimaced. We both looked to Usagi.

She pensively scanned the circumference of the lake, landing on the tall, white trees at one end.

"Earth to Usagi?"

She snapped out of her reverie. "Sorry…"

The three of us tiptoed across the lake, inches from one another. Tension crackled between us. The eerie silence around us didn't help matters. The only thing I could hear was the quiver of my breath. Nervously, I concentrated on each step. The ice looked thick enough to hold us, yet part of me expected it to cave in at any moment. One couldn't blame my nerves. Even Usagi looked paranoid. Her face turned pink as though she held her breath with each step she took.

"Remember," she said, exhaling a white mist. "We find it and get out as soon as we can."

"Pity we can't stay longer," the hatter murmured.

Spreading out, we scanned and scanned the surface. Several minutes passed by, and we still couldn't find anything in the dark, murky depths. I heaved a sigh.

"This could take forever, Usagi."

"Not if …" She glanced in the direction of the distant trees again. "Can you two wait here? I'll be back."

Boushiya narrowed his eyes. "What's going on, Usagi?"

"Nothing, I just…need to check something."

"But—"

"It's just for a minute! Please."

Not heeding our protests, Usagi skittered off the lake and disappeared into the distant trees. A minutes passed, then another. We waited and waited, but there was no sign of her.

"It's been over ten minutes."

"Shall we go after her, Chibi?"

"I don't think we have a choice."

Partly relieved to be off the lake, we made our way into the cluster of towering, white firs. I scanned the landscape until…

"There!"

I pointed to a depression in the snow. As we neared closer, I saw it was a fresh footprint. A familiar footprint.

"She was just here," I said lowly.

"Lead the way, Chibi."

We followed her footprints. They took us deeper and deeper into the snowy woods. A soft, yet high pitched sound filled the air.

"Did you hear that?" said the hatter. "It sounded like a…"

"Jabberwock," I whispered darkly.

Boushiya put a gloved finger to his lip. With all our stealth, we neared the source of the voice. Another voice interrupted.

"That's Usagi," I said. "It sounds like she's talking to someone."

Boushiya went smoky-eyed. "Why the flake is she with a Jabberwock?"

"Let's find out."

We edged closer until the voices were only a few feet away.

"*You have shards?*"

"*Only one. Do you remember where you hid the other?*"

The question made my heart pound. Betrayal coursed through my veins. First Deanna with the invite, and now this.

Anger gripping me, I faced Boushiya. "On three, okay?"

He gave a fierce nod.

"One, two—three!"

We sprang out from behind a towering tree, cornering Usagi and the Jabberwock against theirs. Usagi looked at us, startled. "Alice, Boushiya, what are—"

"Fess up, Usagi." I thrust my finger in her face, then the Jabberwock. I blinked. She was tied to a tree. "What's going on here? Why are you saving that—that *thing*."

"Alice, don't be rude."

"Metanoia have name," the Jabberwock replied.

I glared at the struggling creature, then rounded on my traitorous "friend."

"You're working for her," I said coldly.

"What?" Usagi's eyes swelled. "No. Alice, I—"

Boushiya's face hardened. "I knew you knew too much. 'Just trust me. Take my word as gospel.'" He barked with laughter and tried to throw his top hat to the ground, but found it still frozen to his head.

I gasped. "You...wanted me to get caught."

"What are you talking about, Alice?"

"When you made me skate!" I neared closer, leaving inches between us. My words misted her horrified face. "As soon as I landed in Winterland, you brought me straight to the Snow Queen."

"Only because—" She choked, cut off by Boushiya's shaking fist.

"You left Sangatsu behind to die."

The whisper cracked my heart. Usagi stepped to the side, tripping on a tree root and crashing into the snow. Boushiya approached her, pressing heavy footprints into the snow.

"No," she croaked, scrambling backward. "Boushiya, I didn't. We had to run. The queen was too close."

"Then why are you rescuing one of her monsters?" I demanded.

"Metanoia tied herself to this tree," said Usagi. "I'm not saving her... She doesn't want me to."

"Of course not." Boushiya's tone dripped with sarcasm. I didn't blame him. I balled up my hand.

"No more keeping secrets, Usagi. Tell us what's going on."

"Fine, I'll answer your *truth*, Alice." She rose, dusting the snow off her legs with misdirected umbrage. "How do I know about the Looking Glass? Well, because I read."

"You already said that before," I snapped.

"Well, I didn't lie. I told you the truth. I read about everything...even though I wasn't supposed to." She exchanged a dark look with the Jabberwock, then glanced up at us. "I worked for the Snow Queen."

"I knew it." I gritted my teeth like a dog. "You..."

Before I could add any expletives, Usagi cut me off. "*Worked*, Alice. Past tense. I was the Royal Keeper of Books."

"The *what?*" said Boushiya.

Usagi's gaze drifted to the right. "It meant I never left the library. Day after day, the Snow Queen made me sort though the books—arrange them, clean them, and select the finest sections of the finest tomes for her to read. She imprisoned me in the library…which, truthfully, I didn't mind."

I folded my arms. "Clearly."

"Books were the only thing that kept me going," Usagi said quietly. "They gave me strength. Without them…I don't even want to think about it."

"Then why leave all those precious books behind?" Bitterness clung to the hatter's every word.

"I was forced to. *You know how she is!*"

I stilled at her outburst. A distraught expression came over her. Her braids whipped her shoulders with erratic movement. Seeing the usually composed Usagi exposed before us, the raw emotions playing on her face, I wondered if we were being too hard on her.

"In all my time at the palace, the Snow Queen gave me two rules," she said shakily. "Adhere to my daily tasks and make sure no one—not even I—entered the West Wing of the library. As long as I followed that, I'd have nothing to fear.

"But one day my curiosity got the better of me." A shadow of guilt surfaced on her face. "I couldn't resist the temptation of reading new books. I waited until nightfall and snuck into the corridor I was supposed to be guarding. When I opened the doors to the wing, I was greeted by the most beautiful books I'd ever seen." Despite her pink eyes, her face radiated with ill-concealed delight. "Sitting on those perfect crystal shelves with their perfect silver spines...the moonlight spilling through the glass dome ceiling, bathing the books in an ethereal glow...and the smell of the pages—"

"Usagi," the hatter groaned.

The rabbit kemonomimi flushed. "I spent the whole night reading until I came across a peculiar tome. One more worn and musty than the others. Of course, I flipped through it. At first, I thought it was some mythical story about the Looking Glass. It stated that, in times of peril, the mirror would restore balance. According to the book, this is a constant cycle that has continued since the dawn of time." Usagi frowned. "I started to ask myself why the Looking Glass hadn't shown up yet—unless of course it *was* a mere myth—but slowly, I realized it was right under my nose."

Her nose twitched as she spoke. I wondered if it was false showmanship or an honest reflex.

"The queen had a mirror," she said quietly. "She'd stare into it everyday, transfixed, sometimes for hours. Even though it looked like an ordinary hand mirror, it was one of her most guarded possessions in the palace... or so I thought."

"What do you mean?"

"I heard a crash one day. Outside the library. I snuck a glimpse through the door's crevice and saw the queen looking the angriest I'd ever seen her. Below her glass heels lay the broken shards of her precious mirror. She ordered the Jabberwocks to get rid of them."

Usagi closed her eyes. "Everything began to click. In my heart, I knew that broken mirror had been the Looking Glass. If the Looking Glass was no longer a myth, then the stories of the Mirror Princess weren't likely to be myths either. Holding onto that hope, I decided to flee that night—with the book." She fidgeted with the hem of her skirt. "In retrospect, I should've come up with a better plan. The Snow Queen discovered the missing book and knew I had snuck into the West Wing. She banished me to the ice dungeons at once, but I gave the guards the slip and escaped before they could imprison me."

"I bet someone tipped her off." Boushiya eyed the immobile Jabberwock with distaste.

"No. Metanoia had nothing to do with it." Usagi swallowed hard. "She was on the run herself. That's how we met."

The hatter lowered his lids. "Usagi, how can you trust a Jabberwock?"

"Metanoia was the one who told me about the shards' whereabouts. Open your eyes!" Usagi pointed to the wriggling Jabberwock. "Do you see those rope marks on her arms? She tied herself to this tree—because she no longer wanted to heed the queen's orders." Metanoia glared at me with small, craggy eyes.

"And why the sudden change of heart?" I demanded.

A shadow crept across the Jabberwock's face. "Queen make Jabberwocks hide shards. Metanoia looked into shard. Shard showed who Metanoia was. What she turned into."

"I still don't trust it," said the hatter. "All Jabberwocks are merely an extension of the Snow Queen."

Usagi's knuckles turned white. "Boushiya, Alice, do you see her wings?"

I squinted. The Jabberwock flailed under the ropes, trying to escape, but as it turned, I could make out no wings.

"A wing-less Jabberwock?" I asked.

A pained look stole over Metanoia.

"She tore them off," Usagi whispered. "To rid herself of that cursed heart symbol—and her ties with the Snow Queen."

I crouched down to the Jabberwock until I was eye-level. As I gazed into her struggling face, my hard demeanor chipped away. "Is that why you tied yourself to this tree? To ensure you never did any harm again?"

She gave me a feeble nod. "Usagi tried to free Metanoia, but Metanoia no let her." Her small, beady eyes went glassy.

The hatter lifted his hand to his hat and made to remove it, before remembering that it was still glued to him. "But why must you imprison yourself if you no longer serve the queen…?"

"It is like top hat say," the creature said. Boushiya frowned at the synecdochical nickname. "We part of Snow Queen. Even with no wings, Metanoia want to do bad, bad things." A droplet trickled down her small face. "This why Metanoia must imprison herself. Even if forever."

As I listened to the miserable creature, an idea crept into my head. It may have been hurtful, but I needed to settle this once and for all.

"Usagi," I whispered. "Show us your mark."

Usagi blinked hard. She opened her mouth as if to protest, but closed it. Slowly, she pulled up her sleeve. The hatter and I stepped back.

Her mark had grown lighter.

I repressed panicked breaths. The hatter and I stared our own marks. They looked three shades darker than hers.

My heart sank. I should have been relieved, but I felt like such a fool. Worse than a fool. I was a bad friend. I shut my eyes tightly.

"Usagi…" My voice shook like the bare branches of Metanoia's tree. "I'm sorry for doubting you."

When I opened my eyes again, I saw my friend's small, sad face grappling with forgiveness. I had to offer something better. Something tangible.

I glanced at the Jabberwock. "Is there some way we can help her?"

Usagi's face softened. For once, I had said the right thing.

"Find shards," the Jabberwock croaked. "Only way to save Metanoia."

"Metanoia hid one of the shards in the Treacherous Lake," said Usagi. "I was just asking her if she remembered *where* when you two interrupted." The hatter and I exchanged guilty glances.

Usagi turned back to the Jabberwock. "Please, try to remember, Metanoia. We want to help you."

"Dropped shard middle of lake. Lodged in ice... somewhere."

Sighing, Usagi rose to her height. "We just searched there, but I suppose we have no other choice but to try again."

The Jabberwock violently shook her head. "No go! Rabbit and friends be swallowed."

"By the water? I don't think the ice was that thin," said Usagi. "It looked thick enough to hold us."

"Take from Tum-Tum tree," she rasped. "Herb to eat."

Usagi followed Metanoia's frantic gaze to a strange looking plant growing around the base of the barren tree.

Boushiya shifted his feet. "If you don't mind, I'd rather stick with my tea, thanks."

"Um, I'll stick with the hatter's frozen tea, too."

"No be foolish. Take herb! *Take!*" My eardrums shuddered against Metanoia's trill.

Usagi stepped toward the Tum-Tum tree. "Boushiya, Alice, help me pull it out."

"Are you serious?" I asked.

"Yes."

"Unbelievable," said the hatter.

I agreed with him, of course, but even if I wasn't one hundred percent on board, we did owe Usagi.

The three of us knelt in the snow. We pulled the plant with all our strength until we heard a snap. I stumbled backward, gazing at the dark, viridian foliage in my hand. A bitter smell emitted from it. "This thing doesn't look edible at all."

Metanoia raised her voice. "All will use?" It was a question, but sounded more like an order.

I took the so-called herb and broke it into three pieces. I gave one to Boushiya and Usagi, leaning in to whisper. "I don't know know about you, but eating a weird plant from a Jabberwock who still wants to 'do bad,

bad things' doesn't strike me as all that appealing." The hatter nodded his agreement. Usagi didn't.

"There, we all have the herb now." I gave the Jabberwock a saccharine smile.

"Now can go," Metanoia said.

Usagi's eyes slanted with determination. "We'll save you, Metanoia. I give you my word."

"Thank you," Metanoia whispered under her breath.

Eager to be out of the creature's presence, I retraced my snowy footsteps. "Let's get going, guys."

The duo followed behind me. After several minutes, we had trekked back to the Treacherous Lake. We inched our way to the middle of the lake and surveyed the dark, frozen depths.

"At least we know it's somewhere in the center now," said Usagi. I could tell she was trying to raise our spirits. Unfortunately, it wasn't working.

"What a relief," I deadpanned. "We only need to search about 3,000 square feet now."

Ignoring my jibe, she frowned at her feet. "If only we had some sort of a light."

I gasped. "A light...Oh my gosh, yes. That's exactly what we need."

"Alice, are you okay?" The hatter glanced at my hand. "You haven't eaten that thing from the Jabberwock, have you?"

"No," I said, grinning. "Usagi just sparked a light bulb idea in me."

I scavenged through the pockets of my skirts. Please be here... Please be here... My fingers glided over a smooth, cold surface. *Voila.*

I whipped out my phone.

Boushiya squinted. "What is that?"

"The answer to our problem." I pressed a button. The inbuilt light shone bright at the duo. "Can I get a watt watt?"

Usagi's face lit up as I handed her the phone. She tilted it down. A beam of light permeated the ice, revealing the rippling currents underneath. We took turns with the light, each of us scoping out a section of the lake.

When Usagi's third turn came, she went rigid. She tossed the phone back to me. "I think I just found it." She pointed near my feet.

"There."

I caught a hint of glitter beneath the blue ice. My heart skipped a beat. Anticipation mounting, I rushed over and stamped my foot on the surface. Thinner than the rest of the lake, it had probably frozen over more recently.

Usagi joined me. After an exhaustive series of stamps, we broke though the frigid waters. I knelt down and plunged my hand into the freezing depths. I groped around until something smooth and jagged pressed against my palm.

My chest stirred with exultation.

The second shard.

"We did it," I singsonged. Grinning, I grabbed the shard. I hadn't even pulled it all the way through when the hatter made a sharp sound.

Usagi spun around and placed a finger over her lips. "Sshh."

"Usagi, I think something's wrong." I fixed my gaze on the hatter. His lips quivered on the precipice of speech. "What is it, Boushiya?"

"M-m-mm. "

"What?" I lifted a brow. The hatter's body shook as if he had succumbed to hysteria, but his eyes stayed rooted in horror.

I did a 360 around the lake but saw nothing. I frowned. Maybe the stress of losing Sangatsu had gotten to him. I hoped the hatter hadn't really gone mad.

"Mm-m…t-there."

I followed his gaze to his feet. My chest rose sharply. A throng of livid faces stared up at me through the thick sheet of ice.

"*Mer.*"

Usagi had barely breathed the word when the floor beneath our feet started cracking. The ice gave way. Jets of water shot up from the fractures.

"Eat it, now!" Usagi stuffed Metanoia's herb into her mouth.

As I bit down on the bitter plant, scaly hands coiled around my ankles like tentacles. I plunged into the lake. The sound of rushing water filled my ears. I screamed from the top of my lungs, but only a line of air bubbles came out. The cold water burned my lungs, but the sensation soon faded. I was…breathing underwater?

Deeper and deeper, the icy fingers dragged me into the dark depths. An unearthly melody rose from below. A song filled with wrath. No, not a song. *Voices.*

I stopped descending. Harsh swish and flicks of tails forced me upright. Merpeople with elfish ears encircled me in every direction. A phantasmagoric version of the little mermaid paused in front of me. A mane of dark, red hair flowed around her, tangling with my own. Her cerulean eyes fixed me a piercing stare. She looked like she had swum straight out of a Tim Burton movie.

"You dare disrupt the Ningyo?" Despite her mellifluous voice, the fury behind her words rolled through the waters.

I shook my head as quickly as I could, my hair swirling around me like ink.

"*Liar.*" The word was half scream, half song. "This territory belongs to us." A chorus of ethereal, incensed murmurs echoed her cry.

My eyes darted to their swaying tails. Eyeing the heart shaped marks on them, I knew I couldn't reason with her. She had been consumed by queen's spell. They all had.

A merman swam to her side. He reinforced her words with a challenging glare. "Trespassers are not welcomed." Raising his aquiline nose, he gestured a silent entreaty to the others.

The merpeople swarmed me. They seized my hands, legs, torso—and pulled. I twisted, I kicked, I thrashed. But I remained anchored in place.

"Please," I screamed. "Stop it!"

The merpeople fought the burbling waters for control over me—until the water eventually won. The fish-like hands slipped away. The lake churned me, tossing and turning me like a rag-doll. Gasping, I floundered in the current, desperately scanning the water's surface. Not a hint of a top hat or rabbit ear.

"Usagi, Boushiya, where are—" A sharp pain seared through me. Something was cutting into my palm. A jagged piece of ice. My grip loosened. Just then, Usagi emerged from the water. Her voice resounded despite the chaos.

"Alice!" She swallowed a mouthful of water. "Whatever you do, don't—" I could hear her distress in between bouts of water. Her voice rose an octave. "Don't let it go!" I forced my hand up to my blurred vision. My fingers tightened around the shard.

"I won't—" The icy waters obliterated my words. A current forced me under again. Every inch of me succumbed to numbness. The air in my lungs seemed to freeze solid. *Shimatta.* The herb's effects were wearing off. Feeling the onset of a panic attack, I tried to steel my mind—but the current's grip on me proved too powerful. The more I tried to fight the waves, the stronger it pulled me under.

I resurfaced again. "Oos—" Gasp. "Sawg—" Sputter. "Ee—" Cough. No reply. My heart hammered. *Where were they?*

Another eddy pulled me down, and I forced my eyes open underwater. The saltwater stung but I kept them open as long as I could, gazing through the bleak waters. At a distance, I spotted them: flanked on each side by an enraged assemblage of merpeople.

Usagi and Boushiya screamed, but the waters veiled their guttural pleas. I struggled to swim toward them. Against the wild, unpredictable current, my limbs felt encumbered, like they were attached to weights. The icy water burned my lungs, and the herb's effects grew weaker.

As I propelled myself to the surface with the last bit of energy I had, I made out a hazy figure swimming toward the fray. The silhouette didn't belong to a Ningyo. Or did it? I squinted.

A *boy*—?

A leviathan of a wave crashed into me, slamming me against a mass of dark ice. Usagi's distant cries faded. The shard slipped from my fingers. Everything swirled around me, then blurred.

I drifted into oblivion as the lake's inky nothingness swallowed me whole.

CHAPTER 5

The Garden of the Chrysali

Deeper and deeper I fell. My hair tangled around me like tendrils of black seaweed. Somewhere in my subconscious, I felt a band of steel encircle my waist. It lugged and hoisted me to the surface. I gasped. A burst of salt-laden air invaded my lungs—icy, clean, and fresh.

I sagged sideways, the energy drained from me. Long, slender fingers caught me. My hands grasped a fistful of fabric. I coughed and sputtered as my rescuer wrenched off my ice-sodden outerwear. Cold air bit through my shirt.

For a second, I considered ridding myself of that as well, but the effects of the herb were still warming me enough that I didn't need to strip completely. My frosty, damp shirt clung to my shivering body, but it did not freeze me. Since I wasn't about to die from hypothermia,

I figured it was a decent tradeoff: the discomfort of a cold, wet shirt for salvaged pride.

Something large enveloped my body, and glorious heat seeped through me. I struggled to open my eyes. Through my bleary vision, a concerned face peered down at me, framed by sopping flaxen hair.

"Andrew…"

As soon as the whisper left my mouth, a pair of elfish ears came into focus. My breath caught. I recognized my rescuer not as Andrew, but as someone else equally attractive and familiar. *Akihiko the Winter Prince.*

He hovered above me, his shoulders rising and falling. "Are you okay?"

"Y-yes."

"Good." He finished wrapping his cloak around me while holding my gaze. I dug my nails into the warm cloak as he rose to his full height. His drenched clothes clung to his frame, revealing his eye candy swimmer's build: broad shoulders, lean torso, and…really toned legs.

My cheeks warmed at the way the wet fabric hugged his glutes to perfection. Rebuking my inner fangirl, I forced my gaze up. The Winter Prince rested his hand on the sheath of the Vorpal sword, striking the same pose as the poster in my room. I bit my lip. God, he looked hotter than a Bunsen burner.

Akihiko glared at the Ningyo. "Cease your attack. Need I remind you, this territory is *mine*." His fury echoed across the inky lake. At once, everything went still. In the sudden silence I overheard his mumbled disclaimer. "Or was mine until the Snow Queen took over..."

The Ningyo released Boushiya and Usagi. Despite their biting stares and sulky faces, the creatures forced a bow to the prince. Akihiko held his ground and stood tall. Whatever the technical details of the political climate, he still held some influence over the Ningyo. I didn't know too much about Akihiko's background, but from his elfish ears, it was my headcanon that the prince carried royal Ningyo blood in his veins.

"Go now," he ordered.

The Ningyo plunged into the dark depths, splashing us with icy water.

Good riddance.

The Winter Prince turned to me. He pulled me to my feet and handed me my drenched sweatshirt. "I'm sorry about that..." His eyes dropped to the words on the front, "Fangirl?"

"What?" I blurted. *Oh.* I quickly tucked the garment under my arm, concealing my embarrassing secret. No way was I letting him see that ever again.

"No. It's Alice. Just Alice." My voice came out strained and breathy, but this had little to do with the renewed bouts of oxygen.

The Winter Prince shook his head. "The Ningyo have grown volatile since the Snow Queen froze their dwelling. It may be hard to believe, but they were once the tamest creatures in our world."

"They've fallen to the darkness in their hearts," Usagi said quietly.

A pained look stole over Akihiko. "Allow me to escort you."

The prince treaded lightly across the ice floes, leading us to land. Usagi and Boushiya followed close behind his heels. Akihiko kept his spine straight, his chin slightly lifted, shoulders poised. He looked every inch the fairy tale prince.

"Alice, pay attention," came a sharp voice.

"Sorry," I whispered back, picking up my pace so that Usagi wouldn't step on my heel again.

Boushiya, Usagi, and Akihiko managed the tenuous path, but halfway across, my clunking steps broke through a patch of ice. I yelped, shifting my weight onto my other foot to regain my balance. It didn't quite work out.

"Watch out!" I slipped into Akihiko's tall, sturdy form, my glasses sliding off. Usagi and the hatter gasped behind me. The prince spun around and caught me by the waist before anything could come of my blunder.

"Such heavy footsteps for someone so small." He placed the glasses on the side of my ears. My vision swam back into focus. Arresting sea green eyes ensnared my own. This close, I could see Akihiko's long, thick lashes and faint freckles across his nose. It took all my restraint to suppress fangirl noises. The body pillow of him I had at home paled in comparison.

I tore my gaze from his parted lips. "Th-thank you."

"You're most welcome."

Focusing on my feet, I shambled off the lake. We wandered into a patch of woodlands, the wind blowing snow-dust into our eyes. Chilled to our core, clothes dripping in icy water, we were miserable until we finally found a clandestine ice cave.

Usagi squeezed the water from her satchel. The hatter eyed a group of small, wooden mugs in her belongings.

"S-some tea now would be marvelous." His teeth chattered.

"I'd offer you some if conditions were different." Akihiko seated himself beside me. He dried the water off of his prized Vorpal sword. Slowly, he ran a piece of steel wool over the length of his blade and back. I chewed my lip.

Someone's been reading too many plot-without-plot fanfics.

"Shut up," I hissed to my inner fangirl.

Akihiko's hand stopped moving. He looked at me like I had an extra head growing from my neck.

Heat swiped my face. "I, um, can light a fire. For tea."

"You can?"

"With that." I pointed to the steel wool resting on his sword. "May I?"

"Of course."

Fingers quivering, I took the material. With my free hand, I rummaged through my pocket. Spare change, Jiji keychain, a crumpled envelope, and...*yes.* I fished out my cell phone. Carefully, I removed the battery and rubbed the steel wool on the end of it.

"I learned this in Physics class. You touch this part to a positive and negative contact point to create a charge and then—" I yelped. The steel wool began to smolder. I hastily dropped it onto a pile of twigs. In seconds we had a campfire. Its flames blazed and flickered orange and bright.

Hallelujah, science.

Usagi and Boushiya went open-mouthed. Akihiko gazed at me, an inexplicable look in his eyes. After a long moment, the side of his mouth curved.

"That was brilliant...Alice."

I shivered at the way my name rolled off his tongue. Not to mention, that was the first time a non-internet boy had complimented me. As much as I was fangirling inside, I could only reciprocate a brief, tiny smile. If only he knew about my inner fangirl's musings a moment ago. I suppressed a cringe.

Usagi placed her wet satchel near our makeshift campfire. She sat close to the flames, holding out her hands for warmth. Boushiya hung his tailcoat by a branch. He also hung his hat, which the water had somehow unglued from his head. I draped my sweatshirt over a smaller bough. Arms stretched, Akihiko tugged off his drenched outerwear.

Unlike the rest of us, he wore nothing underneath his robe. Just a bare chest beaded with cold water. I tried to stare at the campfire but secretly peeked at the V-shape half hidden by his breeches. I couldn't remember the last time I blushed this hard. He looked just like every fanfiction described him. Lithe and sculpted and all kinds of glorious. Unbidden, a shirtless image of Andrew at swim practice snuck into my mind.

Don't. Be. A. Freak, my inner fangirl chided.

Look who's talking, I shot back.

Concentrating on baby penguins instead, I played with a lock of hair and watched steam waft off our drenched clothes. Boushiya brewed an earthy, fragrant tea, and Usagi poured it out into her mugs. I snuggled up inside the prince's cloak like a cocoon and stared at the flickering flames. After that disaster of a mission, this small respite was much welcomed.

Akihiko passed the tea around our little circle. When he handed me my cup, our fingers brushed.

"Sorry," we said in unison.

Flustered, I fumbled with the earthenware.

If only I could copy and paste fictional boys into real life, I thought—for the millionth time that month.

I lifted my teacup and sipped the tea. Heat trickled through my body, and the rich, fragrant liquid made my taste buds dance. Mm. Better than butterbeer. A deep sigh escaped me as I lowered the cup. For the first time since arriving in this AU, my mind felt at ease.

I wished I could've said the same for the hatter. Not even the warmth of the tea cured him of his doldrums. Eyes vacant, chin sunk to his chest, he stared into his teacup. My gaze drifted to his other hand, the only part of him that showed emotion. His fingers cradled a crushed green carnation.

"Sangatsu would have loved this," he whispered to himself.

Before I could say anything to alleviate his melancholy, Akihiko rose. "Now that we're settled, perhaps one of you would care to explain what foolish thought made you venture into the Ningyo's dwelling?"

I turned but found myself unable to look at him. My eyes dropped to my teacup instead. "We're searching for the Looking Glass."

"The mirror that belongs to the princess?"

"You've heard about it?" asked Usagi.

"Only from rumors. I always thought it was a mere myth." His eyes narrowed. "It likely is."

"It's not a myth." Usagi balled her fist up, her ears going straight. "Trust me, the Looking Glass is real."

The hatter nodded in agreement. "Usagi has seen it for herself."

Usagi's face softened. I knew it must have meant a lot to her to hear the hatter confirm his trust. The prince pursed his lips.

"But how—"

"That hardly matters now," said Usagi. "We need to find the remaining shards of the Looking Glass if we want to imprison the queen once and for all."

"We already found..." I couldn't complete the sentence. Oh. My. God. My knees trembled as I realized my folly.

"Two shards," Usagi finished. She raised an eyebrow at me.

"Is that so?" asked Akihiko in a crisp, controlled manner. "In that case, I beg your pardon. Most admirable of you to embark on such a valiant quest." As if caught up in his own spell, he lifted his chin. "Most bold to venture where others retreat. Most..."

His gaze settled on us, his eyes gleaming like gold. "Truth be told, I have been wanting to break this cursed spell for some time now, but no one—not even the fierce Ningyo I rule—will assist me. Perhaps, that can change now..." He searched our faces as if studying us for signs of competency. When his gaze focused on me, I blanched.

"I-I lost it," I burst out. "I dropped the shard."

"You what?" Usagi cried.

"I couldn't help it! Everything was pure chaos, and I blacked out."

Bet she wished she hadn't recruited me onto her team now. Boushiya's face went stark white. I couldn't look at him. At any of them.

Numbness spread over me. I dropped my head into my shaking hands. We had so much riding on this...so many people depending on us. I had let all of them down. And *home*...How would I even return home now?

"I've failed everyone." A cold droplet trickled down my face, but a warm finger wiped it away.

"You didn't," Akihiko whispered.

I blinked at him, hiccuping a tear.

The prince reached into the pocket of his breeches and brandished an opalescent glimmer of light. All reason fled me. I threw my arms around Akihiko's bare shoulders. When his hand touched the small of my back, I jerked away.

"This is it then, I take it?" he asked.

"It is." Usagi heaved a deep sigh, relief flooding her features. She took the shard from the prince and pulled the other one from her satchel. She fit them together like puzzle pieces.

"How many more shards do you need to find?" asked Akihiko.

"Only two more." Usagi fixed him a small smile. "From the garden and the labyrinth. Then we just have to find the princess, and our world will be free from this terrible spell." Her gaze went to each of us. "The Ningyo will return to how they used to be, and Alice, you can return home."

"Aren't you forgetting something?" The hatter flashed Usagi a biting glare. He stopped trailing his finger in the snow. An incomplete 'S' was etched in the glittery ground.

"Boushiya, I didn't mean... Of course we'll go back for Sangatsu."

"Sangatsu?" Akihiko asked.

"The queen took him," I explained. "As prisoner. We escaped the ice palace with the shard when she captured him." My voice grew tight. The memory of Sangatsu flickered before me. His stricken face, his eyes desperately fixed on the hatter. So many feels shot through me.

Although they had only known me for short time, I felt a kinship toward everyone here. Their feelings were becoming my own. Their pain, their triumph, their hopes. My characters had always been a source of refuge whenever I read about them. Now, I wanted to be the same for them.

"You need not go on." Akihiko briefly rested a hand atop mine. "You've lost a friend in this fight—though not for good, I promise." He studied our faces again. "You seem truly committed to ending her reign."

"We are." As the prince considered Usagi's firm response, I jumped in.

"Wait, what did you mean, you 'promise'?"

"By promising I'd help save your friend, Sangatsu," said the prince. "I meant I intend to join yo—"

"Omigosh. Yes. Please. Yes." My words tripped out a little too fast. Everyone stared at me. Especially Akihiko.

My cheeks went hot. I quickly composed myself, suppressing my inner fangirl. She couldn't show up now.

Conceal, don't feel.

I took a deep breath and made my voice considerably less enthusiastic. "I mean, we need all the help we can get right now."

A shadow of a smile touched Akihiko's lips.

God, if only he knew what that look did to my inner fangirl. I was pretty sure she had just melted into a puddle of mush. At least that would keep her out of sight for a while.

"Well, we're not going to save Sangatsu by sitting here. Let's get back to it, shall we?" With a burst of zeal, Usagi unrolled the map and jumped into her planning mode. "Extinguish the fire and cover our tracks. I'll need to figure out a shortcut to make up for the lost time."

We followed her instructions to the letter. As we changed into our outerwear, only slightly damp now, the hatter exchanged a feeble grin with me. His gaze shifted to Usagi. Eyes glistening, her face screwed in concentration, she poured over the map. Our path might be filled with hidden dangers and uncertainty, but she was predictable as a Fibonacci sequence. Usagi would always find a way for us. I took comfort in that.

Once she had figured out the quickest path, we headed into the snowy woods again. As we trailed her, I gave Akihiko a guilty glance. His jaw clenched against a draft blowing headfirst.

"Um… here." I started to take off his cloak, cringing at the thought of showcasing my embarrassing sweatshirt again. Fortunately, he stopped me. I thanked my lucky stars.

"You can keep it for now." His eyes traveled from my head to my toes. "It fits you rather well."

A sudden awareness singed down my spine. I knew he was teasing my small frame, but for the first time in forever, I didn't mind being a 'chibi.'

Akihiko resumed his pace, his strides poised as he braved the cold. I couldn't tear my eyes away from him. I fixated on the flaxen lock which blew against his forehead. I couldn't understand how something so small could be so distracting.

Slowly, my inner fangirl crept out of hiding. *The boy may as well be a library book; you can't stop checking him out.*

"Stop it," I whispered.

She rubbed a finger across her chin, her smug smile broadening. *Bet you'd even let him fold your pages.*

"I said *stop it.*"

"What?" came a voice.

I snapped out of my thoughts, only to find Akihiko staring at me. Oddly. My mind raced, trying to salvage the situation.

A shout sounded nearby. To my relief, Akihiko's attention pivoted to the hatter who was pointing at his feet. This time, however, nothing so ominous as the Ningyo appeared. Beneath our feet, grains of snow glistened like a fine powder of diamonds.

"The Chrysalis Garden," Usagi said darkly.

Ice-kissed flowers towered ten feet above our heads. Snow-coated tiger lilies, frostbitten roses, shivering daisies, icicled larkspurs, and powdered clusters of violets trembled in the wind. From the tops of the flowers hung silver cocoons.

"The chrysalises live in cocoons?" I asked.

"Chrysali," corrected Usagi. "And their marks are strong. Maybe even stronger than the Ningyo's."

I stared at the heart markings on the massive cocoons. Now that she mentioned it, the hearts did look a lot darker than the ones on the mer's tails. I swallowed hard.

A sniffle brushed the air.

"We'll go back for him, really." I lent the hatter a comforting hand. "I'm sure Sangatsu's holding up."

"It's not that…right now. It's just, well, I'm rather sensitive to flowers." He rubbed a finger under his nose.

"For goodness sake." Usagi apologized to the prince, ripped a piece of his cloak off my arm, and secured it over Boushiya's nose and mouth. "The Chrysali may be beautiful, but if woken during hibernation, they can be deadly." Usagi glared at Boushiya. "Whatever we do, we cannot wake them from their slumber."

"Perhaps I should go around the garden...?" Boushiya's voice came muffled under his makeshift respirator. "I can meet you on the other side."

"The garden's too big," said Usagi. "We don't have that kind of time. The rest of us could probably find *two* shards by the time you rejoined us. Either stay behind or keep it together."

Boushiya's face reddened at her chilly tone. I knew he was thinking about Sangatsu. Finally, he hung his head.

Usagi sighed. "Just pinch your nose if it gets bad."

Boushiya feebly nodded. He and I exchanged anxious glances, hardly daring to breathe. If only the accio spell worked in this AU, we could've collected all the shards by now.

We inched our way through the silent garden, searching the petals for a glimpse of the shard. I passed by each sleeping pod with careful, light steps, my eyes alert for any hint of glimmer. Though Usagi and Akihiko, with their River-like grace and hobbit-like steps, had little trouble walking in silence, Boushiya and I had a harder time with the task. He kept sniffling while I kept half-tripping and clunking more than my petite frame should have permitted. A hand tightened on my shoulder.

I froze.

"Just preventing potential blunders." A warm breath buffeted my ear.

My heart thudded. Akihiko was close. So close that if I hadn't walked in front of him, no doubt, he'd see my glasses start to fog. Ignoring the fluttering sensation in my stomach, I concentrated on my footsteps. The simple task proved more difficult with every second that passed by. But not because of the slippery ice.

Akihiko's hand continued to steady me. Warmth radiated against my goose-pimpled skin. His long, slender fingers lingered along the base of my neck, and for an instant, part of me wished he would just leave them.

"There."

Usagi's voice jolted me out of my less-than-innocent thoughts. She pointed to the top of a towering larkspur.

A shard. And next to it: the largest cocoon of them all.

Lovely.

"How exactly do we get it?" Exasperation filled my whisper. "I take it you don't have a ladder in that satchel of yours, Usagi."

"Well, no. But maybe we could make a ladder."

The prince rubbed a finger below his lip, a gesture I found more distracting than I should have. "The only way it is to haul one of us up to it. The lightest one, preferably."

"Not preferably—definitely." Usagi crinkled her nose. "I can't hold the hatter on my shoulders."

"Then ..."

"The Chibi," Boushiya whispered.

I stared at his red, watery eyes, then turned. Everyone's gazes had landed on me.

Oh, heck no.

"Hang on," I stammered. "I don't think that's such a good—"

"I won't let you fall."

Akihiko focused on me with dark, intent eyes. I don't know how he did it, but being near him gave my electrons a positive charge. I inhaled a long breath.

"Fine. I'll do it."

Mustering my courage, I raised my arms and gestured a reluctant affirmative. With a huffy heave, the trio lifted me to the top of the larkspur.

"Careful," Usagi whispered.

"*I'm trying.*" Feeling like a circus performer on a tight rope, I raised my hand higher. A whole foot remained between my fingers and the shard. "I still can't reach it."

"Use this." Akihiko lifted his Vorpal sword to me.

Taking it, I raised my arm up once more. The tip of the sword brushed against the shard. Just a bit more... Like an arcade crane, my hand carefully moved an inch.

Closer...Closer ...

"Got it—" I gasped.

The slight shift made me loose my bearings. The sword knocked the shard to the snowy ground. Stifling a shout, I grabbed a large petal to regain my balance. My legs swayed left, right, then crashed into each other. The cocoon started to shake.

My pulse raced as if I had downed an extra large Starbucks doubleshot. The cocoon rattled, and a whirring hum came from within. The petal dipped. My body swung up and down and all around town.

Magnificent idea. Pick the most disaster-prone member of our squad for this task.

The Winter Prince caught one of my flailing legs, and I released the petal. The silver cocoon's shudders slowed to a stop as I plummeted below. The trio caught me like cheer squad.

Usagi held a hand to her chest. "That was close. Too close."

"You think?" I breathed hard, handing the sword back to Akihiko.

"At least we have the third shard now, Chibi."

The hatter bent down and retrieved the fallen shard, then handed it to me. My hand curled around the cold, jagged object.

Better watch yourself, Snow Queen.

Usagi gave us a tight smile and led us forward. My paranoia dwindled away, and a surge of optimism replaced it. I took light, confident strides past the sleeping Chrysali's pods. When the far end of the garden glittered into sight, a wave of relief washed over me. But that moment was short-lived.

"AAAAAaaaaaaaahhhhhhhhchoo!"

The hatter erupted into a paroxysm of sneezing. I watched in horror as the cloth around his nose and mouth fluttered to the snowy ground. Boushiya clamped his hands over his mouth, but that hardly quelled his fit. He sneezed again. And again. And again.

A violent whirring filled our ears. The cocoons shook with force. A slew of cracking sounds echoed from every direction. I felt all the color leave my face. Now, we'd done it.

We had woken the Chrysali. All of them.

I gripped Akihiko's arm for dear life. One by one the buxom creatures shot out of their silvery husks until a maelstrom of transparent wings swooped over us. The Chrysali glistened, looking like animated ice sculptures. They varied in over fifty shades of blue, with no two Chrysali sharing a hue.

Ethereal, lucent veils covered their heads. Their skin seemed to merge with their scanty robes. When my gaze lowered, my face grew warm. Thin gossamer robes clung

to their alluring forms and draped around their hips in a
V-shape, leaving little to the imagination. Between their
sensual beauty and cruel, vengeful faces, they exuded a
femme fatale aura stronger than a Veela's.

The Chrysali swarmed in a circle above our heads.
Their looming shadows fell upon us and engulfed our
own. The largest and most beautiful Chrysalis, from
whose larkspur I had climbed, plunged down. She had
spotted it—the shard in my grasp.

"Alice, run!"

Adrenaline pumping through me, I dove out of the
butterfly monster's way. A sharp gasp escaped me.

"Alice!"

I grunted. A spasm of pain shot through my calf
muscle. I had twisted my leg, but—I double-checked—
my hand still clutched the shard. This time, I wouldn't
let it of my sight.

The leader of the Chrysali screeched and dove again
like a harpy. The sudden movement broke a cluster of
icicles hanging from a larkspur. I yelped, dodging them
as they shattered around me. Eyes smoldering behind
her veil, the Chrysalis curved her lips. Akihiko grabbed
his Vorpal sword by the hilt.

"Hide," he whispered. "I'll distract her."

"But—"

"She wants *you*. You have the shard."

Shimatta. I knew he was right.

Ignoring the shooting pain in my leg, I threw myself into a patch of iced shrubbery and constructed a protective snow barrier to conceal myself.

"Why—not—try—me." Akihiko's glare pierced the Chrysalis' narrowed eyes as he swung his sword in the air. "Back—off." His punctuated grunts grew muffled.

I grit my teeth. I hated that I couldn't help him, but what could I do? With a sprained ankle and the sought treasure in tow, anything I contributed to the fight would only put everyone in greater peril.

My gaze flicked to Usagi and Boushiya. Two Chrysali swooped down to attack the hatter while a wild Chrysalis sprang in front of Usagi. They were barely holding their own. My eyes widened as Akihiko dodged a Chrysalis's razor-sharp nails by millimeters. The Vorpal sword flew out of his hand. The creature curled her sultry lips as she glided toward him.

A tidal wave of helplessness threatened to submerge me. No. *No.* It couldn't end like this. There had to be *something* I could do.

I took in the flurry of the fight. A Chrysalis dove at Usagi, maneuvering her wings behind her back at an odd angle. The Chrysalis assailing Akihiko and Boushiya did the same thing as they attacked. It was almost as if…

"Protip," I whispered.

My hands plunged into the ground. I scooped up two massive fistfuls of snow and packed them tightly. Mustering all my strength, I hurled the snowballs at the nearest Chrysalis. One hit her smack in the wings, sundering their intricate, delicate weave. The Chrysalis twisted in the air, then crashed in a heap of snow.

"Guys—snowballs—aim for the wings," I shouted. "It's their point of weakness."

Usagi, Boushiya, and Akihiko jerked their heads and saw my second snowball careen at an attacking Chrysalis' wings. The projectile broke through them. The Chrysalis lurched and crashed into Boushiya's Zaffre-blue attacker, knocking her out of the way.

"Hurry up! Throw as much as you can." Despite my breathlessness, I projected my voice with authority. "It's our only chance!" I hurled more snowballs, missing the largest Chrysalis by mere inches.

Usagi and Akihiko ducked out of their attackers' paths. They gathered as many snowballs as their arms could carry. Then, they launched them. Boushiya pushed himself off the snowy ground and brandished silverware from his tailcoat. Deftly, he hurled a dozen forks and knives at the wings of the femme fatales. One by one, their beautiful forms fell around us.

We were totally slaying.

The remaining Chrysali retreated. But, the largest one swooped over us, still energetic and strong. With a deafening screech, she dove again and again at Akihiko. The prince narrowly missed her clawed fingers. He grabbed one of the fallen icicles and threw it at her. Using the last fork in his possession, Boushiya joined in. They managed to make a hit, but the small tears in her wings did little to affect her balance.

"It's not working on her." Usagi looked around in panic as she threw futile snowballs at the descending beast. "We need something bigger."

"Leave it to me!" I grabbed the fallen Vorpal sword buried in the snow, then darted in front of Akihiko. I pushed him out of the way, saving him from another strike. The Chrysalis's claw-like nails slashed a hole in my cloak. I swore under my breath.

"Alice!"

Contorting my twisted leg, I flung my body into a full-throttle throw. The sword spiraled out of my hand, whistling through the air as it flew. With a satisfying rip, it slashed through the Chrysalis's wings, disfiguring her perfect form. She crashed to the ground and remained motionless.

Panting, I stared at my hands, hardly believing my own strength.

"Chibi!" Boushiya quirked his brow, impressed.

"That was incredible, Alice." Usagi threw her arms around me in a colossal hug.

Akihiko didn't say anything. He looked at me the way Dee looks at old books. Slowly, his gaze drifted to my ankle. "May I?"

I gave an unsteady nod. He drew me close and slid his arms under my wobbly knees. Nestled against his chest, I clung to his wonderful warmth while hiding my flustered face.

I couldn't recall the last time I had fangirled so hard.

CHAPTER 6

Stargazers

The cold night soon fell upon us. Unable to journey in the darkness, we set up camp to regain our strength. I settled onto a pile of snow, resting my sprained ankle.

"Not here, not here. Oh, where is it?" Usagi sat cross-legged, rummaging through her belongings. A small, worn book peeked out from inside the satchel.

"Are you looking for that?" I asked.

"No," she said at once. She stuffed the worn book deep into her rucksack until it went out of sight.

I raised a brow. "What is tha —"

"Here, it is." She retrieved a different book, thicker this time, that looked like a 101 guide on how to survive in the wilderness. "Red and sweet are good to eat, but take heed from this sonnet: green will make you vomit." She closed the book with a flourish and separated the green berries from the red ones she had gathered.

Behind her, Boushiya architected a makeshift tent in between sourpuss glances at Akihiko.

"Truly, Usagi, I think the more experienced tea aficionado ought to prepare the tea. Instead of some fish boy…"

"*Boushiya.*"

The hatter folded his arms, giving Usagi the cold shoulder. His irritability had increased tenfold since we arrived here.

Usagi sighed and cast an apologetic glance at the Winter Prince. "Sorry. He has a bad case of saudade."

"Saudade?" Akihiko asked.

She lowered her voice. "A nostalgic longing to reunite with someone distant…or lost."

"He is not."

Boushiya whirled around, jaw clenched. He placed a hand over his chest, his thumb grazing his green carnation. "Sangatsu is not lost. He is with me. *Always.*"

"That may be." Akihiko passed Boushiya a steaming mug. "Nevertheless, a cup of tea can bring much comfort in trying times. Why not see for yourself?"

Reluctantly, Boushiya stepped away from the tent and took a small sip. A shade of wistfulness clouded his features. He closed his eyes and sighed a white mist as though reminiscing on some distant memory. I could only imagine which.

I wrapped the torn cloak tighter around myself and reclined against a snowy laurel tree. We all needed this R-and-R, especially Boushiya.

"The darkest nights bring out the brightest stars."

I jerked to my side. Akihiko caught my eyes, then directed his gaze above. I followed his line of vision. Curtains of black clouds rolled aside to unveil a cluster of stars.

"Don't you think the way they flicker is beautiful?" he mused.

"Actually, stars don't flicker," I said, pushing my glasses up. "They *scintillate*." Usagi flashed me a look of approval.

Waving my hands, I launched into an animated explanation. "Stars just look like they flicker because their light is refracted anytime it hits a pocket of cold or hot air in the atmosphere and then ..."

Akihiko tilted his head, sea green eyes glowing with humor. "And then?"

My cheeks grew warm. Great. I was doing that nerd thing again. Changing the subject, I smoothed my hair and pointed to the most scintillating star. "Er, does that one have a name?"

"That's the constellation of Cygnus—the snow goose." Usagi passed around the red berries, sat next to me, and stared above. "Don't the skies look especially *stelliferous* tonight?" She paused when no one answered. "That means filled with star—"

"We don't care what the blast it means, Usagi."

She flinched at the hatter's icy whisper. I chewed my lip. In all the manga I had read and anime I watched, Boushiya *never* acted like this. He was the character who provided comedic relief and fanservice. I never considered he had a somber side to him. Bit by bit, his mask was chipping away, revealing what had been simmering under the surface.

Usagi fidgeted with her braids. "Words to me are like what a cup of tea is to you. They distract me."

The hatter looked away. Tentatively, Usagi reached for his hand. "Look up, Boushiya. Both of you are under the same starry sky, bound by the Red Thread of Fate."

"That what?" I asked.

"It's a magical red thread," said Usagi, "which bounds two people together. The thread may stretch and tangle, but never break."

A resigned sigh escaped the hatter. "I hope you're right."

"At times like this, we need to throw our cares to the stars." Akihiko stared at the star-studded skies. "Ever you wished upon a star?"

"No." The hatter's face seemed to deflate. "Before our world became a winter land, I never had a reason to. I had everything I ever needed."

Usagi's gaze wandered to the constellation of Cygnus and fixated on the brightest star. "I wish Winterland will return to what it used to be."

My voice grew tight. "I wish for a way back home."

"I wish for …" The hatter's fingers tightened around a red berry, squeezing the liquid out. A strong, sweet scent perfumed the air. Glassy-eyed, Boushiya touched his carnation.

Tactfully, Usagi shifted to the Winter Prince. "And you, Akihiko?"

"I'd rather not say. Such is the rule of wishing upon a star, is it not?" His sea green eyes swept over us, lingering on me for a few extra seconds. My fingers curled in my lap. I held my breath—a move I knew would dissipate my blush. I never thought a detail from a young adult romance novel would ever prove so handy.

Self-conscious, I snapped my head away from him like a turtle retreating into its shell. I fumbled with my berry. Whatever hint of expression on Akihiko's face faded. Wordlessly, he bit into the fruit. He didn't look in my direction for the rest of the night.

After our pitiable dinner of forest mushrooms and scavenged leeks, each of us slumped on a patch of white heather, staring at the flickering campfire. When we finally retired for the night, I gazed at the night skies from the flap of our tent. I reached for the crinkled envelope in my pocket and held it against the starry backdrop. The silvery initials, A.L., gleamed at me. A bittersweet feeling washed over me. If my wish came true, I'd soon be going back to my own world. Back to being the geek girl extraordinaire. Back to being the social outcast excluded from parties.

Back to being the…weaboo.

So I made another wish. One which had nothing to do with Winterland. A wish big enough I had to wish on every star in sight. If the cosmos listened, I'd be the happiest fangirl at Charles Dodgson High. A spark of hope filled me as my eyes drifted close.

When the maelstrom lifted, Artemis snapped open her eyes. Her heart raced. Everything in the young cadet's sight was encased in a thick shell of ice. The rows of trees, the abandoned cars in the parking lot, the frosted monkey bars she had once loved to play on. The small girl gazed at the dark, leaden skies.

Only they could have done this.

The Ice Dancers.

Artemis backed up against another girl.

"I can feel you shaking," her comrade whispered.

"I'm just cold."

"We'll be fine. Promise." Cadet Venus extended her pinky to her fellow cadet warrior. Artemis curled her own pinky around it and cracked a smile.

The two girls resumed their posts. They stood tall, every inch alert as they waited. The wind howled in their ears. A line of holly trees rustled in the distance. Like a flicker of a candle, a shadow darted past one of the trees.

Venus narrowed her eyes and whispered, "They're here."

Her words chilled the young Moon Warrior's blood. Artemis watched her determined comrade plant both feet firmly on the ground.

"Come out. We know you're there."

An Ice Dancer jumped out from the snowy branches. With her long and sinewy legs, she performed an elegant twirl. It was as if a beautiful ice sculpture had come to life. Spellbound, the cadets watched the Ice Dancer's bewitching performance. When she finally stopped, she stared at the two girls. Her eyes pierced through them, like a snowstorm waiting to be unleashed. Artemis watched in horror as the creature took a deep breath. Her icy lips curved and opened wide. No...not that.

A blast of flurries and ice jetted from the creature's mouth.

Artemis scrambled out of the way. "Watch out! Venus!"

Venus ducked, blonde curls spilling over her face. Deftly, she maneuvered her fingers. A stream of glowing hearts emitted from her forefinger. The creature tried to evade it, but the glowing chain wrapped around her. It coiled tighter, constricting her more and more. The Ice Dancer writhed, then grew still. Everything went quiet.

Heaving a sigh of relief, Venus made a victory sign. "I told you we'd be fin—"

The Ice Dancer broke out of the restraint with vengeance. She inhaled the biggest breath of air she could.

"No! Venus!" came a scream.

A powerful wintry gust sent the small girl flying against a snowy tree. Daggers of icicles pinned her outline. The Ice Dancer's eyes glinted as she glided forward.

Venus snapped her head up. Her cherub cheeks were strained with effort. "Help me. Hurry…"

Hurry… Artemis needed to hurry. Only she could save Cadet Venus now. Only I could save her.

I had to hurry…

"Hurry up."

A cold draft whistled in my ear. I stirred and groaned. A *dream?* Dim morning light filtered through the snow-clad birch trees, spilling upon the figure in front of me.

"Hurry, Alice!"

My bleary vision made out a twitching nose. "Oo-sawgi?"

Usagi crossed a finger over her mouth and shushed me. It was far too early to deal with her drill sergeant mode. Annoyed with her — and with my subconscious — I made a face. I hadn't had that awful dream since I was ten.

"Get up," she snapped. "Akihiko thinks he spotted a Jabberwock."

I sat up with a start, rubbing the sleep from my eyes. "You can't be serious."

Usagi steeled her face. "Wish I wasn't. We couldn't find it again, but it's best to err on the side of caution. If the queen sent her Jabberwocks to track us, we need to leave. *Now*."

I shook my drowsiness away. Hovering over me, Akihiko took down the tent. Dark circles framed his eyes. It looked like he hadn't slept well last night.

He helped Boushiya clear the rest of the space, ridding all remnants of tea and berries and anything else that could have revealed our presence. I rose to help them, but a sharp sensation lanced through my foot. I stifled a cry.

Usagi jerked her head. "What's wrong?"

"It's my foot." I tried to take a step but plunked onto the snowy ground.

"Let me see." Concern etched across his face, Akihiko kneeled and gently tugged off my sneaker. He trailed a finger over my instep. A shiver ran through me. It was a mere whisper of a touch, yet my muscles tensed.

"That'll be problematic." His gaze focused on a patch of skin at the ball of my sprained foot which had turned an ugly shade of purple. Well, that looked attractive.

"I suppose I'll have to carry both our weight." Akihiko's dark eyes found mine.

I had always considered the twisted ankle trope cliché in romance books, but his voice sounded so melodic, and he smelled like a wonderful sea breeze... A fangirl like me really couldn't complain.

Fidgeting with a lock of hair, I managed an unsteady nod. Akihiko attempted to slide my sneaker back on, cupping the ball of my foot. When his fingers grazed the arch of it, I flinched and retracted my foot. Akihiko stared at me, his face unreadable.

"It's fine," I said shakily. "I'll do it mysel—"

"*Jabberwocks.*"

Boushiya's whisper made my blood freeze. Through the white mist, I made out a dozen tiny figures floating in the far distance, the hearts on their wings prominent as ever.

How did they find us here?

"Hide!"

Boushiya gestured to a large, thick bush. We ducked behind it and watched the creatures near closer and closer. So wild was my heartbeat that my inner fangirl hardly registered I sat sandwiched between the hatter and Winter Prince. Hands clammy, pulse speeding, I watched in horror as the vile little creatures began to inspect a line of holly bushes. They took their time, scrutinizing each bush. A shiver crawled down my spine. They *knew* we were here.

"They're going to find us," I whispered in terror.

"Not if I can help it." Careful not to rustle the bush, Usagi yanked a cluster of green berries from it and smashed them in her hands. "Hold your breaths."

A ghastly smell spread through the bush. I slapped a hand over my nose, trying not to inhale it.

"How is this helping?" I hissed through clenched teeth.

Usagi didn't reply. She fixed her attention on the Jabberwocks. Her eyes gleamed in that way they did whenever she had a stroke of brilliance. I held my breath. The second the Jabberwocks turned their heads away from us, she hurled the squished berries to her far right.

The Jabberwocks snapped their heads up. Like a horde of angry bees, they swarmed around the fallen objects. I could still smell the pungent odor from our hiding place, but the berries were no longer close enough to affect us. I couldn't say the same for the Jabberwocks. Their tiny bodies grew paler and greener; their wings drooped. All at once, they started to retch.

"*Now,*" Usagi ordered.

We sprang into action. The Winter Prince hoisted me up. I hooked my arms around his neck, and we bolted from the bush.

Screeching, the Jabberwocks flew at the bushes. We ran like dementors were chasing us. I chanced a look behind Akihiko's broad shoulders. The Jabberwocks hastened behind us, but the effects of the berries proved too much for them. They flew high, then plummeted low. The entire horde swayed in a drunken stupor. Two of them crashed into each other. Then three.

One by one, they spiraled into the snow, their beady little eyes glaring daggers as we gave them the slip.

CHAPTER 7

Labyrinthine

After what seemed like eons, we slowed down and regained our breath.

"That was close," the hatter panted.

"Tell me about it." I inhaled a ragged breath. A rich scent of the sea, fresh air, and a hint of musk flooded my senses. Because of my sprained ankle, the prince still carried me. Though this was no time for romantic thoughts, I couldn't help feeling self-conscious at our proximity.

I had never been this close to a boy before. I leaned closer, my face against his hair, soaking in his essence. He smelled as intoxicating as the smell of books. I wish I could've bottled his scent. I imagine it was what an Amortentia potion would smell like to me.

Usagi's voice scattered my fangirl musings. "Do you realize how close we are? Only one more shard left."

"But it's the labyrinth, Usagi." Anxiety tinged the hatter's voice. I gave him a wary glance—was it really that bad? Sensing my unease, Akihiko brushed my arm. The motion was so subtle and quick that I nearly registered it as a figment of my imagination.

"I'm sure it'll be fine," he murmured against my temple.

I averted his steady gaze. Akihiko was naturally heroic —a prince, for Pete's sake. His version of 'fine' probably meant harrowing and dangerous.

Usagi consulted the map and marshaled us forward. The wind howled, and snow blew into our faces. Shivering, we hiked through slippery, slushy snow and trudged through unpleasant sinkholes. By the time we reached a steep hill, we found ourselves completely out of breath.

The hatter doubled over. "There must be an easier way, Usagi."

"Maybe...maybe there is." Breathing hard, Usagi looked around. Her eyes lit. She crouched down and picked up two giant slabs of bark. "We can use these as toboggans. But grip it tight. You don't want to be sliding off the end."

That's what she said.

I took a seat, and Akihiko sat down behind me. His arms blocked me on either side; his torso touched my spine. I dug my nails into the rough birch. Down and down we skid, picking up speed. Ice-laden trees blurred past us. My stomach grew queasy. It reminded me of the times I felt carsick reading fanfiction on the bus. I squeezed my eyes shut and leaned against Akihiko's protective arms. When we reached the lichen-covered permafrost at the bottom of the hill, I exhaled a sigh of relief.

"Alright there?"

"Yeah…"

A half smile on his lips, he signaled me to clamber onto his back. Making minimal eye-contact, I awkwardly hooked my arms around his neck. My body pressed against his back. Each time I slipped, Akihiko hitched me up, and I wrapped my legs tighter around his torso, supporting my weight. My breathing grew uneven, and his fingers tightened under my thighs. A strange, fuzzy feeling welled up within me. Not fangirling…but something else. Something more.

As we navigated across the frosty carpet, we fell into a lulling rhythm. His steady pace, the ghost of my breath on his neck, slender hands adjusting their grip on me every few minutes. Despite the cold, the prince's aura enveloped me like a warm blanket. My eyes drifted close. Everything felt tranquil, still. And then I was falling. Deeper and deeper…

The dark-haired girl tumbled into a pile of snow. The Ice Dancer had aimed for Artemis, but the young Moon Warrior careened out of the way just in time. The creature returned her attention to the struggling blonde. Her mouth inched open.

"Get away from her!" Reacting fast, Artemis pressed a finger to her forehead and flexed her arm. Like throwing a frisbee, she hurled her magical tiara with all her might.

The shimmering disk slammed into the ice monster. A scream pierced the air. Prismatic light erupted as the Ice Dancer disintegrated into smithereens of ice.

Relief flooding her, the girl rushed to her fallen comrade. "Are you okay?"

"Thanks to you." Venus took her friend's hand and staggered to her feet.

The young cadets surveyed the landscape. The frozen trees around them began thawing, returning to their springtime forms.

"We did it!" The Moon Warrior raised her gloved hand for a high-five, but her comrade didn't meet it.

A bright flash broke in front of them. And another. And another. The girls shielded their eyes. Tall, hazy figures hid behind the frozen trees.

More Ice Dancers?

Color drained from the blonde's face. She turned her back.

Beyond Artemis' outstretched hand, Venus's outline blurred. The girl disappeared with the Ice Dancers, leaving her confused and colder than ever.

"Alice."

A gentle pressure nudged me. Akihiko's face swam into focus. I blinked my grogginess away. Ugh. Why couldn't I obliviate that unpleasant dream from the deep recesses of my mind? I never had a problem repressing things before. Until now, I had considered myself a pro at it.

"We're here, Alice," he said. "Look."

I didn't know how long I had been asleep, but the surroundings had changed. A labyrinth made of ice towered before me. Two imposing entryways, both identical, faced our diminutive forms.

I swallowed. "Is that—"

"The final obstacle," whispered the hatter.

He and Usagi examined the icy walls as Akihiko helped me down.

"Blast it, which one?" Usagi tugged on her braids as she paced back and forth. "I didn't know there'd be two entries."

"Then it can't be helped. We'll need to divvy up. Into pairs." Boushiya glanced around at us. His mouth parted a fraction. My stomach did a trapeze artist level of a flip.

"Usagi and I shall take the right one, and Alice and fish b—Prince Akihiko can take the left."

How convenient.

My legs wobbled like Jell-O. Usagi seconded his suggestion by winking at me with a mortifying lack of discreteness. I pivoted my attention to my feet, flushing from head to toe. I had read enough manga to know where this was going.

Akihiko moved closer. "Is your ankle better now? Or should I…" He stretched out his hand.

I swatted it away with a spaztastic reflex. "I can I think. I mean, I think I can."

Why, oh why, did I keep doing that, *that awkward thing?*

"Of course." His hand fell to his side. He backed away, his face blank, but I could read the confusion in his eyes. How could I be equally terrified and desperate to be near a boy I liked? No matter how hard I tried, I just couldn't bring myself to face him.

I winced and took a step. A slight pain flared at first but dimmed with each subsequent movement. "I'm good now." Well, my foot was at least. The rest of me…not so much.

I meandered after Usagi and the hatter as they scuttled to their entryway.

"This is it," she said quietly.

Clouds of thick mist enveloped her outline. For a moment, she looked like she was disappearing into a thin mist. Then, she stilled. She retracted her foot and spun around. Catching me off guard, she tackled me in a hug.

"Wha—"

"Alice." Her forehead brushed mine. "I'll see you two outside the maze, okay?"

Something in her voice made my breath catch. "You too." I squeezed her back and watched her return to the narrow, icy entrance. Boushiya forced a wave as he and Usagi disappeared from our sight, the passage's blue shadows engulfing their figures. Akihiko looked at me.

"After you."

"Yeah."

Swallowing my anxiety, I stepped into the shadows of the labyrinth. Cold, eerie, and echoic, the ice walls towered overhead, two stories tall. Small owl-like creatures perched above us, cocking their bobble heads like Kodama.

"Hedwig!" I squealed the name so high that Akihiko flinched beside me. The creature I smiled at flared. Grey eyes glowing, it ruffled its white feathers. A deafening, guttural screech pierced the air. My smile faded. Rimy discomfort prickled across my skin.

"That's a bandersnatch," Akihiko said, massaging his neck. "They're supposed to reside in the outskirts of Winterland."

"Then what's it doing here?"

"Maybe we're closer to the outskirts than we thought." He eyed the snowy bandersnatches, face tensed.

"Akihiko?"

He returned his attention to the maze. "It's nothing. Let's go."

"Okay."

Streaks of dim light cast our disfigured shadows on the walls. As we wandered into the heart of the maze, the passages grew narrower until it could no longer accommodate two people. I started walking in the front, but each time we reached a dead end, Akihiko and I swapped roles. Minutes passed by at a glacial pace. Eventually, I lost track of how many times we switched places.

The more we ventured, the more complex and confusing the maze grew. The passages widened. The white mist thickened. Now we walked side-by-side, taking turns on which path we should go. But the haze grew heavier and neither of us seemed to make good navigational decisions. Though I didn't want to say anything, I knew had gotten ourselves lost in the labyrinth.

As Akihiko and I weaved our way through the glinting ice walls, I snuck a glance at him. Brows furrowed, he walked beside me wordlessly. A whisper of tension settled between us.

We walked on, and my emotions grew more tangled than the convoluted passageways we took. I was consumed in my own thoughts and yet...so highly aware of him.

I expelled a white puff of air. This was *agonizing*.

It wasn't that I didn't enjoy Akihiko's presence—I did. A *lot*. A fangirl like me should've felt thrilled to be alone with him. And I was. But some cold, icy wall stood between us—a wall that I had unintentionally built. Every time he neared close, I retreated into my shell like a knee-jerk-reflex.

I didn't know the first things about boys. Until now, I'd always thought boys were like hard math problems. Confusing and so difficult that you wanted to give up on understanding them. But Akihiko... He was a math problem I wanted to solve. Badly.

I just didn't know how.

I decided to take advantage of the uncomfortable quiet between us, using it as an opportunity to rack my brain for the Akihiko Solution. Of course, I got nowhere —and it was painfully silent. Neither of us exchanged a single word, save for the occasional murmurs of "sorry"; "left?"; "right?"; and "sure."

Finally, Akihiko broke the ice.

Unfortunately, he did it literally.

"Akihiko!" I threw my arms around his plummeting torso. We toppled backward onto the cold, icy floor. Panting, I gaped at the ground in front of us. Or, rather, I gaped at the absence of ground. The large, storm-blue hole gaped back.

In our shock, it took us a while to find words. Even my bearing returned before my speech did. I stood, knees shaking, and stepped toward the edge.

"It goes down farther than I can make out."

Behind me, Akihiko rose. "Should we turn around? I fear falling would mean..." He trailed off. But I understood his grim thoughts. Falling would mean game over. *Permanently.*

I tried to nod, but my head shook itself. "No," I heard my voice say, and I flinched at the sound of it. "If the queen took pains to make this way so dangerous, we must be onto something."

Since when did I say things this confidently? Since when did I act this *brave*? Even if the words were involuntary, brimming up from some deep, hidden, intuitive part of me, I knew they were true. We had to cross this chasm.

"All right," said the prince. "I trust you."

"It connects over there." I pointed at the wall on our right. A skinny ledge of ice separated the wall from the hole. "We could chip holds into the wall for our hands, and…" I clenched my jaw. Shimmying across that ledge would not be easy.

Sensing my anxiety, Akihiko fixed his eyes on me. "I'll go first."

He unsheathed the Vorpal sword and slashed a small fissure into the wall. He swung the sword again and again, until the crack was deep enough to dig the tips of our fingers into. It wasn't much, but it would have to do.

Akihiko wrapped his fingers into the crack and stepped out onto the ledge. Taking care not to look at the hole beneath him, he pressed his lithe body against the wall and inched his way across. Despite the stakes, I couldn't help thinking it was a lucky wall.

A quarter of the way across, Akihiko let go with one hand and slashed open another section of railing. I held my breath. But the prince did not need me to worry for him. When he was satisfied with his second crack, he sheathed his sword, inched farther across, and repeated the action once more. Before I knew it, the Winter Prince was across the chasm. He gestured to me.

Uh-oh. My turn.

I tried to move my foot, but to no avail. It remained stubbornly anchored in place. *C'mon, c'mon. Move already.* I couldn't psyche out now. My fandom needed me.

With a shaky breath, I gripped the climbing hold. It was wet and slippery. I couldn't understand how Akihiko hadn't died.

"You can't rely on them heavily," he said, cupping his hands to shout. "They're only a guide, and they help a bit if you wobble. But...don't wobble."

I gnawed my chapped lips. Helpful.

I curled my fingers into the crack and took the first step. My stomach plunged, possibly to the bottom of the pit. *Shi. Matta.*

I slowed my breathing and slid my second foot toward me. Colorful words swirled through my head. I closed my eyes, plastering myself against the wall as tightly as I could.

"Too deep, Sherlock." I inhaled and forced another step. Then another. Bit by bit, I inched my way across.

When I was a few feet away, Akihiko stretched out his hand, and I reached for it. His fingertips grazed mine, the touch tingling across my skin like static electricity. I registered his smile, his misty breath... My fingers ached to feel the touch of his skin even more. I gripped his hand.

And then, I slipped.

"Alice!" Akihiko tightened his hold.

I swung, bruising myself against the jagged chasm, walls. The cloak caught me in a choke hold. I remembered my sister telling me once about Victorian women and how frequently their heavy skirts drowned them. Would that be me? Death by excess fabric?

"Untie it. Quickly." Akihiko's voice was urgent, but I was surprised by how gathered he seemed. It was a nice contrast to my internal monologue, which was spiraling into panicked gobbledegook.

I lifted my free hand to my neck and tugged at the bow. It came apart. The fabric fell from my shoulders, and Akihiko hoisted me up. As I watched the cloak flutter down into the darkness, I felt a pang in my chest. It was like losing a protective friend, or fighting naked in a war. I felt vulnerable. Exposed.

I threw my arms across my chest, covering my embarrassing sweatshirt, and hugged myself. Another pair of arms wrapped around me.

Akihiko buried his face into my hair. The fangirl in me wanted to breathe the moment in, but I was almost too shocked to register it at all.

"Don't scare me like that," he said, breathing hard. "I thought for sure…"

I quaked, unable to reply. Some defensive part of my brain refused to pay attention to what had just happened. I just wanted to forget it. Repress it.

I tightened my self-hug and found the words. "Can we keep going? Please?"

Akihiko frowned. He probably thought I was pushing myself too far, too quickly, and maybe I was, but I needed to. I needed to not think. I looked at him with pleading eyes until he gave in.

For several minutes, we walked on in silence, save for the scratch of our footsteps and the screeches of the bandersnatches. Finally, my guilt caught up to me. Akihiko had just saved my life, and I'd repaid him by snapping and shutting him down.

"I'm sorry about your cloak," I said lamely.

"Better that than you. But now that you mention it..." He ran a slow glance over me, making me feel exposed. "I've kept something to myself for a while now."

"What do you mean?"

"I know you've been trying to hide it, but your attire..." He chose his words carefully. "It's different. I don't mean to pry, but I surmise you hail from elsewhere?"

"Yeah...elsewhere. I guess you could call me an outsider. I've always been one. Even in my own world." I whispered the last bit under my breath. I fiddled with my hair and segued away from the touchy subject. "The place I come from is er, different. Very different from here."

"Is it cold there?"

I gave a sardonic laugh. "Not like this."

"Then you must not be accustomed to Winterland's climate."

My mind blanked. I didn't want to make small talk about the weather. I wanted to reply with a mysterious air. To come across as demure and sophisticated. To blow him away with my wit. I wanted him to find me *interesting*. And yet I simply bobbed my head and blurted out how the cold never bothered me anyway.

As soon as the corny reference escaped me, I wanted to face-palm myself hard. I probably would have too if not for the fact that this lame quip of mine made him chuckle. The sound traveled down my spine as if he had traced it with a finger. My knees went weak. How did he do that?

"Um, do you have any regions you like here?" My inner fangirl shook her head at my question. *Dull, dull, dull,* she sniped at me.

"Or—never mind. I shouldn't have asked." I forced a laugh. "I know it's like an ice age here—"

"The Treacherous Lake."

I blinked. "What?"

Akihiko glanced above, his eyes clouded. "It used to be my favorite place. I wish you could've seen it before it became the 'Treacherous Lake' to others. Back when its inhabitants were more pleasant. Back when it was home. Back when I wasn't the *Winter* Prince." A melancholy expression surfaced on his face. "The sea breeze ruffling your hair, the soft melodies of the Mer, the most beautiful flowers we'd ever laid eyes on..."

I frowned at the soft tenor in his voice. "We?"

"The Mer and I. We'd bask in the beauty of it all until we'd lose track of time."

As much as I wanted to believe his words, I couldn't. According to face-reading, looking to the left involved using the part of the brain that controlled visually constructing images—in other words, lying. Looking to the right meant recalling a memory. Right now, Akihiko was staring *far* to his left. Jealousy snaked through me, coiling around my heart. Who had he taken to the place so special to him?

"I want you to know that I do not dislike the Treacherous Lake even now."

"What?" Breaking out of my conflicted thoughts, I met his focused gaze.

"If I had to pick my favorite region in this frozen wasteland," he said, "I'd still choose the lake. Though for different reasons now."

Without another word, he resumed walking in front of me. I stared at the back of his head, wishing I could see his face. Did he say that because it was his territory, the place where he had once reigned? Or because...My heart skipped a beat. I tried not to think about. It was far too wishful a thought. And yet there it was, materializing more and more clearly in my mind: did he consider it special because he had met me there?

Instead of vocalizing that question, I returned to the place he had mentioned. "I'd like to see those flowers someday."

"You should," he whispered, slowing his pace. 'They're beautiful."

"I'll bet." My voice grew quiet as I toyed with my scarf. "I love the sea. Reminds me of summer vacation. And summer means no school, no social hierarchies... no Christmas parties." Why was I rambling to him about this?

"You dislike social gatherings?"

"Yes. Sort of. Well...it's complicated." My hands slackened at my sides. "Just forget it. It's nothing."

Akihiko didn't look convinced. "Are you positive?"

"As a proton." I forced a smile at Akihiko. He seemed to get my cue.

He slowed and stepped smoothly back to my side, then shifted the conversation. I made more small talk. So did he. Slowly but surely, our small talk blossomed into something more. We talked about how snowflakes formed, our favorite scents, the ocean, music, and magic. We talked about stars, books, our phobias. We talked about everything and nothing at all.

Akihiko's demeanor changed. His posture relaxed; his gait grew casual. He lost the crisp enunciation in his voice. No longer did he look—or act—like the picture perfect fairy tale prince. Now, he was laughing heartily, one hand slung in his pocket as I explained to him how the city of Syracuse had once tried to make snow illegal.

Akihiko suppressed a snort. "Your world seems most intriguing."

"You have no idea. That's just the tip of the iceberg."

So absorbed in our conversation, I hardly noticed that the passageway around us had grown narrower—a fact I didn't mind at all.

My face heated as we brushed shoulders. Heart hammering, the subtle touches that felt like currents passing between us, butterflies in my stomach, releasing breaths I did not know I'd been holding… I felt like I was experiencing all the instalove symptoms I had read about in my young adult novels.

Nothing about this was 'insta', of course. I'd been crushing on the Winter Prince for ages in my own world. I was the girl who talked about my fictional crush the way other girls talked about actual crushes. Not expecting anything to come out of my nonfictional feelings for a fictional character, I had resigned myself to a state of *la douleur exquise*. One of Deanna's lingual factoids, the phrase described the exquisite pain of wanting someone unattainable. But here was my prince. Walking in tandem with me...so very attainable.

So what kept stopping me?

Just tell him you like him already, cajoled my inner fangirl. Woo him with your awkwardness. *That's the solution.*

I considered seducing Akihiko with every pick-up line in my arsenal.

I want to form base pairs with you, Akihiko. To integrate our curves and increase our volume. To be the variable to your coefficient. To change our potential energy into kinetic energy.

I giggled to myself. Okay, maybe that's laying it on thick. Of course, *I* would never say something that outlandish, but my inner fangirl...well, she might actually go through with it.

"Alice?"

I jumped. In all my mega-nerdy internalizing, I didn't notice Akihiko staring at me. My heart thumped at his smoky eyes. I pivoted my attention to my feet instead, praying he couldn't read my embarrassing thoughts.

"Is something wrong?" he asked.

I let out a nervous laugh. "No…it's nothing. Nothing at all." I stepped in front of him, fiddling with my scarf.

The prince grabbed my hand. "Nothing usually means something. Two nothings make that more definitive."

"Well…"

"Alice." Akihiko spun me around to face him. He studied me carefully. I fought the need to retreat from his penetrating gaze. After searching my face, he released my hand. His Adam's apple bobbed. "I think I understand now."

"You do?"

He gave me a wan smile. "You do not enjoy my company the same way I do yours."

My eyes widened. No way. He couldn't be serious. I wailed inwardly. *If only he knew the truth.*

I tightly coiled a lock of hair around my finger. "It's… it's not that."

"It's not?" His eyes bore into mine, once more seeking out my most guarded thoughts. I wanted to answer him, but I couldn't move my lips. Ugh. Why couldn't I be smooth just once in my life?

"I'm sorry," I blustered as we came upon a fork in the road. "It's not you. It's me." The words tumbled out of my mouth before I could stop them. Suppressing my nervous stimming, I stopped playing with my hair. I took a full breath, my poker face crumbling. My lips quivered on the brink of revealing my deep, dark secret.

"I'm a—"

Akihiko stopped me, pressing two firm fingers against my lips. I froze, ready to melt.

But Akihiko's face was concerned—not tender. "Don't breathe," he whispered. "Something is off here..."

I held my breath and looked around. The passage we'd just been walking through was normal by all accounts, but the two passages before us held an eerie vibe. Both were covered with icy roofs, a feature we hadn't encountered before. The right-hand passage emitted a thin, lavender mist. The left-hand passage glittered with large, static flakes of snow. And then I noticed the labyrinth was silent. No horrible screeches. I stared above. No Hedwigs, either.

Exercising caution, Akihiko approached the lavender mist and drew his sword. He raised it and prodded the haze. Instantly, ice shot up the blade, encasing the metal in sharp crystals. When he withdrew it, the ice did not melt.

"So much for that passage."

Following his lead, I rummaged through my pocket and pulled out my Jiji keychain.

"Sorry," I whispered to the smiling anime cat. Holding my breath, I chucked it into the passage with static snow.

Nothing happened.

"Can we breathe yet?" I asked. "I mean, normally?"

"I don't know how to tell. The snowflakes could be nothing..."

"Or they could be more toxic than Britney," I said warily. "But...we have to try." No way had I crossed that ice ledge for nothing. And even more importantly: no way was I crossing it again.

Akihiko still looked uncertain, so I went first. I tiptoed into the left-hand passage, trying my best not to touch any of the flakes. The air was cool and sweet. It smelled like Lori's garden tea parties: vanilla and floral rolled into one. The snowflakes tinkled lightly as they shone.

A wave of relaxation swept over me. I stopped fidgeting with my hair. I felt happy, at peace...like I could say anything.

"I'm a fangirl," I whispered dreamily.

"Pardon?"

Akihiko's question made me jump. Why had I said that? *How* had I said that? I hadn't even meant to talk.

"A *fangirl*," I said, louder this time. I slapped my hand over my mouth.

Akihiko's expression melted into a languid smile as his gaze dropped to my sweatshirt. "A girl who is a fan?"

"It goes beyond that," my mouth explained for me. "A fangirl is a girl who obsesses over fictional characters. A girl who devours fanfiction like candy...a girl who squeals at fanart of her favorite ships."

Akihiko's head flopped in a sluggish stupor. "I sailed a ship once."

"She's a girl who lives in her imagination," I continued, unable to control myself, "which can make her come across as a bit awkward to others. A fangirl can get like that when she spots her OTP or..." My voice grew hoarse in my attempt to restrain it. "Or something she really likes."

The moment my double meaningful tripped out, I wanted to crawl up into a little ball. The cringe factor was escalating fast.

What the flake was wrong with me?

"I suppose I can't deny that." Akihiko fixated on me, his eyes like the ocean's mist. "You *are* a rather awkward one, Alice."

"What?" I whispered. I could hardly believe my ears. Granted my entire existence had been a series of awkward moments, but this one took the cake.I couldn't deny I was a cringe-worthy mess in general, but did he have to be so direct about it? It was so un-princely of him. Maybe I'd been wrong about him.

Akihiko angled my chin to his face. I stopped breathing.

"We cannot change who we are," he said, his voice lilting like a gentle wave. "Whether you like to hear it or not, you *are* a fangirl. Awkward to the core and yet... strange in all the right ways."

My voice cracked. "You—you really mean that?"

"Must you ask?" he said softly. "I don't think we're able to lie right now." His languid eyes surveyed the flakes. "I think their fumes are forcing us to speak honestly."

Holy lasso of truth. Veritaserum-saturated snow? I considered his theory for a moment. It definitely felt right. My mind was lucid, but my tongue was so loose.

A slow grin crept Akihiko's lips. "Truth-flakes or no truth-flakes, you must never apologize for what makes you *you*. There will always be those who will hold it against you, but they're not worth bothering with." He leaned in, his whisper a rich tenor. "Because there will also be those who like it."

His disarming words struck me like a wave. My fingers dug into my sweater. I never thought a nerdy fangirl like me would hear those words. The words that captured my essence so perfectly. The words that made me feel all warm and fuzzy inside. The words I had desperately wanted to hear for so long.

"Being around you," he murmured, "I feel like I can just be myself. Not the Winter Prince, not the leader of the Ningyo…just Akihiko. Just *me*. I never had that before."

My heart leapt. But it also ached for him. I couldn't imagine a life like that. After all, didn't I already have someone who I could always be myself around? My eyes pricked. I thought of the photograph on my nightstand. Deanna and I smiling at last year's cosplay convention.

"I'm so sorry," I whispered, searching for the right words. "It's such a rare, beautiful thing, to have a friend like that…"

"A friend," Akihiko repeated. "But maybe something more…"

The small gap between us began to close. In a moment meant for fanart, my foot popped, clinking against a snowflake with an echoic ding.

"Watch out!"

The world around me spun. I inhaled a sharp gasp as I watched my hair and scarf fall above me toward the floor. Akihiko and I stood on the ceiling, looking down.

"Holy OTP, we're right-side up." I clamped my jaw tight. I had meant to say the opposite.

"I know what happened." Akihiko furrowed his brow. I inferred that he had no clue.

"We can only speak the truth now." I shook my head. "I mean, the *truth*." I clenched my fists. "The *truth*." What I really meant was lies.

"What about questions?" I sighed, relieved. The question came out neutral. Akihiko nodded, noting this loophole.

"What do you think we should do?" he asked.

I shook my head. Even if I could tell the truth, I wouldn't know what to say. But before I could think on it for very long, Akihiko pointed.

"Alice." An odd hitch filled his voice.

"What is it?" I said, watching my words.

Akihiko squinted behind me, his eyes keen and restless. I spun around.

A thick, impassable block of ice towered before us. I would have cursed my luck, but Akihiko stared with such rapture that I had to look closer.

I edged toward the wall. Patterns of fractals, faint and intricate, were etched into the ice, forming the shape of...a door? Akihiko's voice contradicted my thought.

"I think it might be a dead end." He swore, then laughed. "I mean, do you think it's a gateway?"

I smiled, enjoying our game of "opposite day." Could I nod? I moved my hands to my head to enforce the proper motion. It worked. *Yes*, I gestured. *Definitely a door.* Akihiko grinned.

We stepped toward it, each grazing a few snowflakes with our moving limbs. The world spun again, more wildly this time. When it stopped, the door was gone.

Akihiko and I looked at each other.

"One plus one is two," I offered. The truth rang out.

"We've found the Mirror Princess." Akihiko frowned.

"Did you mean to say we seek her?"

Grimacing, he nodded. I sighed. This grey world of truths and lies was even harder to navigate. I was about to touch another snowflake, hoping to get us back to pure truth, when Akihiko gave a shout. The door had reappeared.

Taking pains not to touch any more snowflakes along the way, the prince inched forward and reached out. Euphoria danced in his eyes. As he traced the fractals, the patterned ridges under his fingers grew more and more distinct. I held my breath. The air grew thick with mist. Through it, a strange glow outlined the fractals of the gateway.

A high-pitched laugh erupted. The snowflakes and icy roof splashed down around us, filling the passage with freezing water. I squealed. My knee-high socks were soaked. The water climbed higher and higher...

"Climb onto my shoulders!" Akihiko knelt and I clambered aboard. My feet dangled above the rising sea, which was now up to the prince's waist, up to his chest... Akihiko inhaled, ready for the plunge.

But instead of diving, he threw his arms wide, knocking the wind out of the air. In seconds, the water level fell—parting in a perfect circle around his feet. My mouth dropped.

"How did you—?"

"Being part Ningyo has its advantages."

I stared around. Except the spot where we stood, the passage was still a cold, frosty sea. I lowered myself from the prince's shoulders. A foreboding silence filled the air. I didn't know what was coming, but I preferred to be grounded for it.

Then, I caught it. A strange shape appeared on the glowing wall. Before my shout could disperse into the air, furry ears materialized. Then came feral violet eyes, an attractive face, a well-defined torso, and a long, luxurious white tail.

The snow-white cat kemonomimi eased in from the mist. A Cheshire smile curved his lips. I could hardly believe my eyes.

Shiroi Neko.

Not only did I recognize him from my *Winterland* manga, but I also had cosplayed the cheeky guardian of the Ice Labyrinth at Winter-Con last year. Still...something about him looked uncomfortably familiar. Oh Mylanta.

"*Catpernicus?*"

The kemonomimi's eyes crinkled with amusement, but he didn't answer.

"F-Fur Elise?"

This time, the kemonomimi tittered. "What laughable names. I prefer Shiroi."

The gateway stopped glowing behind him, reverting back to a wall of patterned ice. Tall and wispy, the androgynous figure gallivanted toward me. He placed his hand on his exposed midriff, grazing the heart mark on his skin. A purple vial-locket bobbed from his neck, creating a stark contrast against his pale skin and white, tight garb that showed off everything a fangirl wanted to see.

Blushing, I forced my gaze to his tail, which moved with frenzy. Deanna had told me that cats flicked their tails when they were angry, but this half-feline looked... excited. Too excited.

Shiroi tilted his head at me and purred. "My, aren't you a pretty little thing?"

Akihiko raised his hand, creating a barrier between the kemonomimi and me. Shiroi met the prince's glare with a smirk. "Quite the looker yourself."

"Enough. We need to get across."

"I can let you across, certainly."

I cast the prince a sidelong glance. "Er, great then."

As soon as I stepped forward, Shiroi blocked my path. His tail wrapped around my hips, and he whispered into my ear, "You didn't think it'd be that easy, did you, love?"

I shivered. "Well…"

He chuckled, his breath clouding the air. "I shall allow you entrance, provided you answer my riddles first —correctly, of course."

I gulped. So he was the riddle master of this labyrinth. So much for hoping for another way out. I tried to obliviate Usagi's words from my mind.

No one has answered the riddles to date.

My pulse skittered. No use psyching myself out now. We could do this. We had to.

"We'll answer them," I said. "Your riddles, I mean."

"Of course you will." Shiroi curled his lips into a puckish smile until his mouth resembled a sideways 3.

Dear gods of anime.

"Let's begin with something simple, shall we? Tell me, what does one call a vampire in winter?"

My shoulders relaxed. Hardly an impossible riddle. Quite the opposite, in fact. My mouth parted to answer, but to my surprise, Akihiko beat me to it.

"Frostbite?"

Shiroi's smile faded. "Correct..."

I glared at the disappointment in his voice. Geez Louise, did this ridiculous kemonomimi want us to fail that badly?

Without batting an eye, Shiroi moved to the next question. "Where can one find an ocean without any water?"

The prince consulted me. "A frozen ocean? No, that doesn't make sense. Ice *is* water."

"Maybe...a moon crater?" I offered. "Like the Sea of Serenity." According to NASA, the massive crater had held water eons ago before it dried up. But could anyone really call that an ocean now—even by Winterland logic?

My eyes widened.

That's it.

A spark of hope shot through me. Who needs Winterland logic when you have real logic? Maybe we didn't need to answer the riddles. Maybe we could find our own path and solve the maze by ourselves.

"Spatial reasoning," I said, waving my hands.

Akihiko looked startled. "Come again?"

"The ability to understand spatial relations among objects. It's this thing my math teacher told us. You can imagine spatial images and manipulate them in your mind to get a map."

"Correct," came a murmur.

Akihiko lifted a brow at the kemonomimi. "Correct?"

Shiroi sighed. "Yes. One can find an ocean without any water on a *map*."

Akihiko and I exchanged a glance and broke out into massive grins. We had *so* lucked out on that one. Shiroi didn't join in our small victory but shot the next riddle at us with unceremonious haste.

"What type of cake does a snowman consume?" he demanded.

"Anything with icing," said Akihiko.

"Or frosting," I added.

"Fine, fine, either of those will suffice. But...I have one final riddle before I can let you pass." Shiroi inched closer, his face contorting before us. His peeved expression transformed into a borderline-maniacal grin. Sharp, feline teeth glinted at us. I swallowed. At once, I knew he had been saving the hardest, most twisted riddle for last.

Shimatta.

"What eight letters does one find in the lakes of Winterland?"

Akihiko and I faced each other. Our mouths teetered on the edge of speech, but the wretched cat got our tongues. The prince swore under his breath. I saw my frustration and anxiety mirrored in his expression.

Shiroi purred, relishing our stumped faces. Even Schrödinger's cat theory didn't perplex me as much as this cat's riddle.

I ruffled my tresses, adrenaline racing. We were so, *so* close. We couldn't throw in the towel now. I'd stand here shivering and mulling it over forever if I had to. But apparently, Akihiko didn't feel the same way. He rounded on Shiroi.

"You are going to let us through." For the first time, I heard raw visceral anger in his voice. It unnerved my core.

"But you haven't answered my riddle," Shiroi drawled.

I glanced at Akihiko nervously. "Is there any other way you'll let us through?"

"I suppose I can accept other means of payment."

Okay, progress. I offered a business smile. "Like?"

A devilish gleam touched Shiroi's eyes. His gaze drifted to my lips. A tight knot formed in my chest.

"A kiss," he whispered.

My nostrils flared. "I'd rather stick with my otome games at home, thanks." My mind flashed to my stupid Shiroi cosplay. With Deanna springing the tickets on me last-minute, I had planned on reusing the costume for

Winter-con, but not anymore. If I ever got out of this maze in one piece—or back to my own universe, for that matter—I'd shred that costume.

Akihiko grabbed the cat kemonomimi by the shoulders, his composed princely self flying out the window. His face twisted, his jaw clenched. I could feel the fury rolling off him in waves. For a second, I didn't even recognize him.

"Akihiko, calm down." I jumped beside him, but he pushed me away with an unexpected roughness.

"Stay out of this," came a snarl.

I gaped. If I hadn't seen the Winter Prince utter those words from his lips, I wouldn't have believed he had addressed me so harshly. Sure, the initial trigger had been real enough, and he was valiant for wanting to defend me, but this had grown into something beyond that. My eyes flicked to his neck. The heart mark had grown darker, matching his blackening eyes. My mind roiled with anxiety.

Shiroi cocked his head at me, then returned his gaze to Akihiko. "My, hasn't this gotten interesting?"

"Silence." Akihiko lunged at him with full force. The Vorpal sword out, he slashed the air. Shiroi's grin tapered as he dodged the frosted blade.

"Stop it!" I screamed. "Please Akihiko…"

Akihiko didn't slow down. Rather, the opposite. He maneuvered his sword in fierce, deft movements, missing the cat kemonomimi by millimeters. I swallowed at the silver blurs. His body moved like an angry sea that wanted to wipe out everything. This was not the Winter Prince. At least not the one I knew.

"You—feral—imp." Each assault of Akihiko's sword was punctuated by a heavy grunt.

The kemonomimi dodged a direct attack, eyes slanting. "Compliments will get you nowhere. Though, I suppose if the girl turns down my offer, you'd do." Slowly, he ran a tongue over his lips.

Akihiko turned scarlet. "You dare…"

"I do." Shiroi crept closer to the Winter Prince. The purple vial-made locket bobbed against his chest. In one languid motion, he removed the locket.

"What are you doing?" I demanded.

"You'll see, love."

Akihiko slanted his eyes. Ready for anything, he clutched the Vorpal sword with both hands, pointing it at the kemonomimi.

Shiroi appeared unfazed. With two fingers, he dangled the locket in front of Akihiko. The liquid inside the vial, purple and luminous, danced in sluggish swirls. Like a lava lamp, the purple globs stretched, compressed, and floated in a hypnotic spectacle. Despite the relaxing visuals, panic seized me.

In the original Winterland manga, Shiroi had put intruders in a trance so that they'd become hopelessly lost in the vast maze, sometimes never finding their way. I never knew how he did it. Until now.

Akihiko lowered his sword, but his gaze didn't drop from the locket.

Shimatta.

"Put the sword down," said Shiroi.

In moments, the prized Vorpal sword was lying on the ground, utterly forgotten.

"Come closer," Shiroi whispered. "I won't bite."

Face devoid of emotion, Akihiko closed the small distance between them.

Every inch of me shuddered. *Shirohiko* shippers from the Yaoi-After-The-Dark panel would have a field day if they saw this. With the equal fervor I shipped my OTP, I titanic'd this pairing.

"Hail no," I yelled, intercepting them and grabbing the vile locket from Shiroi. As much as I refused to have my first kiss stolen, I couldn't watch a crackship become canon.

With all my strength, I hurled the locket to the ground. The vial didn't break, but Akihiko's trance did. He stirred, catching his head.

Shiroi scrambled to the ground and cradled his locket, flashing me an irate look. "If this broke, I would have *actually* gone through with that."

The Winter Prince clutched his sword. A bead of sweat glistened along his cupid's bow. Fury burned in his eyes. He didn't hold back.

Panting, he slashed, twisted, and thrust his icy sword. Shiroi narrowed his feline eyes and scratched Akihiko's face with his long, sharp nails. Grunting in pain, the prince stumbled. The Vorpal sword pierced the ice wall. Its ice-case shattered. Akihiko wrestled it out. He turned to the kemonomimi, sword in hand. The blade glinted.

"Enough cat and mouse games." Akihiko's pupils swallowed his eyes.

"A shame. I was only getting started." Shiroi parted his lips into a devilish smile. "Play things like you are so difficult to come by."

I took in their contorted faces, slit-like eyes, and domineering stances. I couldn't believe how out of character the two were acting. No longer were they the heroic prince and playful kemonomimi I knew. These weren't the characters I wrote fanfiction about. These weren't the characters I loved.

My eyes flicked to their heart shaped markings. A sick feeling knotted my stomach. They were growing darker by the moment.

Without blinking an eye, the duo lunged for each other.

"Stop it!" I screamed.

Mid-jab to each other, they did. But not because of me. A blood-curdling scream echoed through the maze's icy walls.

"What was that?" Akihiko asked sharply.

My eyes darted to my feet. The ground was vibrating. It sounded like a stampede of footsteps rushing toward us.

"Alice."

That voice. My head snapped back.

"Usagi, Boushiya!"And behind them...

Packs of guards poured out of a passageway.

"Alice!" Usagi and Boushiya's high-pitched voices carried through the chaos, weak but adamant. I watched their eyes take in the ice water barrier. Without Metanoia's herb, there was no way they could cross it safely. But this was Usagi. She was born to be composed under pressure.

"Go—go *now*, Alice." Usagi heaved her satchel at me. The bag flew through the air and skidded on the ice by my feet. Then, she grabbed Boushiya's arm and pulled. Together, they dove into the icy water.

"Usagi! *Boushiya!*"

"The satchel," yelled Akihiko.

I made a hasty grab for it, then rounded on him.

"You're part Ningyo! Swim back to help them—or part the waters!"

But he didn't seem to hear me. His heart mark pulsed as it darkened to a sickly storm blue.

Shiroi smiled. "Even if your boy toy was here, he couldn't do more than that silly circle. He's not the Snow Queen, you know." He cocked his head. "So, what will it be, love?"

I half-closed my eyes, feeling him approach. A misty puff ghosted across my face. His mouth hovered inches from my cheek, but he made no move to near closer. My lips went taut. *No way in hail was I offering him my first kiss.* I sidestepped him and took in the fray looming behind him. I only had one way out of this.

I pulled at my tresses. *Think, Alice think.* What eight letters did one find in these lakes? Like a whirlpool, the question swirled in my mind. M-e-r-p-e-o-p-l-e? No. Nine letters. Maybe c-o-l-d-n-e-s-s? But that would amount to two "S's"—seven individual letters... Gah, did that even matter?

My mind raced as two of the guards dove into the water. They were fast swimmers, gaining on my friends every second.

"At least repeat the riddle!"

Shiroi obliged but spoke with less enthusiasm. "What eight letters does one find in the lakes of Winterland?"

"If the cat is any indication, the answer must be something too nonsensical to figure out." Akihiko's eyes turned rueful and bleak. "I didn't think it would end like this." His mark still shone prominently. It seemed his darkness took multiple forms.

"Don't say that." My voice rasped as I stared at the shell of the prince.

Trapped in his own ennui, Akihiko stared into the skies, expressionless. His cold hand grazed mine. "I'm sorry I couldn't protect you, Alice."

As his energy lagged, the wall of water around us wobbled. A small, cold puddle trickled around our feet.

"She doesn't need you to protect her," interjected Shiroi. "Anyone with wits can protect themselves." The kemonomimi stepped closer until he stood in the same puddle as me, invading my personal space yet again. His gaze dropped to my feet. "You see, but do not observe."

"Is that supposed to be a cryptic message?" I asked exasperatedly.

"Use your wits, love."

Shimatta. I rubbed my temples in fast, furious circles. I couldn't blank now.

You're supposed to be an INTP, my inner fangirl hissed. *The logician type for flakes sake.* Answer with something. *Anything.*

When nothing came to me, my thoughts flickered to the famous logician of Baker Street. Oh, what would Sherlock Holmes do?

Usagi yelped as a guard grabbed her ankle. Boushiya moaned, barely conscious. Desperate to shut out the fracas around me, I withdrew into my mind palace. The chaotic atmosphere came to a slow until time itself seemed to freeze.

I glanced past Akihiko's bowed head, past the attacking guards, past Usagi and Boushiya's horrified faces. The only thing that moved was the water lapping my feet. My eyes fixated on it. Something in my gut told me it held the answers I sought.

But it's just a stupid puddle, I shot back. Just a meaningless puddle. What answer could I possibly deduce from it?

You see, but you do not observe.

I concentrated harder at the puddle and froze. Like a tidal wave, the illogical answer struck me.

Eureka.

My mind palace broke. I tore my gaze away from the puddle and grabbed Akihiko by the collar. "Water—the answer is in the water!"

The prince eyed me as if I had gone batty, which at this point, I possibly might have.

"We can't answer wrong, Alice. How certain are you on a scale of 1-10?"

I bit my lip. "Like…a nine and three-quarters."

His eyes hardened. "Very well. I trust you, Alice."

At least one of us did.

Regaining his energy, Akihiko spun around. He plunged into the water to fight off the guards. My nerves shook like the water wall, which was falling apart in the absence of its maker.

I spun around to face Shiroi. "The chemical formula of water is H_2O," I bursted, "which using Winterland logic translates to 'H to O.'"

The cat's eyes glinted, oblivious to the mounting tension around us. "And so?"

My voice grew shriller as a guard hiding underwater swam toward Akihiko. "The eight letters found in the lakes are H, I, J, K—elemeno!"

Erupting in a fit of laughter, Shiroi unblocked my path.

The gateway behind the cat kemonomimi glowed with a blinding brightness. The guards shielded their faces. Seizing her chance, Usagi kicked and twisted her leg, forcing her captor to release her. She crashed out of the depths and onto our circle of shallows, Boushiya in tow. Akihiko clambered behind them, swinging the Vorpal sword at the waves.

But he chose the wrong battle. The true threat was in the sky.

Like a plague of locusts, the snowy bandersnatches swooped down. They seemed to grow in size as they lunged. Three of the largest bandersnatches grasped Usagi by her coat, digging their talons into her side. She cried out in anguish. Akihiko spun on his heels and hurled the Vorpal sword at the bird-like creature. It sliced through the air, but another bandersnatch swept in and snatched it away. Screeching, the creature flew off. I could only imagine what that sword meant to the prince, but I knew what it meant for our fate.

Boushiya shook away his torpor and pulled at his friend. "No, let her go!"

He held onto Usagi's ankles as tightly as he could. I held onto him. Akihiko held me. The bandersnatches lifted the chain of us into the air, then lurched in sync. Akihiko and I crashed to the ground, but the hatter flew forward into a wall. It cracked, and I swore. A hiss of lavender haze trickled through.

"Boushiya, look out!" But it was too late. Ice wrapped around him, encasing him in the same sharp crystals that had once covered Akihiko's lost sword. The guards seized him.

My vision blurred. Without thinking, I sprinted to him. The guards snapped their fingers, and a bandersnatch landed between us.

"You know where to take them," said a guard, mouth curling.

With a piercing cry, the bandersnatch unfurled its wings and took off. I watched helplessly as the hatter, Usagi, and the wicked, snowy creatures faded into a small, hopeless dot. Soon, the skies swallowed even that.

"Boushiya... Usagi!"

I screamed their names until my throat went raw.

The prince grabbed my arm with a vise-like grip. "Come on!"

He kicked off on his legs, and we flew through the glowing portal. Bright light washed over us. Through the swarm of guards, I glimpsed the chuckling kemonomimi disappearing into the misty nothingness. Before his disembodied tail faded out of sight, it flung something at me. A glint of silver.

I slowed to catch the object, and the nearest guard lunged at me. The tips of his sharp, jagged fingernails scraped the nape of my neck.

"*Alice.*" Akihiko yanked me against him. The guard snatched at the air as my long, black tresses flew through it, but I whipped it away in time. A *smack* echoed as a guard ran into the closing wall.

As the gateway swallowed us up, I tightened my grip around a tarnished silver frame—attached to the final shard.

CHAPTER 8

A Sprite's Tidings

As the icy gateway closed behind us, Akihiko slipped. His grip on my hand tightened as he took me down to the floor. We crashed onto the cracked, frozen earth. My head landed on the crook of his neck. The hard snow crunched beneath us, leaving an imprint of tangled legs. I pushed myself up. My long hair draped about his face, curtaining our gazes.

"I'm sorry." Akihiko loosened his hold on me. "Back there, I...don't know what came over me."

"You weren't yourself," I said quietly.

His eyes burned. "I don't want you to see me like that ever again."

"Then let's finish this."

Brushing the snow off my legs, I picked myself up and surveyed the barren outskirts of Winterland. Of course, there wasn't much to take in. A desolate sky stretched across an endless expanse of bleak white. Not a creature stirred, but the wind hissed in our ears like a ice serpent. Arctic air lashed against my goose-pimpled skin.

Behind us, the walls of the labyrinth stretched up and up. They looked even taller from this side. I took in my pale and weary reflection, warped by the wall's subtle waves. I hardly recognized myself.

The girl in the icy mirror wasn't nervous fangirl Alice Leira from Charles Dodgson High. She was battered and bruised, strong and determined. She had been on a quest, and come out of it with the prize she sought. She had crossed chasms and survived icy seas. She had spilled her secrets and borne bad dreams. She had fought demons and lost close friends...

Friends.

That last memory struck harder than all the others combined. I scrunched my face, searching for the thing that could end this nightmare.

A few feet away lay Usagi's satchel, half-opened and crumpled. My stomach churned as I went to retrieve it. Would Usagi and Boushiya hold up? Could I find the Mirror Princess in time to save them? My mind whirled like a raging snowstorm, but as I touched the satchel, something within me calmed. I trailed my fingers against its soft, velvety fabric. The only warmth I had in this blasted cold. With the satchel in hand, I felt as though I had a little piece of Usagi with me. The thought comforted my nerves. Everything would work out.

I drew in a deep breath. The moment of truth. With mounting anticipation and an unsteady hand, I fished the frame and shards out of the bag.

"Shall we?" asked Akihiko.

I turned to him. His eyes, no longer clouded and dark, gleamed with a newfound determination.

"Let's."

Taking turns, we began piecing the shards together like a jigsaw puzzle. "For Sangatsu." Akihiko touched the piece that shined inside the tarnished frame. An image flashed through me: my OTP's private tea.

I smiled. "For Boushiya."

As I lay the second piece in the frame, my smile faded. A hollow yip echoed in my brain: Sangatsu's anguished cries. I cursed the Snow Queen for separating him from the hatter, then squeezed my eyes shut, blocking the picture out.

Get a grip, Alice. *You will never reunite them if you lose it now.*

Akihiko sidled close to me, his voice soft. "For Usagi."

He picked up the third piece. The one Usagi had found in the frozen lake. I touched my wrist, wincing as I remembered its sharp edge and sudden absence. Akihiko fitted it between the other two shards, and a barrage of memories tumbled through me. The bleak lake, the icy eddies, the sensation of drowning…

The Ningyo's wrathful voices played on repeat, growing louder and shriller. *Repress it.*

I turned to Akihiko.

His eyes smoldered. "One more, Alice."

My pulse ignited as my hand found his. "For us."

"For us," he whispered back.

Together, we reached for the final shard. I thought of Akihiko's words in the Labyrinth. My confession. The blazing look he had given me then. But Usagi and Boushiya's voices melted those sordid feelings away. *Go —go now.* How could I forget their self-sacrificial insistence that we save ourselves instead of them?

My breath hitched. I tried to collect my thoughts, reminding myself that once we set this piece down, we would set things straight. The mirror would be complete. The Mirror Princess would imprison the Snow Queen and save Winterland. Sanbou would be reunited. All would be well.

Everything we had fought for had lead us up to this moment. Together, we pieced the final shard into the frame. "We did it."

Hope flooded me as I took in the completed Looking Glass. Akihiko and I waited with bated breath. A minute passed by. Then another.

Slowly, my nerves started to creep back in. Okay, this was getting anticlimactic.

"Nothing's happening."

Akihiko inspected the Looking Glass. "Odd. Perhaps it won't work until we bring it to the Mirror Princess firs—" He swore under his breath.

My anxiety accelerated. "What's wrong?"

Racking his hand through his hair, he didn't reply. He didn't need to. I followed his line of vision, and all rational thought fled me. A tiny space, barely visible, blemished the middle of the mirror.

A shard was still missing.

My spirit shattered into even tinier shards. I couldn't breathe. An avalanche of emotions assailed me. My entire body trembled. I rocked back and forth, the memories of Winterland—and my own world—pouring in against my will. This time, I didn't even try to block them. I blinked in the icy air, eyes burning. We had made it this far, sacrificed so much, only to find no ice palace, no princess...no Looking Glass.

How would I even return home now?

A shadow swept over Akihiko's face. He intertwined his hands with mine, gripping them as if they were the only things pinning him to this arctic wasteland. I hiccuped against his shoulder, my tears freezing against my face. He rubbed the nape of my neck in soothing ministrations and kept whispering, "It'll be okay." I surmised he was telling himself this more than me.

I latched onto him tight, so tight that I could feel his heart beat against my chest. He was just as terrified as I was.

"What's going to happen now?" I couldn't keep my voice from shaking.

"We'll...we'll just keep looking." Despite his resolve, I heard the strain in his voice. I glanced down at our tangled hands, then his tired, yet fervent eyes.

"Alice," he whispered, angling my face to his. "We'll find it. Together."

Akihiko caught a tear from my lash before it could fall. I looked up into his face, and the bleak world around us blurred. Our failures, our harrowing journey, the Snow Queen—I forgot them all as we stood facing one another, aware of nothing but each other.

The distance between us shrunk as though a magnetic force had ensnared us. Akihiko's deft hand slipped behind my head, gently tilting it. My mouth parted. We exhaled in sync, white puffs of air mingling with each other. Like tectonic plates, our lips drifted toward each other. Closer and closer. Tears obscuring my vision, I closed my eyes, bridging the inch between us.

"Who goes there?"

We broke apart from each other. I wheeled around to face the owner of the delicate, whispery voice.

A dainty creature, the size of a miniature figurine, hovered in a soft, white haze.

"A sprite," Akihiko whispered.

The sprite tilted her head, almost dropping the oleander wreath in her hair. Her small face, pale as a pearl, looked confused by the sight of us. "Visitors?"

"We're searching for the Mirror Princess." I yipped out my answer in a single breath. The words piled over each other in a jumbled, incoherent mess.

A knowing gleam touched the sprite's eyes, as if she knew exactly why I sounded so frazzled. Something about her enraptured me. An aura of mystique and perceptiveness exuded from her. I felt I could tell her anything, but also that she already knew. She looked so delicate and unassuming and yet …

"Why you seek princess?" The sprite was barely audible over the harsh, hissing wind, but I could make out her gentle tone. Her speech sounded somehow comforting and disarming all at once. Coaxing, I think, would be the right word.

Unable to bottle my emotions, I spewed. I told her about the missing shard. The Snow Queen. The guards capturing my friends. Everything.

She listened with a solemn expression, bobbing her head every time I needed a moment to catch my breath. Word by word, I felt lighter.

When I finished our tale, the tiny sprite fluttered her snow-coated wings and hovered above my palm. The effect it had on me was hypnotic.

"You brave much turmoil. Most noble to take road less traveled. To embark on quest no one else has." Her eyes dotted with emotion. "You come far. Very far."

The mellifluous words danced about me with a calm, metronomic effect. I thought of Clefairy, or Luna—the gentle, otherworldly allies. I took comfort in knowing we had her assistance on our side.

The sprite studied our faces. Something flashed in her eyes as they met mine.

My pulse picked up. *She knew.*

The notion grew sharper and brighter in my mind until it shone with crystalline clarity. "You know where the last shard is," I whispered. "Don't you?"

The sprite tilted her head at us, askance, making sure only our ears would hear her. She flapped her wings closer to us, as if she feared her words would be swept away in the wind. Anticipation mounting, I leaned in.

"Last shard," she said softly, "lies with princess."

My heart thumped. We were close. So close I could taste it. I whirled around to Akihiko, my cheek muscles hurting from grinning like mad.

His eyes glittered above his pink, ice-kissed nose. "Where can we find her?"

"In secret cavern," said the sprite.

"Take us there. Please." My voice oscillated with fervor. The seesaw of emotions had taken a toll on my nerves. The pendulum in my mind swung back and forth, from near-capture to nearly-there to hopeless disappointment to renewed hope. Now, I just wanted to get going with vehemence.

Great. I was turning into Usagi.

A kind, seraphic smile touched the sprite's mouth as though she picked up on my jittery eagerness. "Will show shortcut if both follow."

Akihiko bowed his head. "We cannot thank you enough, ah…"

"Yuki-onna," the sprite replied. "Yuki for short."

"Yuki." I gripped the sprite's tiny, cold hand in my two fingers. "I don't know what we would've done without you. Thank you."

"Yuki must thank you," she said softly.

Beckoning us, she fluttered away, leaving only a trace of powdered snow in the air. I trailed close after her, my chest swelling with gratitude.

Things were finally looking up.

Akihiko and I hiked through the outskirts, following her like a pair of overgrown ducklings. A light shower of flurries enveloped us. As we trekked ahead, a montage of Christmas specials and their romantic, snowy scenes filled my mind.

Tilting my head back, I caught a snowflake on my tongue. "Mm."

Akihiko's eyes glittered dark. Seeing Yuki a few feet ahead, he leaned close to my ear, his voice low as the sea. "You have snowflakes stuck in your hair."

I reached a hand to brush them off, but Akihiko caught my eye. "No, leave them. They suit you."

A thousand butterflies fluttered through me. "Really?"

"Really. Each one stands out like a white star against the night skies." His spoke in soft, velvety drone that made me melt.

"You know," I whispered back, "a single snowflake isn't white. It's a matter of reflection."

"Oh?"

"Light beams bounce around and wavelengths are reflected, making snowflakes white, but a single one clear." I leaned closer, feeling his breath on my ear. "Kind of like sugar crystals."

A deep, rich chuckle left Akihiko. I shivered, the static-like sensation traveling from my scalp to the back of my neck. I think I had just found my favorite ASMR.

Yuki turned around, and we sprang apart. The sprite took in our red faces, then gave us a gentle smile.

"Close now," she said.

"How close?" asked Akihiko.

"Very."

But her idea of "very" didn't match mine. We traveled further and further as the snow picked up. Thick and heavy, snowflakes descended upon us, pelting our frozen cheeks. All romantic musings fled me.

"Well, this is less than ideal." Akihiko walked in front of me, acting like my personal snow shield.

My teeth chattered. "I'm sure we'll be there soon."

We trekked deeper into the storm, and Akihiko's outline blurred in the swirling frost. Snow sank past my ankles with each step. The wind howled with ferocity. Arctic blasts struck my face with knife-like sharpness. It was as though we had discovered the very heart of winter.

"This is horrible," I shouted. "I-it's freezing."

"How much farther?" The wailing wind swallowed Akihiko's words, but the ever-perceptive sprite understood him.

"Close," she called back.

I trudged after her crude form. Within a few minutes, the blizzard started to subside. The air cleared, revealing a lone bandersnatch and clusters of winter cherry in the distance. At last, some sign of life.

I exhaled a misty breath in relief, but Akihiko stopped me with his arm.

"What are you—"

He silenced me with a finger to my lips. His gaze turned dark, his pupils enlarging. A fresh surge of panic flared through me.

Something was wrong.

I followed his line of vision to Yuki. With the snowfall tapering away, I could see her much more clearly now. She appeared dainty as ever, her wings fluttering in graceful movements.

Her *wings*.

I froze. My rose-colored glasses slid off.

A small mark peeked out from underneath the snow that coated the fluttering lace—half a blue heart. Fear seeped into my veins.

"We've been led on," I whispered.

Akihiko and I looked at each other in panic-mode. We had been rickrolled by a Jabberwock.

The blizzard had now reduced to a light dusting, showcasing our surroundings. Lines of hedges, ice sculptures, and… My stomach twisted. The Snow Queen's courtyard.

So much for a shortcut.

The "sprite" spun around.

Yuki twisted her small, pink lips into an impish smile. Her disguise melted away. Her porcelain skin turned into a harsh blue; her soft, ethereal expression hardened into something menacing. With a cruel trill polar to the sprite's honeyed lilt, the Jabberwock announced our presence.

"Seize them!"

Within seconds, two guards emerged behind the ice sculptures. They charged at us.

"*Alice.*"

"Akihiko!"

My palm grazed his. We scavenged the courtyard for something to fight with, but it was all we could do to back up against each other. The prince flashed me a dark look. "I'll hold them off. You run."

"You don't even have your sword!"

"I don't care." He gave me an unexpected shove. "*Just go!*"

I clenched my fist. "I'm not leaving you, Akihiko."

The guards lunged at us. I sprang out in front of Akihiko before he could stop me. With all my might, I kicked the nearest guard hard enough to knock her off course. I issued another blow, but she quickly recovered and seized my are. The other guard free to tackle Akihiko to the ground.

Oh, where was a reset button to this game?

My eyes darted around. And widened. A horde of Jabberwocks were diving into the fray, led by Yuki.

I screamed as the vile creatures yanked my hair and tossed us around with startling strength. Akihiko and I punched and kicked, but even our most calculated jabs did little in this stacked fight. I writhed and butted up my head against a guard's solid chin to no avail. My best efforts couldn't save me. As I looked dishearteningly at Akihiko, I realized his couldn't save him, either.

Somewhere between our naïve faith in pretty words and gentle wings, and my failure to keep up in gym class, we had lost.

Bruised and battered, I glanced up. I couldn't resist anymore. The guards unceremoniously restrained our hands to our backs and dragged us—along with the incomplete Looking Glass— into the Ice Palace.

Game over.

CHAPTER 9

The Mirror Princess

The guards hauled Akihiko and me through the castle's icy halls, careening around twists and turns. Their vise-like grips on us tightened whenever we uttered a protest. And so we stopped. My mind tried to calculate escape routes and tactics, but energy sapped, I could think of nothing to free us.

My insides gnawed with guilt. Usagi, Boushiya and Sangatsu had sacrificed so much for nothing. Soon, they would know everything. How I hadn't found the Mirror Princess. How the guards had confiscated the useless mirror that we had failed to complete.

Still, an ounce of warmth flooded me. They would see me, and I would see them.

Cradling that small comforting thought to my chest, I let the guards jerk me around an ice carved corridor. The translucent walls radiated cold, washing over me as they rubbed against my sore, bruised arm. I clenched my teeth against the ice burn. We must have been getting close to the icy dungeons.

The guards dragged us into a hall filled with colossal mirrors. Supported by pilasters of ice, their arches bore intricate heart symbols. But the mirrors themselves were either cracked, covered, or turned around. My gaze traveled to Akihiko's right. Every mirror there was turned to its side.

"Eyes forward," barked a guard.

Unrelenting hands shoved me forward, forcing me to increase my pace. A frosty door, intricately carved with snowflake shaped hearts, stood at the end of the hallway. Blue shadows emanated from its depths. Propelled by the guards, I stumbled through the opened door, straight into an ice chamber.

Draconian beauty enveloped me. Ice sculptures of snow nymphs lined the walls. A bluish glow bathed them, making their faces look sharper. I peered above. A staircase in a Fibonacci spiral reached the floor. In the center of the spiral, a mural of a beautiful, somber-faced woman in billowing robes decorated the high ceiling. Echoes of fluttering wings resounded against it. Wonderful. More Jabberwocks, I thought bitterly.

I squinted through the shadows. A long, narrow carpet of unperturbed snow stretched across the space that led up to a glinting throne. Fear paralyzed my limbs. The guards hadn't taken us to the dungeons after all.

"Did you miss me?" Venom dripped from a soft, feminine voice.

Panic robbed my breath. Pinioned by guards on both sides of my arms, I craned my head to see a sleek figure floating down the spiral stairway.

The Snow Queen took slow, deliberate strides. She moved like a symphony of grace as she seated herself in her throne of ice. Her gaze drifted to the domed ceiling I had been staring at. "Do you like that? That mural is of Chione. A mortal princess who became the goddess of snow and winter." The queen languidly crossed one leg over the other and extended her hand. "Let's cut the pleasantries, shall we? One of you, hand me that."

A guard approached, bowed, and handed her Usagi's satchel. I reacted with an involuntary jerk. The grasp on my arms tightened.

The queen pressed forward, sneering. "Accept it. You are trapped."

Helplessly, I watched her pull the Looking Glass from Usagi's satchel. She turned it over in her hands, set it down in her lap, and flashed me a piercing stare. "I've had my eye on you, Alice, since the moment you dared to infiltrate my kingdom. I've been aware of your whereabouts through *all* of this." An evocative smile touched her lips.

I eyed the crystal globe she lifted. Her loyal Jabberwocks swarmed around it, their wings beating against the viewing glass. Cloudy images whirled from within its depths. Images of a frozen lake, a snowy garden, and then...our campsite. My insides churned.

"You tracked our every movement," Akihiko said darkly.

"Of course," she replied.

"Why?" My jaw clenched. *"Why would you..."*

"Well, I suppose you could say I needed something to pass the time."

Her gaze swept across the room, landing on a kemonomimi statue to my right. My chest tightened. Had it suffered the same fate as Boushiya?

"All these pitiful inhabitants of Winterland," the queen began, "falling so easily... falling into my every net. Throw a banquet, invite the 'elite'—suddenly they're all jumping through hoops to gain my approval...It's pathetic. It's *dull*. I wanted a game. A real game—with you."

I stood there, dumbstruck. She was doing all of this because of she was...bored? No. That didn't make sense. Her manipulation and moves in this game were too calculated, too elaborate if done solely to amuse her from boredom.

Something was off.

Her pearly teeth glinted as she stroked the crystal globe. "I wanted to see how far you'd make it. How close you'd come to the outskirts." She gave a nonchalant wave. "Of course, I could have stopped you at any time, but that would have spoiled the fun. I wanted to play with you first." Her fingers stopped drumming the delicate crystal sphere. She dragged her gaze away from the globe and refocused it on Akihiko and me. Her slit-like eyes glowed like embers in the shadows, as if deliberating what she wanted to do with us.

I couldn't take the oppressive silence. Anger coursed through my body. "Don't you feel the slightest bit terrible for what you're doing?" My voice rang out, sharp as like a silver bell.

The queen's eyes widened a fraction at my outburst, then lowered. Slowly, she rose. "Terrible? You started all this."

"What are you talking about—"

Her eyes flashed at me. "Sticking your nose where it doesn't belong. Infringing on my territory. Stealing my most valuable possessions. *Trying to destroy me.*" She released a hollow laugh. "Take a cold, hard look at yourself, Alice. The only terrible one here is *you.*" Her eyes bore into me, their depths raging with spite. "I'll do everything in my power to protect my world from you."

A shiver ran through me. She didn't see herself as the villain. She genuinely thought I was in the wrong. I didn't fear the Snow Queen the most until now.

"Don't contort your face like that—it's awfully unflattering." She coiled a lock of hair around her finger. "I also suppose you thought I wasn't aware that the Looking Glass could imprison me. Did you know, *I* broke the Looking Glass, Alice? *My* Jabberwocks hid the fragments in the four quadrants of *my* kingdom."

"We knew that already." Akihiko clenched his fists.

"So you did? And yet..." The queen tilted her head, studying him. There was a hungry look in her eyes. "You harbor a question. Why not ask it?"

Akihiko lifted his chin, unfazed. "You could have entrusted the whole mirror to any one of your loyal monsters. Why break it into shards?"

The Snow Queen's smiled faded. "That is none of your business," she said coldly.

"I know why. The Mirror Princess scares you." I gathered the courage to continue, bidding myself not to show fear. "To go through all this length... Admit it, you're terrified of her. If we'd found her in the outskirts..." My voice came out a dark whisper. "You wouldn't be sitting there right now."

Shrill laughter hit my eardrums. "Foolish girl. The Mirror Princess sits right before you."

My entire body froze. "What...?"

"You heard right. Your Mirror Princess only exists in the form of a perpetuated myth—a myth concocted by yours truly."

A *myth*? I felt sick to my stomach. "I-it was all a lie?"

The queen smiled, relishing my sudden smallness. "I suppose so. But if it's any consolation to you, the final shard's whereabouts wasn't a lie. My sprite told you she would take you to it, did she not?" Her voice went soft. "Well, she kept her word."

Akihiko glared. "What do you mean?"

"I have the last piece of the Looking Glass," she whispered.

"But we stole the shard in your—"

"Not that one. Obviously not that one." Her eyes cut through me, like sapphires set in snow. "You truly think I would safeguard my most important treasures in a barely-secret chamber even runaway servants can access? No. I've hidden the final shard elsewhere—somewhere you cannot hope to find it." Her lips twisted, and she fell back in her seat. "Not that it matters. Your plan still wouldn't work, you know, even if you had the last shard."

What was she saying? Was this part of her twisted game to shake my psyche even more? Had Usagi somehow been *wrong*?

"So much fuss over this." Languidly, the queen held up the incomplete Looking Glass. "You truly think an eternal winter can be stopped with a simple mirror? My spell is more sophisticated and complex than that—not something a mere Looking Glass can break. Even if you manage to imprison me with the mirror, it still won't end this eternal winter."

My body trembling, I stared at my feet. The chibis stared back, mocking me with sinister Spitzbub smiles. "So you're saying our whole quest was pointless?"

"Essentially."

The floor under me crumbled.

We never even stood a chance.

The Snow Queen stroked her lip, her face softening at my defeated expression. "Come now. It wasn't *completely* pointless. It has been ages since I've been entertained so thoroughly. For that, I commend you."

"No... No..."

My gaze darted wildly between the queen and Akihiko. Her guard tightened her grip on my arms, spun me with force, and marshaled me toward the exit. Another guard joined us, grabbing me by the hair to stop me from writhing so much.

"Wait."

I snapped my head up.

"I do not wish to leave you with the wrong impression, Alice. I am a fair queen, after all. You might be interested to know that your friends—Boushiya, Usagi, and Sangatsu, was it?—will shortly join me in the courtroom. Yes, even treacherous, treasonous criminals deserve a fair trial. Of course, in their case, it will all be rather pointless. But, you know, formalities matter to the people, so..."

My breath cut my lungs. "You can't do this."

"Watch me." The Snow Queen rose from her throne. "I think we're quite finished here." She threw Usagi's satchel behind her. The clay mugs within it cracked, and something inside me cracked as well.

I craned my neck, but yelped as the second guard tightened her grip on my hair. Needles shot through my scalp, and strands snapped. The queen chuckled at my strained, feeble position. The familiar feelings of humiliation ravaged through me.

"Leave her alone!"

The queen shifted her attention to Akihiko, her laughter tapering.

"Let him go," she ordered the guard holding Akihiko.

The guard looked at her, hesitant. "Are you quite certain, your majesty?"

"Are you questioning me?" She spoke in a soft whisper that gave me the chills.

"Of course not," said the guard, releasing the prince. "I just thought—"

"Step away from him."

Sensing the danger in her voice, the guard bowed and backed away.

Akihiko stood feet apart, his stance wide and strong. "Chione," he whispered. "Stop it."

Chione?

The Snow Queen smiled. Her voice dipped to a rich, silky timbre as she stroked her crystal globe. "I don't think so, Aki."

"Aki?" I whispered to myself.

With a flick of her hand, a beam of ice soared in the prince's direction. His feet froze on the spot, just enough to hold him in place.

"Akihiko!"

The Snow Queen faced me, reveling in my turmoil. "What's a queen without her king?"

"Historically, better off," I whispered, thinking of Cleopatra, Victoria, Cixi, and countless other female monarchs.

I watched the queen glide toward the prince. Her hips swayed with each step. With provocative slowness, she trailed a finger along his clenched jaw, along his neck, along his heart shaped mark. My heart brimmed with revulsion.

"I knew you'd come back to me." Her lips grazed his earlobe.

I swallowed hard. "Back ...?"

"Did he not tell you?" A slow, serpentine smile crept her mouth. "We were betrothed."

A wave of shock rippled through me. I looked to Akihiko, desperate for a contradiction. His eyes bore a pained expression.

I felt like I had been slapped in the face.

"Alice," he began, "listen to me, you don't understand—"

"Oh, I think I do." I couldn't hide the betrayal drenching my voice.

The queen draped her arms over the prince's shoulder and wetted her carnelian lips. "Soon you'll be completely mine," she whispered. "Again."

My skin crawled. The mark on the prince's neck darkened before me until it was completely black.

Watching my expression in relish, the queen dropped her voice to an icy whisper. "Poor girl, you've lost the game."

She snapped her fingers. Without further ado, the guards dragged me into confinement. This time the thick ice door they unlocked and shoved open actually led to the dungeons. Circular, silvery ice cells glinted menacingly in the murky shadows. Though the entire palace was made of ice, this was the first room where I felt truly cold.

The guards shoved me down a spiral stairway. We passed cell after gloomy cell until…I strained my eyes. Yes—there they were. Each imprisoned in their own icy cell.

My friends.

"Usagi," I choked out. "Boushiya. *Sangatsu.*"

At the sound of my tremulous voice, two thirds of the trio grasped the bars of their circular prisons. The hatter was still a frozen statue of a man. Only his eyes moved, melting my heart like I wished I could melt his curse.

I took in the trio's battered faces. They took in my bound hands. Anguish clenched Usagi's face. She watched the guards thrust me into my own circular cell and slam the door shut.

Usagi faced me. "What happened?"

"The Snow Queen. She tracked us all along. We only made it this far because she let us…" Unable to swallow the lump in my throat, I couldn't speak more.

Sangatsu and Usagi didn't reply. Boushiya's eyes widened and flicked about like he wanted to speak, but with his mouth frozen shut, he could only stare at me. Before I could tear my gaze from him, he blinked hard.

And again, as though trying to gain my attention. What was he...?

He repeated the gesture, emphasizing each blink. *Morse code?* But if it was, it was only two letters. I focused on his lids. B...S.

B.S.? Was he calling the queen a liar? But I had *seen* the viewing glass, or crystal globe, or whatever it was called. I had watched the regions fade in and out. I had seen our campsite for flake's sake. No. Boushiya's message was either coincidence or plain wrong. The queen hadn't lied about that.

Tears streamed down my cheeks. "Akihiko and I tried so hard. But in the end, none of it mattered. There is no Mirror Princess. The Snow Queen concocted the entire tale." My voice faltered. "She has the Looking Glass now."

Usagi made a strangled sound. "Alice, I don't know what to say."

"Then don't say anything." My tone came out harsher than I wanted. An unexpected burst of anger consumed me. I couldn't look at her. How could she get so many facts wrong? How could she lead us on a pointless, perilous journey? She was *Usagi.* The confident, competent character I had always admired. Out of everybody, I never imagined *she* would let me down. When her tears dropped to the icy floor, something inside me broke. And yet, I clenched my fists tighter.

"This whole mission has been one epic fail," I said acridly. "And now Akihiko is—" I couldn't finish my sentence.

"Chibi…" Boushiya and Sangatsu exchanged a desperate glance from opposite ends of the prison chamber. Despite my venting at her, Usagi looked at me with a crestfallen face. "I'm so sorry, Alice."

"So am I. In fact, I wish I never came across Winterland in the first place." A blind rage swept over me. "I-I wish…I wish I never met any one of you." My words sounded so foreign to me. Why had I said that? *How* could I say that?

"That makes the two of us."

I stared hard at Usagi. "What?"

"All my life I've done things alone. Me, myself, and I were all I relied on. I thought I should change that, but I was wrong." Her gaze traveled to each of us. "Maybe if I retrieved the Looking Glass on my own, we wouldn't be here right now."

The hatter's eyes burned with frosty tears. He couldn't speak, but his expression was clear. I whispered his question for him. "Do you truly mean that, Usagi?"

Her parted lips trembled. "I do."

"Sorry we held you back," Sangatsu said coldly.

"I'm sorry too," she replied.

I stared at my shaking hands. The heart on my wrist was clearer and darker than ever. I glanced at the trio. Usagi and Sangatsu's heart marks had grown to the same inky-black as Akihiko's. I couldn't make out Boushiya's under the thick encasement of ice, but from his smoldering eyes I knew he was in the same boat.

We had fallen to the darkness in our hearts.

A jangle sounded nearby. The door swung wide open, and a pair of guards stormed in. They eyed Sangatsu, Boushiya, and Usagi. "The trial will commence shortly. Her majesty will start with you three."

Protests echoed off the walls as the guards wrestled the trio from their icy confines and pinned their hands behind their backs. Boushiya's stiff body clanged against the frozen floor, making me cringe.

"Alice," came a strained voice just before the door slammed.

I didn't reply.

I couldn't reply. My throat burned. A tsunami of emotions crashed down on me. I crouched to the floor and hugged my knees to my chest. My long hair spilled over my arms, covering me like a safety blanket. For a long time, I stayed like that until my feet started to cramp. I shifted, my bleary eyes drifting above. Brown straps were coiled around one of the prison's bars.

I rose to my feet and yanked the straps from the bar, pulling the thing they were attached to into my cell.

Usagi's satchel.

How did it end up there?

Not that it mattered. Surmising one of the guards must've thrown it there during my containment, I kicked it to the far side of the wall. A clock and pieces of broken clay mugs spilled out. A small red book peeked out from among the shattered odds and ends. Almost of its own accord, my hand reached for it. I ran a finger along the worn spine, then opened the cover.

A diary?

I flipped through the pages. The entries chronicled her lonely days at the palace, the weeks spent as a fugitive, the months spent in isolation, save for the few books that kept her company.

I skimmed a few of these, then skipped ahead to the recent entries.

Day 331

Is it strange that despite the unrelenting cold and the constant turmoil that follows me, I do not feel half as miserable as I used to?

But I don't know that I'm quite happy yet, either. I fear it is a case of kairosclerosis—when you become aware that you're happy and try to drink in the feeling, analyze it, and put it in context... only for it to dissipate until you're left with a bittersweet aftertaste.

I still have far to go, but I think I'm getting there.

<u>Day 332</u>

Collecting the third shard today was no easy feat, but it made me realize something. Individually, we are snowflakes, but together, we are an avalanche. A force to be reckoned with.

<u>Day 333</u>

No longer am I alone. I have them. And they have me.

After years of searching, I think I finally found something I love more than books—friendship.

A deluge of tears gathered onto my lashes. I blinked, and they gave way. Warm liquid ran down my cheeks and fell upon the page, blurring the ink. For a moment I felt a ping of guilt, but it faded. What did the diary matter now? What did any of it matter anymore?

I couldn't suppress myself anymore. The raw emotions within me spilled like an overflowing river. I shouted my frustrations to no one at all. My frustrations with this world, my own world. Myself. Racking sobs rattled my chest. In response, an arctic wind swept through my confines, howling like the cold laughter of Father Winter. I was spiraling, imploding, my despair turning into a pool of tears.

A faint chuckle mixed with the laughing wind. I rocketed to my feet.

Smirking, a familiar kemonomimi eyed me through the bars of my cell's circular window. "Ugly sobbing doesn't suit you."

"H-how the h—"

"Deus ex machina." Shiroi quirked his lips. "Looks like you found yourself in a full circle."

"Very punny." I rubbed my stinging eyes, too exhausted to play his puerile games. "Just leave me alone."

"Mm, someone's salty," he tittered. "Honestly, I didn't think the queen would manage to *round* you up that easily."

"Spare me the cattitude." I gripped the bars of my circular prison until my knuckles turned white. "Help me out. Or get out."

"I suppose I could release you."

"Really?"

"I could, but what good would that do?" He tilted his head with unnatural flexibility. "Tell me. Do you even have a plan?"

"Well, no, but—"

"Then," he purred, "it's rather pointless, isn't it?"

As usual, he acted rational as Pi. But deep down, I knew he had a point... I had no plan.

Squeezing my eyes, I backed into the slippery wall and slumped onto the icy floor. "You're right, it's pointless. Even if I come up with a plan, it's too late for that." I stared at the blackish-blue heart on my wrist. Like assailants in the shadows, my mind assaulted me with Usagi and Sanbou's exchange. Akihiko's lie. My harsh words. "The darkness has already taken over us."

"You say it like it's all bad," he purred.

"Because it is."

"But you need darkness to see the stars, love."

"Don't call me that," I said coldly. "If you can't be useful, just go away."

"As you wish."

Stunned, I watched him back away. I didn't think he'd listen to me that easily. Bit by bit, his body melted into the icy backdrop. A sting of panic gripped me.

I stuck my arm through the cell's bars. "Wait, come back." His tail vanished into nothingness. "I'm sorry," I burst out. "I didn't mean—you can't just leave me like this!" The last remnants of his body disappeared.

He was gone.

I seized the bars of my prison cell and pressed my forehead against the ice, hoping the cold wetness would numb my frustration. It didn't.

Squeezing my eyes, I yelled from the top of my lungs. "Why does everything I do just make things worse and worse?"

"Sometimes wrong choices guide us to the right place."

From the canvas of nothingness, an opaque outline formed. Gleaming amethyst eyes appeared followed by a devilish smile. The rest of the kemonomimi's body filled out.

I put a hand to my chest, breathing hard. "Don't mess with me like that."

"With you, it's tempting not to." Shiroi flashed me a feral smile, eyeing me as if I was nothing more than his play thing.

My mouth twitched as I tried to control my anger. As much as I wanted to tell him off, I bit my tongue. No way was I making the same mistake twice. I needed find a way to appeal to his good graces.

I took a full breath, hardly believing what I was about to do.

Slowly, I peered at the ridiculous kemonomimi through my lashes. Like the middle notes of a violin, I made my voice rich and smooth. "Shiroi."

His eyes slanted. "Hm?"

"I...never realized how handsome you are."

"*Oh?* Do tell me more about myself." He sauntered closer.

"You have such long, flowing hair. And er, cute feline teeth."

I winced at my words. *Suppress the cringe.*

"Go on, love." Shiroi went heavy-lidded.

"And your tail... It's so *twisted.*" I twirled my finger in a circle and swallowed the last scraps of my dignity. "You're the cat-ion to my anion, Shiroi. You've stolen my heart."

The cat kemonomimi curled his lips into a Cheshire grin. "Mm. Flattery will get you everywhere right now.

Everywhere except this." He flicked his long tail against the lock of my cell. "Try again, love."

I gritted my teeth. "You. Have. To. Help. Me."

"My, always so demanding. I don't have to do a thing."

"Okay, you don't, but *please*. I'm begging you—help me."

The amusement deepened in his eyes. "Since you used the magic word, perhaps I can be of assistance." A sliver of hope flickered through me. "But," he added, "only under one condition."

Of course. I should have expected some string attached to his offer. Nothing would come easy with this ridiculous cat.

"Name your price."

"Oh, nothing too taxing." He exhaled as he spoke, letting his moist breath ghost through the ice bars of my cell, and to my face. I shivered.

Please, not a kiss.

"I've been regretting how easy I went on you last time. So..." He wetted his lips. I gulped. No, no, n— "You merely need to humor me with one more riddle."

I blinked. "Again with the riddles?"

"Well, there's always the other alternative." His gaze dipped to my lips. I shuddered.

Why couldn't he understand the urgency of the situation? I wouldn't have minded if it was a favor that actually benefitted him, but to waste time like this for his entertainment? It was all so absurd. Pointlessly, maddeningly absurd. Just like him.

Feeling my face redden, I drew a deep breath. *Keep calm and carry on, Alice.* If this was his ridiculous currency, then so be it.

I jerked my head up and down. "Deal. Give me the riddle."

"What is the name of the Mirror Princess?"

"But that isn't a riddle at all. It's just a question."

"So, your answer?"

"The Snow Queen. Or whatever her non-title name is." I gripped the icicle bars in front of me and spat the word out, "*Chione.* There. Now, how exactly do you intend to get me out?"

"I don't." Shiroi flicked his tail and hummed. "Try again, love."

What? How could my answer be wrong? Maybe the cat wanted her alias. "Princess Ariel—I mean Ariel Ecila." Silence. "*Princess Ariel Ecila,*" I repeated. "Now let me out already."

Shiroi lazily curled his tail around bars of my confines. "I don't think so."

Drat and blast him. I balled up my hands. My patience was wearing thinner than a sheet of ice. Did he really want to help me, or was this whole thing a ploy to stall me until I froze over?

With infuriating indifference, Shiroi traced his sharp nail against the wall of the icy cell. His finger scrawled something in the moisture.

My eyes flicked to the name he had written on the ice cell: Ariel Ecila. Maybe Ariel was pronounced the way Sebastian said it—*Ah-ri-el* instead of *Air-iel*. A ridiculous nuance? Yes. But given the ridiculousness that made up Shiroi, it wouldn't be too much of a stretch.

I repeated my answer a third time, even throwing in a slight Jamaican accent like my favorite crustacean did.

The kemonomimi didn't look amused at all. "No, no, *no*." He tetchily eyed the name he had scrawled. "I'll give you only one more chance."

A sarcastic laugh escaped me. The irony. He was losing patience with me.

Muttering some colorful words, I fell back against the icy, wet wall and crossed my arms. I stared at the written letters, long and hard, then at the moisture dripping from them. A small, thin puddle collected at the base of my prison. I went rigid.

My mind flashed back to the puddle in labyrinth. If the riddles were anything like before, the answer to this one wouldn't be straightforward either. I'd need to flip my usual logical process upside down and inside out if I wanted to solve this.

An onslaught of word plays assaulted me. Puns, anagrams, spoonerisms, oxymorons, riddles. My mind raced like an engine, racking for the correct answer. Nothing was clicking.

My frustration dwindled to anxiety, then despair. And then into nothingness. A familiar numbness spread over me, chasing out any remnants of hope. I was falling. Falling into a dark, bottomless shaft…

Don't you dare give up now, screamed a voice inside my head. You've camped out just to meet your favorite voice actors, endured years of waiting for the new season of Winterland, *pulled all-nighters to finish a cosplay costume, painstakingly written a 394 page fanfiction as a labor of love; you've relentlessly thrown yourself out of your comfort zone since landing here… This is nothing.*

I balled up my hands. If my inner fangirl wouldn't give up on me that easily, neither would I. She was right. I had come way too far. The online sorting hat hadn't placed me in Ravenclaw for nothing. I could solve this.

My brows slanted into two lines. I straightened up with determination. Using the puddle as a point of focus, I withdrew into my mind palace. Balancing my mind the way I balanced chemical equations in class, I repeated

Shiroi's question to myself. *What is the name of the Mirror Princess. What is the name of the Mirror Princ —?* My concentration broke. I drew in a sharp breath.

Mirror.

Something within me cracked. I staggered back as if someone had pulled a rug out from under my feet. The room around me spun like the truthflake passageway, and the answer struck me with full force.

Lips trembling, I turned to Shiroi. "Alice...Leira." My voice came out a shaky whisper. "The Mirror Princess is *me.*"

I stared at the scrawled letters on the icy wall and saw the answer confirm itself on the floor. Like a mirror, the puddle reflected the letters Ariel Ecila in reverse. My name, *Alice Leira,* danced at me in the water.

"I've been searching for myself this whole time," I whispered.

Shiroi curled his lips. "And now you've found yourself."

He dug a long, sharp nail into the lock and turned. The door opened with a flourish, and I stepped out of my icy confines.

I was finally free.

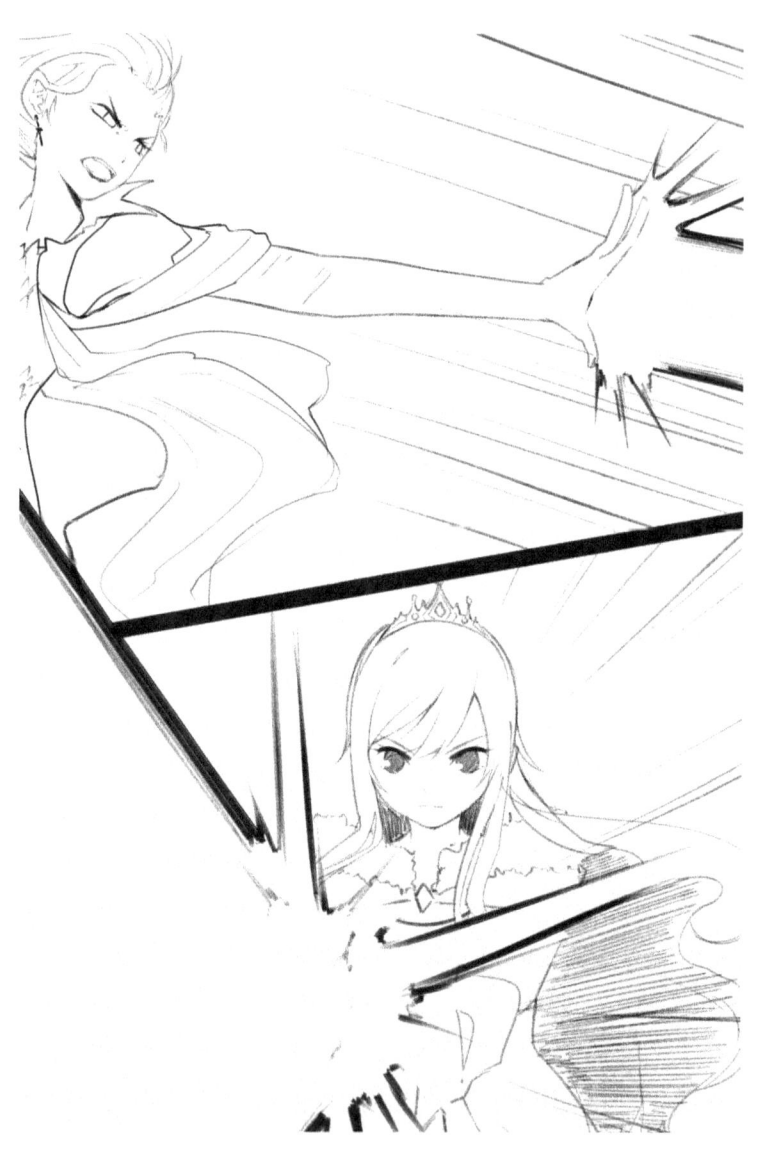

CHAPTER 10

Through the Looking Glass

Shiroi vanished piece-by-piece. Soon, only an arrow of a tail remained in the air, followed by a soft cackle. When all of him had disappeared, I gave a start.

The trial.

I turned to leave, then stopped in my tracks. Usagi's satchel. I couldn't leave without it.

As I picked up the satchel, a long snow white strand fell from its strap. The three-foot hair could only belong to one person. A smile touched my lips. Maybe I didn't need to burn my cosplay after all.

Slinging the strap over my shoulder, I bolted out of the prison chamber. Veering right and left, I blundered through an empty corridor. Slick with ice, the floor kept slipping under my feet. But each time, I caught myself from falling. Looked liked the ice skating rendezvous with the frostmaidens had paid off. Still, I struggled to move quickly but quietly—something that was *so* not my forte. One false move, and the guards would throw me back in the dungeons. But if I failed to get there in time... *No, don't think about it.*

I couldn't get lost in my negative thoughts now.

Keeping my knees bent, I moved my center of mass forward, maintaining my speed and balance. I maneuvered around a corner, passing a line of mirrors that were all turned around. A wisp of concentrated light filled the shadows. I blinked a couple times until my eyes adjusted. When the spots and blurs cleared, a hallway came into view—like none I had ever seen. I hadn't been able to appreciate its beauty when I was being dragged by the guards. But now, it was all I could do not to ogle. Soft, blue rays of light spilled down from three staggered lines of small, square windows, checkering the floor in dim, glowing squares.

Instinct kicking in, I started hopping between the squares with soft, rhythmic steps. I pictured them lighting up like DDR arrows. Suddenly, all the years of invitation-less Saturday nights had paid off. I hummed a K-pop song under my breath to calm my nerves and darted through the hallway with quick, light steps.

Careful, careful, I whispered to the beat. *Slide to the right. Slide to the left.*

I skirted past the throne room and stepped onto a long stretch of smooth, Zamboni-ed floor. I backed up for a running start and found myself skating down the rink-like tract. My soft yelps bounced off the ice walls as I zipped by. Bit-by-bit, the ice under me disappeared. A large, open archway shimmered into view. From within it, a din of protesting voices spilled out. I stumbled onto the frosty ground.

Breathing hard, I propped myself up and peeked into the space. Two twin guards resembling Anastasia and Isabella flanked an entryway. Behind them, I could make out a stark white courtroom filled with kemonomimis. All ears and eyes were preoccupied with the task of silencing the riotous dissenters. I caught my breath, calculating my next move. I needed to find a way into the trial. But how...?

My attention dropped to Usagi's satchel. Maybe it had something I could use. I stuffed my hand into the pouch and rummaged around.

Sweet, sweet serendipity.

I pulled out the small, brass clock. Quickly, I set the alarm and crammed it back into the satchel. Then, I hurled it into the courtroom and backed up against the wall.

My haphazard plan seemed to work. Seeing the object in midair, the guards gave a shout. The Isabella-look alike took the bait, flying after the satchel, but her twin narrowed her eyes in my direction.

Please don't see me, please don't see me.

Gulping, I watched her near closer until—*brrriing, brrriing, brrii*—a shrill ringing pierced the air. Usagi's alarm clock sputtered on the floor, screeching its mechanical heart out.

The queen's voice echoed from the courtroom. "What is that sound?"

A swarm of Jabberwocks whirled out of the archway, searching for the din. They circled the satchel—and the twins, blinding them in a flurry of blue, leathery wings. It was a small diversion, but it was enough for my first step. I inhaled a deep breath. Now was my chance.

I flung myself through the archway. A Jabberwock swooped past my head but was too distracted to notice me. I ducked beneath a frosty ice bench before it could turn back. The ringing ceased.

"Finally."

Seated in her throne, the Snow Queen towered over the crowd. Her ghastly shadow bathed their outlines. "Now, let us come to the verdict. The fates of our treasonous trio…"

"This is absurd!"

"*Unreasonable.*"

"Unjust!"

"Order, order," cried a royal attendant, but the volume of the objections didn't change by a decibel. Usagi and Sangatsu's discordant voices bounced off the high-domed ceiling. Their cries of dissent piled on top of each other like music playing from three tabs at once. Then, the din subsided into a series of muffled yips. I peered up from my hiding place.

I stilled. The Jabberwocks began gagging them into silence. When they finished, the vile creatures fluttered back to their mistress. Her gaze swept over the mute, struggling kemonomimis, the frozen hatter, then the young man by her side. Akihiko's face was withdrawn, his eyes clouded. The queen took him in, smiling like it was Christmas morning.

Anger bubbled within me, ready to explode. It took every ounce of restraint to bottle it up and maneuver through the chilly pews with all my stealth. Inch by slippery inch, I army-crawled my way to the front of the room.

"Much better." The queen curled her lips and returned her attention to the parchment in hand. The paper spilled dramatically across the room, carpeting the place three times over. No way had we committed that many offenses.

I glowered at the endless list. It was lies. Lies, lies, ridiculous B.S lies—

My eyes widened.

B.S. So that was what Boushiya had meant.

"Usagi," the queen drawled. "The jury of royal supe-riors has found you guilty of aiding and abetting a dangerous insurgent, leading a tyrannical faction, pilfering royal property, injuring the royal guards… etcetera, etcetera, etcetera." She tossed the parchment over her shoulder. "You are hereby sentenced to the only punishment befitting your crimes." Her eyes blazed at Usagi's trembling ears with cold vengeance. "*Off with her ea—*"

"No!" I jumped out of hiding, my own body shaking with rage. Gasps came from every direction.

"Ah-riss—dohn't." Sangatsu shuddered and stared at me in horror. He blustered an incoherent warning, but a Jabberwock tightened his gag.

Usagi craned her neck to see me, but with her mobility limited, she could only flit her glazed eyes my way. I could tell she was torn between her belief in me and her desire for me to escape. But before she could make up her mind about what she wanted me to do—as if I'd even listen—the guards on either side of Usagi's chair tightened their grip on her arms. She released a cry of pain.

"Usagi!"

Immobilized by the guards, she signaled to me. Her eyes flicked to an exit nearby. She wanted me to save myself.

No, I mouthed to her. *I have to do this.*

She seemed to echo Shiroi's question. *Do you even have a plan?*

Well, no. I faltered a step back. No longer startled, the guards eyed me like prey. So this was how a fly caught in a spider's web felt.

The guards began to round on me, their muscular arms reaching for mine. The Snow Queen drank the scene in. Her eyes smoldered like blue flames.

Flames.

In one jerky motion, I plunged my hands into my pockets and withdrew the phone battery and a few strands of steel wool. *Please be enough.*

I touched the material to the positive and negative sides of the battery. It lit. The guards retreated with a shout. I hurled the material on the parchment-strewn floor. The flames licked their way along the paper. The fire blazed, then spread. The icy pews and walls began to drip.

Chaos ensued in every direction. Throughout the room, court-goers leapt up, yelping. They stormed through the aisles, making for the exit.

"What is this?" shrieked the queen.

"*Physics.*"

"Take care of it," she hissed to her Jabberwocks.

They shot off to douse the flames, when a sharp sound resounded from the defendants' chairs. Boushiya jumped to his feet. The fire had melted his curse.

Mustering all his strength, he punched Sangatsu's guard, and the two of them abandoned their posts. The duo ripped their gags off and tackled Usagi's guards. Working in perfect sync, they brought the guards down and freed Usagi.

I waved my hands to her. *Get Akihiko.*

Usagi understood my message. She rushed to Akihiko's side. After grabbing an abandoned, blazing tail-coat, she melted the ice around his feet. The prince, however, made no effort to move. He stared at her, expressionless. She ushered him to follow her, but he merely fixated on the queen's silhouette. Usagi chewed her lip and looked at me helplessly.

I was too late. He had been consumed by his own darkness, left only with a shell of himself. He was in the queen's control now. I steeled my heart.

I...couldn't save him.

Tears pricking my eyes, I shook my head. Usagi gave a painful nod. Through the chaos, she followed after Sangatsu and Boushiya.

The queen shouted in frustration. "Up! Over there— get her... No! They're getting away—stop them! Don't just *follow* them!" Her orders only confused her Jabber-wocks more. A few of them followed her erratic hand movements, then crashed into each other right before her face.

Seizing my chance, I slipped behind the queen's throne and reached up with a stealthy hand. I snatched the incomplete Looking Glass from where it sat, woefully abandoned, on a frosty armrest.

I bolted away, catching a glimpse of my Picasso-self in the discordant mosaic of shards. My eyes flashed back at me in the fractured reflection. Wait a minute. I was the Mirror Princess. I could work the Looking Glass, couldn't I? I could imprison the queen and save everyone… if only I could find the last fragment.

Before I could mull over the shard's whereabouts, a stream of ice flashed across the room. The Snow Queen had caught on to my stunt. Her face convulsed with white-hot fury.

"Give that back!" she snarled, arms raised.

"When hail freezes over!"

I cringed. Okay, not my best comeback.

I jumped as her ice magic grazed my foot. A blizzard raged overhead, matching her mood. Thick flurries obscured my vision. I could only see black strands of hair whipping my face in the wild, whirling whiteness.

Another attack.

My scarf fell to the ground, cut from me by a blade of ice. Before I could catch my breath, I dodged another blast and another. By her third attack, I was panting for air. I couldn't keep this up for much longer.

The queen did not appear the slightest worn. She lifted her arms again and again, crashing them down with a violence that could have broken my arm on its own accord, without the added benefit of magical ice. Rubbing salt on the wound, she wore a cool smile on her lips the entire time she assailed me.

"And *this* is why nerds need gym class," I hissed to myself. If only I had a TARDIS, I would go back in time and force past-me to participate in kickball.

The Snow Queen narrowed her wrathful eyes. Power sparked from her like a cut wire. Her hand sliced through the swirling frost. Over and over. An angry vortex of icy shards formed before her, increasing in size. I watched in horror as tendrils of ice crystals collected in her palm. With both hands, she aimed straight at me.

Unable to react in time, I clamped my eyes shut and clutched the Looking Glass with everything I had. Her attack sent me sprawling to the ground. For several moments I didn't move—until I realized not an inch of me had frozen over. I cracked open a lid. And gaped.

A sheet of ice had encased the queen's right hand. She gazed at it with fervid confusion. Together, we redirected our stares to the incomplete mirror in my hand.

The Looking Glass…deflected her magic?

The queen shot me a venomous glare. She lifted her frozen hand and smashed it against a wall. The ice shattered, freeing her. Dozens of Jabberwocks swarmed out of nowhere like a storm of vengeance. Ensconced in a swarm of wings, the queen aimed blast after livid blast. With the mirror as my weapon, I deflected her magic back at her.

One deflected blast of ice headed for the crystal globe in her left hand. At the last second, two Jabberwocks intercepted it. They plummeted into the snow, helpless and immobile, their leathery wings encapsulated in ice. The queen blanched at the sight of her fallen warriors.

Enthused by the poetic justice of the scene, I couldn't help but smirk. "Looks like the tables have turned."

The queen snapped her head. Her pale skin darkened a shade bluer, and her cold eyes pierced through me. I held out the mirror with confidence. Waiting—eagerly this time—to rebound her spell.

Shaking off the ice bits in her chignon, the queen assailed me again. Once more I deflected her attack. She dodged the rebounding magic and aimed again. This time her ice magic seemed weaker. She moved slower, and yet, with more composure. I squinted. Her wrathful expression had melted, and in its place—apathy. As I rebounded her third attack, I realized she was putting less and less effort into it.

Was she just giving up?

The Snow Queen raised her right hand one more time. Then, she lowered it, slower yet, less forcefully. My brows furrowed at the shift in her demeanor. What did it matter? As long as I had the Looking Glass, I had nothing to fear. Soon this would all be over...

A familiar stream of ice jetted toward me. I raised the mirror to deflect her magic. Quick as a flash, the Snow Queen stretched her arms apart, pointing her hands in the opposite directions.

No...she wouldn't.

"Revenge is best served cold."

"Stop!" I screamed.

"Allow me to deliver your comeuppance," she said softly.

The scene unraveled in slow motion. Each hand emitted a powerful blast of the magic she'd been harnessing this entire time. Icy whorls from her right hand struck Akihiko. The one from her left hand hit Usagi—followed by Sangatsu and the hatter. Ice crawled up their bodies, encasing each one of them in thick, jagged crystals.

I rushed to their sides. "Sangatsu…Boushiya…*Usagi!*"

Over and over, I recited their names like a litany, but my desperate pleas did nothing to change the color draining from their faces. With every passing second my friends looked more and more like ice sculptures.

"A-Akihiko."

"Alice," he gasped, his eyes regaining a trace of his old self. "You changed my world. Since we met…it's been you. Only you." His lips parted open as though they wished to utter something more. But it was too late. They remained paralyzed.

"No…*Akihiko!*"

Tears streaming down my face, I tried to scrape away the cursed ice with my fingernails. But all my efforts gained me were chipped nails, flayed fingertips, and a whisper of a scratch on the ice.

"Look what you made me do," the queen whispered, breathing hard. "Now hand over the mirror before I do something worse." Her pale hands flicked to the horrified audience of kemonomimis.

She knew she had won. I knew she had won.

I collapsed onto the snowy ground. The air around me grew colder, biting deeper and deeper into me. A vortex of darkness pulled at me, threatening to consume me on the spot. My mind went numb. Even the tenacity of my inner fangirl had disappeared. All this time, I had tried to stay afloat, but now I was drowning. Drowning in the icy depths of my own despair. I felt powerless. Soulless. Like an empty shell.

I felt like nothing.

"Take it," I said, holding up the Looking Glass.

The queen smiled. "Now, that wasn't so hard now, was it?"

She glided toward me, her right arm outstretched. As I moved to hand over the mirror, I spied a Jabberwock moving wildly in the throne's blue shadows. The creature flailed its limbs, trying desperately to grab my attention. I squinted harder. Could it be...? My heart skipped a beat.

Metanoia.

The wingless Jabberwock mouthed a single word, but I couldn't make it out. With a shake of her head, she pointed a finger through the air. I followed it to the small object cradled in the queen's left hand. The crystal globe that never strayed from her presence. The queen's own words echoed in my mind. She had watched us through that. Tracked our every move.

My gaze darted back to Metanoia. Her frantic hands kept pointing to the globe, putting my mind in a state of quandary. What? *What?* Frustration barraged me like a hurricane beating against a tarp. What did she expect me to do with a stupid snow globe?

You see, but do not observe.

Taking a deep breath, I calmed my mind. I focused on the crystal sphere with a quiet intensity. Discretely, I eyed the world of Winterland inside the glass. The Snow Queen reached for the mirror in my hand, bending nearer and teetering in her eagerness to attain it. Then, I saw it. A section of the globe's surface didn't match the rest of the glass. My pulse picked up.

An embedded . . . fragment?

A sliver of hope flickered through me. My eyes darted to Metanoia, then to the queen. The Jabberwock bobbed her small head and emerged from the shadows. I lifted the mirror closer to the queen. She leaned in further, sacrificing her balance in her greed. That was all it took.

Metanoia jabbed the queen from behind, causing her to stagger sideways. Instinctually, I swung the mirror over the orb. I brought it down with all my might. The mirror hit the globe, cracking its surface with a crisp *whack*. The queen screamed, and the orb fell the floor.

I scrambled to pick up the fallen Looking Glass shard. Before I even touched it, a small fissure formed in the leaden skies above. A streak of iridescent light erupted from it. Epiphany struck. I felt an invincible summer within me, banishing the cold. A rush came over me, like after a long struggle with a calculus problem, and understanding finally dawned. I knew how to stop this eternal winter.

A guttural sound escaped the queen. Her sharp nails aimed for me, but she wasn't quick enough.

I whacked another crack into the crystal globe. The queen shielded her face from flying glass. The fissures in the skies branched out. More slivers of light penetrated through them. It was as though the queen's spell had kept us contained in a snow globe, and the glass was finally breaking. I aimed again. On my third strike, crystal fragments flew in all directions. I had broken the globe completely—and along with it, her spell.

The fissures overhead gave way. A brilliant light swept over everything. I shielded my eyes against it. Though I could not see my friends in the blinding light, I heard them collapse. There was a muffled softness to their landing that the icy floor could not have supplied. I raised a hand to my face, my eyes adjusting as the light lifted.

The spots and blurs cleared. Usagi, Boushiya, Sangatsu, and Akihiko stirred on the lush ground, the ice around them thawing. Surrounding them was an Elysian vision.

The boughs, no longer bereft, were adorned with blossoming hues. Grasses with purple, feathery plumes blanketed the ground, and gumdrop-colored flowers popped up everywhere. I had never seen so many exotic flora all in one place. A cascade of strange, lollipop-like blooms spilled near my feet. Their intoxicating fragrance made my head swim.

The bleak landscape wasn't the only thing that transformed. No longer devoid of color, kemonomimis glowed with the lively, bright hues of a watercolor painting. The Jabberwocks's harsh blue skins warmed into a sweet powder blue. Their claw-like digits softened into small, dainty fingers, and their leathery wings grew diaphanous, as if spawned from moonlight. They fluttered past me, their faces angelic and delicate. So their true form had been sprites after all. Now, they really were kawaii.

The royal guards shed their thick winter coats on the rainbow flowerbeds and pointed above their heads in awe. Instead of snow, a light shower of stardust sprinkled down from the skies.

The queen slowly spun in a full circle. The more she took in the changes, the more deranged her expression grew. Fury crackled like blue fire within her eyes. She lunged at me, clawing the air as she flew through it. As her nails grazed my shoulders, I jumped to my feet and grabbed the mirror fragment from the pile of shattered glass. Fingers fumbling, I pieced together the final shard.

The moment I completed the mirror, a spark zipped through my fingertips. I gasped. An opalescent glow formed along the cracks between the shards, melding the mirror into a perfect whole. Even the tarnished frame polished itself until it gleamed like mottled moonstone.

And the mirror wasn't the only thing that had changed. I blinked hard, but the reflection I saw in the Looking Glass did not belong to me. The girl who smiled back shared my face, but her eyes were bright and alluring. Every illuminated line of her face was bathed in soft rainbows. She was me, but different: the me I aspired to be. Mirror-Alice smiled at me.

And then, she winked.

And suddenly, I was turning into her.

Reflective circles of light bounced around me. I held onto the mirror, awestruck. My clothes melted away as pink, aqua, and green pastels bathed me. In a transformation sequence straight out of Sailor Moon, ribbons of light wrapped around my hands, arms, torso, and legs. My hair whipped back and forth, a delicate weight entwining in it. When the lights faded, I gawked.

The magic had weaved an outfit tailored just for me. It fitted every curve and matched my boldest wishes. The silvery threads on the bodice shone like scattered stars. My skirt undulated with scallops of candy-colored gossamer. The ethereal fabric burst from the waist and blossomed to the ground like a flower. Akihiko's cloak had returned to me, cascading off my shoulders and kissing the lush, purple ground. Shaking, I took in my reflection in the Looking Glass. A diadem, set with crystals, adorned my hair.

I had finally become the girl I had been searching for.

Untamed power rippled through me, filling every part of me. Following it came a newfound strength that had nothing to do with being the Mirror Princess. I inhaled confidence and expelled doubt. Never before had I felt so sure of myself. I gripped the mirror and felt its energy siphoning through me in waves.

Ready to imprison the queen, I spun around. But, even without the aid of magic ice, what I saw froze me on the spot. A tear trickled down the queen's cheek. I backed up a step, my grip on the mirror weakening. How could I feel pity—for *her*?

Our eyes met. The queen bit down on her pale, chapped lips. She pointed a trembling finger at me. "Because of you, I lost my world. But most of all," she choked out a barely audible whisper, "I lost *them*."

Her manic eyes darted at the non-wintry creatures. The Jabberwocks' blue heart markings had dissolved— and with them, their loyalty to their queen. Her eyes welled. Breathless, I stood there, taking in the Snow Queen: the tears spilling down her face, her distressed gaze...the pained expression her long locks could no longer conceal...

She just wants to be loved, a voice inside me whispered.

… But she doesn't understand what love is.

My chest rose and fell. I knew what I had to do. Slowly, I held out a hand to the Snow Queen.

"What are you doing?" Usagi's hoarse shout pierced the air. My eyes flashed to her. She stood weakly, dripping wet, her arm linked with the hatter's for support. "You can't."

Boushiya breathed hard. "I told you she was mad."

"She isn't worth it, Alice!" shouted Sangatsu.

I pushed their voices—and all logical thought— out of my head. Ignoring their insistent cries, I neared closer, my hand still held out, offering the queen a chance for redemption.

"I'm sorry they changed." The queen didn't respond to my words. She remained rooted in place, staring at the heap of fur hats and white winter coats scattered on the ground.

"It doesn't have to be this way," I whispered. "You have the power to change all of this."

Her head snapped up. Through her tearstained face, the queen glared at me with red, slit-like eyes. She drew in a hissing breath. "Because of you." Venom punctuated her every word. "Because. Of. *You.*"

"*Have a heart.*" I shouted louder than I knew I was able to. Even the furthest kemonomimis looked startled by my volume. I held my ground and gripped the Looking Glass tightly behind my back. "Have a heart or...or..."

"Or what?" she snarled.

"Or else you'll be defeated by your own self."

I held the mirror behind my back, readying myself for the attack. But suddenly, the Snow Queen stopped moving.

A flurry of silky heart-shaped petals showered down on her. Hesitantly, she caught one in her hand. Her brows drew together. I could see the questions and arguments swimming behind her fervid eyes. But deep down, I knew she was considering it. Letting the spring reach inside her. Letting it melt her cold heart.

"That's it," I said softly.

The queen took a reluctant step toward me. Her face began to morph. Her shaking hand extended to mine. She was so close. So close...Her fingertips brushed mine. Then, she pulled away.

The queen sucked in a sharp breath. "How could I forget who you are? You're the Mirror Princess. I saw your face in my globe as warning." Her breath came in erratic bursts. "I know what you're trying to do. You want to undo me. To destroy me. To take away everything. Everyone... I can't let you." Tendrils of icy streams danced around her fingers.

"Please don't do this," I whispered.

The Snow Queen raised her pale hands high and swiped them down. Ice shot toward me, and I whipped the Looking Glass from behind my back. Instead of deflecting the ice, this time the mirror simply melted it.

The Snow Queen froze, ignoring the water pooling on the ground. Her entire body trembled. "I swore...I promised myself...I thought I'd never see that face again," she whispered under her breath.

"What...face?"

"Th-that."

I followed her quivering finger and stilled. Despite the queen's statuesque beauty, the mirror displayed something else. Desperate, sunken eyes. Sallow, murky skin. And the disarrayed hair of someone who had lost all means of control. Her perfect elegance had disappeared.

Realization crashed through me. So that's why she had broken the Looking Glass into pieces. It had shown the queen her true reflection. And she hated it. She hated herself.

The Snow Queen pinned my eyes with hers. "Did you know...I broke and turned every mirror in the palace around? I couldn't stand that person inside me. I never wanted to see her again." A strange expression washed over her. I held my breath. Her face was faltering. Into something that looked like... Was she showing remorse?

My eyes went wide. The heart on her forehead began to fade.

Slowly, the queen lifted her hand. She entwined her fingers with mine. The hard angles of her face softened like a fragile bud opening to the warmth of spring. The face in the Looking Glass started changing too. Her mask was cracking.

"You've finally found yourself."

"I...I'm ..." Struggling to get the words out, she pointed with difficulty to the mirror.

My hand still clutched it with force. I tried to lower the Looking Glass, but a strange sensation had stolen over my fingers. Panic seized me. Shimatta. I couldn't budge them. A powerful band of energy was teetering me to the mirror.

"Stop it," I breathed. *Please.* With every fiber in my being, I bid the Looking Glass to heed my order, but to no avail. My fingers wouldn't relinquish the mirror.

A beam of opalescent light shot out from the reflective surface and washed over the queen. I gasped, shielding my eyes against the flash. A powerful force wrenched her hand from mine. Her scream pierced the air. Through the Looking Glass the Snow Queen went. The mirror swallowed her, imprisoning her eternally in its chasm of shadows.

CHAPTER 11

Wonderland

The energy connecting my hands to the mirror broke. The Looking Glass dropped to the ground. Had that really just happened? And the Snow Queen's expression at the end...I couldn't shake the image from my mind. Despite the warmth and triumph I should have felt, a large part of me just felt numb. It took a long, purple tail curling around my waist to snap me out of my spell.

"You can't save someone from themselves," Shiroi purred into my ear. A vivid purple had completely replaced his white hair and attire, matching the purple vial-necklace bobbing against his chest.

"But she was drowning." My throat went tight. "She could've saved herself by just standing up."

"A good thing you did, love. Or else Wonderland would still be Winterland."

"Wonderland?" Before I could get anything else out of him, his body vanished into nothingness. Only the sound of his chuckle lingered behind.

"You did it."

I whirled around. Usagi stood before me, blinking back tears. "You brought our world back, Alice."

"I didn't." I cracked a smile. "We did."

"Oh, Alice ..." Usagi dabbed her eyes, her broad, gap-toothed smile widening. She flung her arms around me. A warm, fuzzy sensation stole over me. I hugged my friend back.

"I'm so sorry, Usagi. I never meant those things I said earlier."

"I know you didn't." Her voice went tight. "None of us did."

Over her trembling shoulder I saw a melting pot of colors replace the once bleak white. But that sight couldn't compare to the one in the distance. Two figures were running toward each other.

"*Boushiya.*"

"Sangatsu!"

Swarmed by green carnations, my OTP embraced each other. My breath caught at the picturesque scene. A strange feeling welled inside me. No longer did I see them as some ship catering to the whims of a fangirl.

Now, I only saw the ship for what they were. Two halves of a whole.

Lips parted, face flushed, the duo fell into their own private bubble once more, the world around them blurring.

"Kairos," Usagi whispered.

"Definition?"

"A perfect, delicate, crucial moment to say or do something...like, well you'll see."

Holding my breath, I watched the pair entwine their fingers together. The hatter fixed Sangatsu a smoldering gaze. "There's something I've been meaning to ask you for a long time."

"What is it?"

"Would you like to drink tea with me?" Boushiya's voice went soft. "Forever?"

Anticipation stirred inside my chest. I crossed four fingers, concentrating all my attention on the scene. *Say yes...say yes.*

Sangatsu simply stared at the hatter. After a long pause, a droplet trickled down his face, the meaning settling in.

"F-forever? You mean—"

"I do." A tender smile edged the hatter's mouth.

"Then I do too." Sangatsu reached up. He traced the curve of the hatter's cheek down to the corner of his lips.

"If I could reach up and hold a star for every time I thought of you, I'd have the entire night sky in my palm."

Kneeling, Boushiya brought his paramour's hand to his lips. "Sounds like we're written in the stars."

"I don't doubt that," Sangatsu whispered through a smile.

So many feels rushed through me.

The subtext had finally become text.

Boushiya rose to his full height. Sangatsu gently leaned forward, his lips grazing the hatter's forehead. They dipped lower and lower... and stopped against his parted lips. The duo disengaged from each other, catching me staring. They gave an abashed laugh and waved. I smiled back at them, so hard that my cheeks hurt.

My OTP was reunited at last.

Usagi rubbed her eyes. "Best let them be for a while."

Allowing the pair a private moment, I let Usagi lead me to an open space. A swirling mass of colors surrounded us. But it didn't come from the landscape. Kemonomimis of all shapes, sizes, and colors took in themselves and each other, faces glowing at their original forms. Chrysali swooped over them, their wings gleaming with flowery stalks and kaleidoscopic patterns.

I basked in Wonderland. What I had read about it in books didn't even come close to this. "It's the most beautiful thing I've ever seen ..."

"You took the words right out of my mouth."

Like an unseen breeze, someone swept behind me. A pair of arms wrapped around my waist, warm and strong. I didn't need to turn to know whom they belonged to. The fresh scent of the sea swam around me.

"Akihiko."

The prince held me fiercely and breathed into my hair. "Thank you."

"You're welcome," I whispered. Then, I remembered something. "I think this belongs to you..." I reached inside the cloak and pulled out the Vorpal Sword. It glinted against the light.

Akihiko beamed. He took the sword and set it in its sheath. Then, he held out his hand. "Can I show you something?"

Giving me a secret smile, Usagi discretely took her leave. Alone at last, I took Akihiko's hand, feeling equal parts nervous and intrigued. "What is it?"

An evocative smile touched his lips. "You'll see."

I took his outstretched hand and followed him into a bowered pathway of azure foliage. We walked in tandem, not speaking to each other. This time, the silence wasn't awkward. It was the comfortable kind. The kind where you don't need speak to each other because you exist within the silence together.

After several minutes, Akihiko stopped in front of a tall, blossoming tree. "It's up there."

I raised a brow.

"Trust me," he said.

Giving him a wary look, I hoisted myself into the tree. Akihiko followed behind me. Farther and farther we climbed until the branches could barely hold us. They swayed under our weight. I found a seat on a small but sturdy bough. Akihiko chose another nearby. Alone and far away from the lively, bustling crowd, we faced each other.

"Look there." He pointed to a gap in the pink flowers.

A sea by the cliff's edge.

"That's ..."

"Yes," he said, smiling into the backdrop. "*Home.*"

We soaked in the view of his favorite spot in Wonderland. Their scales like the hues of a coral reef palette, the merpeople splashed about in the shimmering waters. They drew nearer and formed a circle. A seraphic melody poured out of their lips. Though the song had no discernible words, I could feel the surge of emotions behind it. Every note swelled. With each arpeggio, the currents rippled around them. Another lyrical voice, soft and rich, introduced itself into the mix. Slowly, I turned.

Akihiko was singing with them.

Closing my eyes, I became lost in the music. His ethereal rhapsody swam in my head. Each cadence flowed like water. It sounded like the most beautiful poetry I had ever heard.

Suddenly, he stopped singing. "Look there, Alice."

Above the sea, iridescent colors streamed like ribbons, reminding me of Aurora Borealis. A swath of stars freckled the cotton candy skies. It looked like dusk and dawn at the same time.

My gaze drifted around the cliff. Everywhere, something new blossomed, and every time we breathed, a new flowery scent perfumed the air. Moonflowers, gardenias, honeysuckle, pink jasmine, and wild roses. Wind rushed through them, and a blizzard of flowers blew around us, the petals decorating my hair.

"Beautiful." Akihiko's voice lingered as a gentle breeze rustled the leaves around us, making an instrument of the tree.

"It is," I whispered.

"I wasn't talking about the flowers."

A charged silence fell between us. Holding my breath, I faced Akihiko. His lips parted like the clouds on a sweet, starry night.

"I finally found someone to share my special place with," he said softly, holding my hand.

I stared at my wrist. My heart mark had vanished, but for a flickering moment my beating heart felt shadowed. "But you had someone."

"I didn't." His dark eyes raked over me, engulfing me. "I told you, Alice. When I'm with you, I feel like myself. Like I can *be* myself. I didn't have that with her. With anyone." He brushed a strand of my hair out of the way and put his lips to my ear. "Only you."

Honey. His words flowed like honey. I closed my eyes, savoring every sweet, golden drop.

Akihiko pulled me close. A tide of emotions came over me. I melted against his chest, reveling in his warmth. My walls cracked and shattered into a thousand pieces. No longer did I want to hide. No longer did I want to hold back. It was time to let my inner fangirl out of the shadows.

"Even without gravity, I'd still fall for you." I cracked a tiny smile.

Akihiko threw his head back in a hearty chuckle. I laughed along with him until our laughter robbed us of our breaths. The prince threaded his fingers into my hair. His other hand angled my face to his until I could see my reflection in his dilated pupils.

Slowly, he traced a thumb across my trembling lips. I closed my eyes. His touch came light and gentle as a sea breeze. I could feel his smile on my lips—the best kind of kiss.

The rich, honeyed fragrance of flowers wafted through the air, mingling with that heady scent of him which always flooded my senses. Euphoric warmth blossomed within me. Eyes still closed, I savored his lingering touch even as he pulled away. When my lashes fluttered open, I saw Akihiko taking in the sight of me.

"Wishing on a star works wonders." He rested his forehead against mine, his eyes blazing. "Penny for your thoughts?"

"Just this." Giving in to my inner fangirl, I flung my arms around him and, this time, kissed him with total abandon. His fingers closed around my tangled locks. We sank into a fervent kiss. The kind that made you forget your name. The kind that felt like stars exploding. The kind I always wrote about in my fanfiction.

His lips parted and closed and parted again. It was as if a magnetic force teetered our lips together, binding us, stealing our breaths. Every color and sound deepened around me. Between the merpeople's lyrical voices, the lush flowers, and him, I felt like I was riding on the crest of a wave. Everything thing about this moment was so perfect, so *right*.

So kairos ...

"Metanoia found them," came a wispy voice.

Two long ears popped up from the branch below us. Akihiko and I jerked apart. Usagi's face came into view. A tiny, colorful sprite flew around her head in a playful circle.

With her doll-like face, cherub cheeks, and ethereal dress, I couldn't help but think Metanoia's original form was super kawaii. If she hadn't interrupted just then, I could have beamed at her forever. However...

The pair took in my flushed lips and Akihiko's mussed hair. They glanced at each other, knowing smiles surfacing their mouths.

"Celebration changing places," said Metanoia.

"If you two don't hurry, you'll miss it." Usagi paused. "Unless, of course, you two prefer to miss it."

My cheeks went hot. *Real subtle, Usagi.*

"We're coming," I said with an awkward laugh. "Right Akihiko?"

The prince's lips twitched. "Wouldn't dream of missing it."

"Well, then come on." A shimmer of mirth danced in Usagi's eyes. She swung herself down and out of the tree, the sprite following after. Akihiko and I glanced at each other and stifled our laughter. After we stole an eskimo kiss, I secured the Looking Glass in the cloak's inner pocket and clambered down the tree.

As we wandered through the blossoming wonderland, new creatures joined in, each adding their instruments and shouts to the jovial clamor. By the time we settled down on the edge of a flowery orchard, my hearing had grown fuzzy.

The celebration commenced in full swing, reminding me of a massive holiday parade. Usagi danced to the Ningyo's melody, humming felicitous tunes with the rest of the no-longer-wintery creatures, who had arranged themselves into a quadrille. Led by Yuki, the sprites collected flowers off the lush ground and performed aerial dances of their own, showering everyone with colorful petals.

"Shall we join them?" Akihiko offered me his arm.

"Let's."

I secured my arm under his and followed him to the festooned dance floor. A group of petite winged creatures took one look at me and stopped dancing. They glanced my way and parted, letting their leader step out. A circlet of rose quartz and ivy graced her proud head.

Akihiko whispered behind me. "The Fays never offer circlets to anyone...unless—"

"*Fays?*"

"Come here," Mirror-Lori said quietly.

Heart quickening, I meandered through the whispers and stares until I stood directly in front of the leader of the former frostmaidens. Her face unreadable, she removed her circlet.

"You think you've proven your worth by restoring Wonderland," said Mirror-Lori. "Well, you're mistaken."

I chewed my lip.

"You were always worthy. Never forget your value— even if others are blind to see it." Mirror-Lori gestured me forward. "For returning us to Fays, we wish to bestow upon you a token of our gratitude." She placed her circlet over my head, even brushing the loose strands out of my face with a surprising gentleness. "You are no Fay, but we would be pleased if you joined us... Alice."

Her softness was so polar to the pride I was used to from real-world Lori. I couldn't help but grin. "Thanks for the honorary membership."

"It suits you," she murmured before composing herself. She straightened up and motioned for me to join her group.

My body swayed to the melody's enchantment, the hem of my skirt swishing against Akihiko's legs. The Fays danced around us in circles. My head was full of colors and lights, and from Akihiko's heavy-lidded eyes, I knew his was too. We glided together, our bodies in perfect sync. No one would even believe I was a total klutz in real life. For once, I exuded fluid grace. I felt confident and bold. Beautiful even.

Over Akihiko's shoulder, I saw Sangatsu and Boushiya partner for the quadrille. Eyes locked, they circled, turned, then parted. Even when the quadrille drew them away for those brief seconds, their eyes never strayed. Transfixed, they turned to look, and look, and look, drowning in each other's gazes.

Meeting Akihiko's dark eyes, I could understand their sentiments.

Amidst the dancing kemonomimis, I caught Shiroi bowing to his dance partner. My jaw dropped.

Usagi?

She lifted her nose and followed his lead, looking both interested and disinterested in him all at once. A hand raised to his, she partook in the quadrille, though she kept a measurable distance between them.

I stifled a giggle when the pair drew near us. "Talk about a ship I didn't see coming."

"Are you calling me a ship?" Usagi asked stiffly. "I've only had a small plate of food so far."

Shiroi wriggled his brow. "I think she means us."

"*There is no us.* Like that anyway..."

Ah, the rare, but refreshing platonic ship.

Usagi promptly increased the distance between the cat kemonomimi and herself, but continued on with their dance.

After a while, I grew breathless from all the dancing. Akihiko and I disbanded from the crowd. We strolled hand in hand, smiling so widely we might have been anime. I brushed my fingers through my hair and felt the rose-quartz circlet. A thought struck me. "Akihiko..."

"Yes?"

"What do you know about the Fays?"

He cocked his head. "Well, like I said. They're proud..."

"How proud?"

"I'm not sure I understand what you mean."

"Would the Fays be proud enough to fight the Snow Queen over, say, an insult? Even when they were frost-maidens?"

Akihiko laughed. "If any of Winterland's creatures would have dared that, it definitely would be them. I doubt they would have rebelled enough to help us on our quest, if that's what you were wondering. But if they were insulted, they likely would have acted up."

My lips twitched. Classic Lori. Launching a full-scale battle over a cut-off performance. It was nice to be on the other side of her self-importance for once. I never thought I'd say it, but her absurd reverence for the arts and "the greats" had actually helped me.

The prince and I kept walking until we came across a familiar alcove. Amidst a tiered cake stand, lacy doilies, and starry tablecloth, Sangatsu and Boushiya were pouring piping hot tea into teacups. I waved to them.

"Chibi," the hatter called out. "Come join us. Fish boy, too."

We sat down and I placed the mirror on the table. Boushiya steepled his hands under his chin and grinned at me. "Did you decipher my code?"

Oh! I had almost forgotten.

"Of course. This is me we're talking about." I winked at him. "It was Morse code, right? For 'B.S.' You were telling me that the queen was lying...but not about tracking us like I originally thought. You meant she wasn't letting us win."

The hatter's mouth gaped a bit. But he didn't speak, so I went on.

"You wanted me to know that she was just trying to save face. Pretending to have played with us out of boredom when, in actuality, we evaded her every time. She tried her hardest to stop us, and we kept getting away. In the courtyard, at our campsite, in the labyrinth..." I grinned. "Knowing we'd bested her three times already, well... It's what gave me the courage to fight her again."

Boushiya stared at me, eyes widening.

I arched a brow. "What?"

"Actually..." He glanced at Sangatsu with a dim smile. "The code was shorthand for BouSang. Our couple name. You looked so miserable back there, I just...I was trying to lift your spirits a little. I wanted to thank you for reuniting us. Even if it was just for our last moments."

I didn't know which was more upsetting: the shame of missing a riddle, or the shock of the un-canon portmanteau. Before I could decide, I felt a pressure on my shoulder.

"You're having a tea party?" Usagi appeared behind us. "Aren't you going to invite me?"

"Oh! Here." I patted an empty seat beside me.

"Thanks." She seated herself and rounded her gaze at all of us. "I can't believe we're sitting here again. It's like waking up after a bad dream. Like nothing ever happened."

A watery smile filled her face. "Our world is ours again, we returned to our original selves, and now..." She caught my eye but didn't finish.

I frowned. "Usagi?"

"You can go home now, Alice. With this." She forced a tiny smile and pointed to the Looking Glass.

"I...almost forgot about home."

"How could one forget about their own home, Chibi?"

My throat grew constricted at the hatter's words. "Maybe I want to forget." I paused, considering my words. "Or...no. I don't really. For a while, I did but, I know I have to go back. I...I want to go back."

"I know it's selfish to want you to stay." Akihiko met my gaze with a resigned smile. "I've known for some time this moment would come, but it won't make it any easier." Gently, he reached for my hand and brought it to his lips. "I'll miss you, Alice."

My voice thickened. "Same."

"We'll miss you too," BouSang whispered.

"Saudade," chimed Usagi.

"I'll miss you too. But I also won't." My eyes stung despite my smile. "Because there will be a piece of you in me. Always."

Usagi sucked in a breath and spread her arms. I embraced her with everything I had. Little by little, I felt more arms enveloping me.

I half-laughed, half-cried. Their touch felt comforting, heartening, and bittersweet all at once. My chest swelled with emotion. Even reading hurt-comfort fics never made me feel this much.

I broke apart from the group hug and wiped my cheek. "Let's get back to some fun."

"Drink this, Chibi." Sangatsu offered us a cup of tea each, then gave me a mischievous wink. "Not iced."

"You don't say." I took a sip and let out a languorous sigh. "Mm. Tastes like bubble tea."

"You think that's good, eat this." Eyes glazed, Boushiya handed me a slice of cake. My tastebuds danced at the rainbow of flavors.

The hatter turned to a heavy-lidded Sangatsu, holding a spoonful of the dessert. The hare kemonomimi licked the spoon clean, his eyes not straying from the hatter's. "It's good. Very."

I swooned in my seat. A bit too forcefully. Akihiko caught my swaying shoulders and chuckled through a hiccup. "Remind me to have tea with you more often."

The hatter turned to Usagi. "You've got to try these," he slurred. "Aren't they the most delicious things you've ever tasted?"

Nose twitching, she took a small sip. "Yes, delicious, but different." She lowered her teacup and reached for a piece of cake. One bite into it, she paused. "This too." Her vision narrowed. "What exactly did you put in them?"

A lazy smile surfaced the hatter's face. He slung an arm around Sangatsu and pointed to a bunch of items strewn across the table: canisters of tea, a teapot wafting with steam, and a small, half-empty vial of purple liquid.

Usagi snatched the vial. "Where did you get this?"

The hatter hiccuped and rolled his eyes. "A fellow offered it to us at the quadrille. Said it might make our tea party a bit more entertaining."

"*You. Dolt.*"

"Calm your ears, Usagi." Sangatsu languidly stood up and stuck two fingers into his long ears. I giggled.

Ignoring Usagi's ranting, the hatter grabbed the mirror in boredom and tossed it to Sangatsu—who tossed it back.

"Stop that," hissed Usagi.

"I'll get it, Oosagi." I set down my cup and stood. My body seemed to liquefy, but I ignored the sensation. "Give it here."

Akihiko joined in. I woozily sprinted to Sangatsu to steal it back, but my unsteady legs slowed me. When I managed to reached him, Sangatsu threw the mirror to Boushiya. They were playing a game of catch. Or, rather, keep-away, now that Akihiko and I were involved.

Boushiya laughed in a drunken-like stupor and tossed the mirror back to Sangatsu. But his throw was a little too strong. Akihiko ambled backward to catch it. He bumped my shoulder, and the mirror whizzed past his outstretched hands.

I flew after it, my fingers scant inches from it. A bit more... I stretched my arm until I grasped the silver handle. "*Got it—*" I tripped over my feet. The force of it sent me reeling forward—into an icy blue passageway. The same passageway I had come from. I gasped.

"Alice?"

"Alice!"

"Alice!"

"Ali..."

The quartet's shouts faded. Their anxious faces grew smaller, blurrier...until darkness swallowed them up.

My eyes snapped open. Pulse racing, I found myself starfished out on my comforter. I peeled the sticky, shiny pages of the *Winterland* manga off my face. A line of anime bobble heads, colorful bookshelves, and fandom memorabilia came into focus.

Home. I was back home.

My gaze drifted to open manga lying on my bed. Bright faces peered up at me, wide smiles plastered on each of them. A wistful sensation settled in the pit of my stomach.

Saudade...

I had lost myself in the world of my book; I had also found myself there. Because of *them.* As much as I ached for my friends, they were with me. Right here. I held the book close to my chest.

A bolt of inspiration struck me. I jumped out of my bed. A faint mirror-Alice appeared on the laptop screen, but she vanished the moment I touched the trackpad.

"I…am…Sherlocked," I whispered as I entered the password.

Everything went back to where it had been. The blank, white finale-less document glowed at me, but no longer did it look threatening. I knew what I needed to do.

I busted out my art pens and cracked my knuckles. *If there's a fanfic you want to read, but no one has written it yet, then you must write it.* And so I would.

With a sip of cold mocha dregs, I typed the night away.

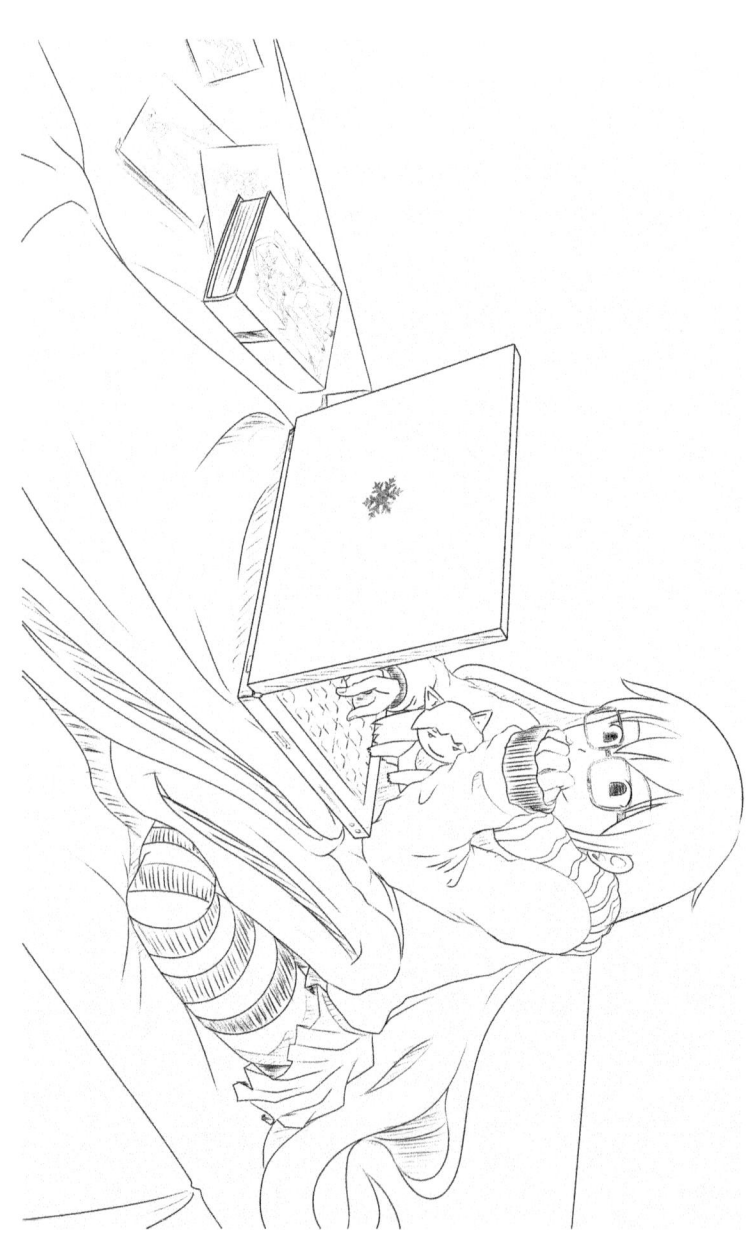

CHAPTER 12

Fandom Nation

I woke up the next morning and hurriedly dressed for school. Then, balancing my laptop on my knees, I typed in my password. My fanfiction homepage greeted me.

The moment of truth.

Holding my breath, I refreshed the URL to my recent update. My eyes flared.

hipster_mermaid, inkmonsta, I_am_Johnlocked, SnowPrincess, MissMangaka, JubJub, W.I.T.C.H, pearlrose, TheDominatrix, Iceman, Sanbou- Shipper, drarry4life, IMADEYOUREADTHIS, sunnyyugi, ClosetOtaku, Nimbus3000, Kingdom- Heartless, starfire, maygirl17j, TeamMikasa, Bughead, SnowAngelCastiel, katsudon_is_vksuno, ThatsSoRaven-claw, polandybananas, Katluvs- Coffee, bookaholic-pixie, chibbimom, Super- woman, winteriscoming, sapphic_poetess, mimsy- borogoves, smol-neko-boy, wordsculpture, seme-

kun, cdawg, onehelluvabutler, ThatMystery-
Writer, aloeverasol, AardvarkArthur, book-
bosomed, tsundere-chan, WhiteRabbitAce,
korrasami, TJLC_is_real, kiyokan, TequilaMock-
ingbird, SuperWhoLockian, TifaxCloud, mimOsa-
not-mimosA, Literati_Lady, MissHolmes,
be_my_waifu, and 15 guests left kudos on this
work.

Oh mylanta. I could have screamed into my pillow. And
then, I proceeded to do just that. Never had I received
that many hits on a chapter. Unable to contain my
excitement, I scrolled through the flood of comments.

booksniffer: 'The subtext had finally become
text.' The words every fangirl waits for.

bandersnatch-cumberbuns:SO MANY FEELS. I don't
usually like reader-insert fics, but I loved
this winter-fic snow much <3 (sry)

Granger+Lovegood-2020: The Sanbou scene at the
end made me asdfghjkl aloud. My mother asked
me what the hell I was reading. I told her it
was a fusion piece based on classic literature
that challenged heteronormative tropes. She
looked impressed. #YaoiFanfiction #SorryNot-
Sorry

panromanticfanatic: *"The prince traced a thumb across your trembling lips. Slowly, he leaned in… You could feel his smile on your lips—the best kind of kiss."*
Me: *out cold*

ElsaFrost: *'Will you drink tea with me… forever?'* Best proposal ever for Sanbou, but I have a bone to pick with you. Hope you don't get offended, but I'm not big on ambiguous endings, which is what happens to the Snow Queen. She wanted to feel love but couldn't. (Is that the reason for her heart symbols?) I need a Snow Queen fic now. She deserved so much better.

I frowned at the review. If only they knew I didn't want that ambiguous ending either. As badly as I wanted to change what happened to the Snow Queen, I couldn't bring myself to fabricate and rewrite her story. It just felt…wrong.

As I re-read the comment, something inside me collapsed. The reviewer was right. All the characters had gotten their happily ever after except the queen. But she had been close. So, *so* close…

Her tear-stained face flashed before me. Her hand in mine. I couldn't forget her grip on me. She held my hand so tightly—as if I was the only lifeline saving from the darkness she had succumbed to. In the end, I had let her down.

A blanket of guilt enveloped me. *No. There's nothing you could have done differently.* I shook my head and forced myself to keep reading.

calculus-is-ʃexy: puns…science puns every-where. I found them sodium funny that I slapped my neon one.

> **JackFrost:** My head hertz from the frequency of bad puns.

> > **calculus-is-ʃexy:** but all the good ones argon.

> > **MissHolmes:** Get out.

> > > **calculus-is-ʃexy:** *NaH.*

Despite my self-reproach, a tiny snort-giggle escaped me. Well, that thread made me feel an inkling better. I scrolled further.

hipster_mermaid: I -knew- something was fishy with that snow globe. The queen *always* had it on her.

dachshund-through-the-snow: the reader's (my) inner fangirl made me cringe but like, in the best way possible.

CurosiTea: Why is inner fangirl RELATABLE AF.

WhiteRabbitAce: *Brava!* You've written this fic with such meraki (i.e. pouring your soul, creativity, or love into your work). As a minor character in canon, Usagi hardly gets screen time and when she does, she has a Mary Sue vibe. She feels more fleshed out here. She's not perfect; she messes up, but despite her shortcomings, she always does her best. She's a flawlessly flawed character <3. The fandom needs more Usagi-fics. She's simply *supercalifragilistic.*

And so are you.

Re-reading Deanna's comment, I smiled like an idiot to myself. I could feel her hug in those lines, reminiscent of Usagi's. The familiar warm fuzzies stole over me. I read through the rest of the reviews.

HungryHungryHippogriffs: THE CHAPTER FANART IS ASDFGHJK; I CAN'T

kiss-me-under-the-light-of-a-thousand-stars:
My fanart on what happened when Sanbou was alone...

aspergirl: Bless you.

Born2ShipVicturi: Brb. Fangirling hard.

no-waifu-no-laifu: my ovaries

smol-neko-boy: Shiroi Neko is bae.

MoonPrismPower: Having some very nonfictional feelings about fictional characters.

nosynonym4synonym: me analyzing a book for school: I guess there's some foreshadowing here…

me analyzing my favorite fanfic: THE LOOKING GLASS SYMBOLIZES DUALITIES. DARK VS LIGHT, THE READER VS THEIR ALTER EGO.

phangirl: Find someone who looks at you the way the Winter Prince looks at you.

XistentialDan: Find someone who looks at you the way Boushiya looks at Sangatsu

hiskMeUp: Sanbou (Bousang?) is GOALS.

tsundoku: Usagi teaches me vocabulary.

WhiteRabbitAce: Lol. I gave SnowBaby23 a book for her birthday ('Totally Weird & Wonderful Words'). Highly recommend it to fellow logodaedalians.

rebelle: *notification squad* SnowBaby23 has just updated a Winterfic. Guess homework will have to wait.

A massive derpy smile on my face, I scrolled all the way to the bottom of the page, scanning for that familiar username. My brows drew together. Weird. I couldn't find it. I probably skipped it.

I skimmed the page again. And again. And once more. A pang of disappointment gnawed at me. Winterpuff...hadn't commented. And they were *always* the first to leave a review. My spirits plummeted. Did they not like it?

The question ate at me as I ate my breakfast. It was only when I heard the whirring of an engine that I broke out of my self-doubts. The school bus had pulled up outside my home.

I crammed my laptop into my Totoro backpack and skittered outside. Out of breath, I hopped onto the bus, swung into a seat, and stole a quick glance around, checking for wandering eyes. When the coast was clear, I opened up a file I had created during breakfast.

A collection of Tumblr screenshots featuring gif reactions to my finale. Some had even reblogged my fanfiction's fanart with reaction gifs. Though it may have been a little vain, reading the compliments cheered me up a bit.

My phone buzzed. A notification on my fanfiction. Brimming with nervous excitement, I clicked on the latest review.

New comment from Literati_Lady.

I let out a tiny sigh. Not Winterpuff, but an interesting user no less. I didn't usually get reviews so...detailed. And *meta*.

Literati_Lady: As a reader of Victorian literature (and owner of *Le Language des Fleurs*) I thought the mirror and flower motifs added a cryptic layer to the narrative.

The Looking Glass reminds me of Basil's painting of Dorian Gray. Basil was so enamoured with Dorian, that he painted a portrait of him. Even though Dorian remained as beautiful as ever, the portrait revealed the secret of his soul. It grew uglier and uglier as he descended into depravity. In the end, Dorian couldn't stand the sight of it. He stabbed his portrait, inadvertently destroying himself. It mirrors the Snow Queen's fate tragically well. She was a victim and villain.

As per the language of flowers, the laurel and white heather (symbols of 'success' and 'luck') foreshadowed that the quartet's wishes on the star would come true. The reader and

Akihiko could have saved themselves some serious trouble had they known what the sprite's oleander wreath symbolised.

But I must say, my *favourite* flower motif was the green-coloured carnation Sanbou wears—a suggestive reference to my favorite Irish author. All I can say, Sangatsu and the hatter are born to be Wilde. ;) I've never read Winterfics before, but reading this has made me a Winterlander (Is that what we call ourselves?)

I let out a squeal. Nothing like converting someone into a Winterlander. Or having them read between the lines.

Beaming, I tucked my phone away. So what if Winterpuff didn't like my fanfiction? With every chapter, every word, I had left a part of myself in my story. And others had liked that part of me. As a fanfiction writer, I couldn't ask for more.

I smiled to myself, brimming with a surge of confidence. I felt invincible—like I had sipped a drop of liquid luck. Ready for anything the day might throw at me.

But when the bus finally pulled up outside our school and I ambled through the main entrance, I had to accept the cold, hard fact that my euphoria wasn't entirely bulletproof.

"Say cheese!"

Ack. Did Olivia's peppy voice have to be the first thing I heard at school? I sighed. The muggle struggle was real.

I flitted past her. She took no notice of me. Flipping her ombre locks and traipsing about like she owned the place, she snapped photos of various groups for the school's yearbook. Drama Club groupies, tennis jocks, and the student council. Skirting around the Mathletes, Olivia trotted to the next group. A group of attractive pretty boys.

The swim team.

I slowed my pace. In the middle of the group stood the head captain. Andrew was only a few feet from me, yet he felt light-years away.

The swim team posed for Olivia, flashing their best pearly smiles. But the smile didn't seem to reach Andrew's eyes. Or maybe that was my wishful thinking again.

Andrew's friend, a boy with a crooked smile and crooked snapback, crossed his arms. "Well, water are you waiting for?"

Olivia giggled as the camera went off. When she finished, she fanned herself and showed the picture to the boys. "That's hot."

"Tell me something I don't know." Snapback boy winked at Olivia. Andrew rolled his eyes at his friend.

"What?" said the boy. "It's not bragging if it's true."

Envying their little charmed sphere, I hugged my laptop to my chest. Only last night, in my crazy Pocky-induced Winterland dream, I had locked lips with some fictional version of Andrew—but the real one still remained oblivious to my existence. An empty void grew in my chest. I had experienced so much with someone who hadn't experienced any of it with me. The whole thing left a bittersweet taste in my mouth.

I drifted to my locker and pensively entered the combination: 221B. I raised a hand above my head to fish out my chemistry textbook when—"Ah!"— someone bumped into my shoulder. I lurched upright, seconds from dropping my laptop.

"Watch it!"

"S-sorry." I managed to catch myself—and my laptop — from falling, though my cheeks must have turned pinker than Kirby. I spun around, whipping a familiar face with my hair.

Olivia.

I gulped. The Queen Bee curled her lips into a disgusted frown. But instead of backing away from me, she leaned in further, invading my personal space until I smelled her cherry ChapStick.

A sinking feeling spread over me as her searing gaze settled on my locker's décor. Olivia took it all in. The poorly concealed heap of Winterland doujinshi, my anime bobble heads, my shippy fanart. Her lips twitched with cold glee. Whatever high I had this morning came crashing down on me like a tidal wave.

"Truly, you've outdone yourself this time, Alice. So much better than I possibly could have hoped for. It's just so...so you." Her eyes flashed at my fandom-decorated haven-away-from-home. "Weaboo books, weeb dolls, weeb toys." Poison seemed to spill through the air as she laughed. My stomach sank. As usual, the girl made Draco Malfoy look like a cinnamon roll.

"What's going on?" asked Anastasia.

"See for yourself." Olivia elbowed me out of the way, exposing my locker to everyone.

Claire clapped a hand over her mouth. "Olivia, maybe you should let Alice finally have her own spread in the yearbook."

"That's savage."

A chorus of hushed giggles enveloped me. The sounds grew louder and louder until I couldn't make out which direction they came from. I stared hard at my feet, on the brink of a panic attack. Pulse speeding, fingers fidgeting with my hair, I struggled to block the voices out.

Skittish, I glanced up and caught Andrew's face in the crowd. Every inch of me froze.

Olivia gave him a coy smile and clicked away. I shielded my eyes from the bright flash as she gathered photographic evidence of my plush characters, horcrux magnets, and Sanbou posters.

"Cut it out it, you Spitzbub," snapped a voice.

Deanna needled her way to the front of the crowd. But before she could pounce, I put my hand on her shoulder.

I drew in a deep breath. "Don't."

Her eyes widened. "What the h—"

"Please, Deanna." This wasn't her battle.

I stepped away from her and faced Olivia. For once, I didn't want to disappear or cry. The lengths I went through to keep my fangirl lifestyle a secret suddenly felt ridiculous to me. Like, Winterland levels of absurdity. Seeing my locker fully exposed before me made me realize something. I didn't see it as a badge of shame. Not anymore. Not ever again. If others didn't like me for being myself, well, I would be myself even more.

"Go ahead."

"*What* did you say?" said Olivia.

"I said go ahead." I matched her glare with full force. "Take as many pictures as you want. I'm not hiding anything. I'm a fangirl. And... and proud of it."

Olivia blinked. She stared at my fangirl sweatshirt, my only armor standing between us. Then, she threw her head back, exploding in laughter. My inner and outer fangirl bubbled with indignation. I straightened up, balling my hands.

"Fandoms bring people together. They're a way for us to create and share our stories. A way to find inspiration in our art—and each other." My voice slightly cracked. "A way to feel like you belong."

Olivia snickered so shrilly this time, I thought her camera lens would break. "God, not a speech. You think you can start a nerdy revolution and be canonized into sainthood? Alice Leira, patron saint of weaboos and fandom freaks."

"Alice is right."

Like a beam of magic ice, the voice immobilized my feet. The whole hallway went pin drop silent. My eyes widened as I turned. Had I fallen back asleep? Down another rabbit hole? Of all the people who might have stood up for me...

Andrew Lewis?

Olivia shared my shock. Her eyebrows sprang up, and her blue eyes went wider than an anime character's. But then, as if aware that she'd need all her wiles working in her favor right now, she composed her face into a smile.

A smile so sickeningly sweet it made me want to swear off Christmas cookies this year.

"Oh, c'mon." Her dulcet tones lilted through the crowd, then wrapped around Andrew like the wings of a femme-fatale butterfly monster. She twisted her hair and peered at him through dark lashes. "It's just a bit of harmless fun."

Andrew didn't reply. He impassively flitted by her and stood in front of his locker. "If you're going to put her locker in the yearbook, you might as well put mine in, too." With one hand, he opened his locker door.

The Queen Bee and I froze. Our mouths went agape as we took in the contents. Anime figurines decorated a shelf. A Hufflepuff prefect badge glimmered next to a pair of swim goggles, and I caught a Game of Thrones paperback peeking underneath a textbook. My gaze darted to the inner door. I stilled. We shared the same poster.

Of the Winter Prince.

Olivia looked horrorstruck as a Pokémon card fluttered to her feet. "Y-you're a fanboy?" she sputtered.

Andrew gave her a cursory glance. "I am. And an active fanboy at that. The real reason I can't make it to your Christmas party is because I'm attending a Winterland cosplay convention this weekend—with my swim team."

Olivia pointed a shaky manicured finger at him, at the swim team, at him again. "Please tell me this is some sick joke."

"It's not." His face hardened. "I just don't get it." He squared his shoulders and faced the crowd. "Why does being passionate about something mark you? And you know what sucks? When you're honest about it, you become a walking target to others." He gave an empty laugh. "I guess that's why we have 'guilty pleasures' in the first place. Because none of us can just come out and say what we're really into without being judged."

"Preach Lewis," hollered a boy on the swim team. The other students broke out in murmurs. Olivia and her squad said nothing.

Andrew turned to me. My heart thudded to a wild, spastic rhythm, but I managed to hold his dauntless gaze.

"I like your scarf," he whispered. His eyes dipped further. "And your sweatshirt."

The words sounded distant, and the moment felt ecstatic, surreal. The gaggle of onlookers blurred beyond recognition. The only thing I saw was him. And his locker.

My gaze drifted to the Winter Prince. "I like your poster."

"Thanks." He ran a hand through his hair, not meeting my stare. He seemed different now. Not the confident jock anymore, but someone unsure of himself.

"Your Winterfic," he started hesitantly. "I read it."

I dragged in a breath. Someone pinch me. This had to be another Pocky-induced dream. Knees knocking uncontrollably, I forced myself to focus, devouring his every word.

"It's like, after a while, I forgot I was reading words on a screen. I felt the character's emotions instead of imagining them. I heard their voices instead of reading them." He shuffled his feet. "It's like I was actually there. And I just..." He glanced up, a strange look filling his eyes. "I wanted to tell you that in person this time. Not behind a computer screen."

"Winterpuff?" I whispered.

Andrew cracked a smile.

A warm rush fluttered through me. And along with it, a renewed glimmer of hope.

Andrew stared at the ground. Slowly, he raised his head. "Maybe...maybe we could get together sometime and write a collaborative Winterfic."

My eyes shyly caught his smile. "I'd like that."

Olivia looked faint.

A freckle-faced girl on cross country team reluctantly stepped forward. "I used to read Han Solo fanfiction when I was in middle school." Her voice grew quiet. "I still do sometimes."

The foreign exchange student beside her fidgeted with her hands. "When I was in Korea, my friends and I made Super Junior dance covers. The band's fans call themselves E.L.F. It means everlasting friends."

"I guess I'm part of a band fandom too." A lanky boy with tinted hair scratched his head. "I listen to Lady Gaga a lot. She's like, my queen. Her fans call themselves her Little Monsters."

"I'm a Potterhead," murmured a small, freshman girl, before extracting a Gryffindor scarf from her backpack and tying it around her Afro.

"And I'm a Twihard," added her friend. Lips twitching, they glared at each other, attempting—with minimal success—not to smile.

A few more Potterheads quietly announced themselves, and from there things picked up. Demigods, Hetalians, Moonies, Shadowhunters, Roomfriends, Scoobies, Lawsbians, X-Philes, Tolkienites, 1-Directioners, River Vixens, Selenators, Disnerds, and Trekkies stepped forth. First reluctantly. Then casually. And now enthusiastically.

Blackjacks, Browncoats, and Buffistas declared their loyalties and to my surprise, some exchanged Tumblr screen names. Even a few Winterlanders I had never met before walked up to me and asked for mine.

"Proud Slytherin in the hous—" Claire stopped short. Her face flushed at Olivia's seething eyes.

"Seriously?"

"Siriusly."

"I can't believe this!" Olivia spun around to the twins. "At least you two haven't lost your sanity."

"I don't know." Isabella gave her twin a side-glance. "I think Ana and I have been part of a fandom too."

"What?"

"Bachelor Nation," Anastasia said with a giggle. "They hold viewing parties for The Bachelor. Bella and I blog about it every premiere. This season's guy is our favorite. The hot, brooding, misunderstood type." The pair giggled again like full-blown fangirls. Olivia looked like she wanted to punch herself.

"I'm obsessed with the guys on Buzzfeed," said a brunette from journalism. "Technically, that counts as an internet fandom, right?"

"As much as Fantasy Football does."

Snapback boy sauntered to us, hands in his pockets. "Last year, Andrew and a few guys from the swim team cosplayed as the Iwotobi Swim Team for Otaku-con." He flashed his signature crooked smile. "We basically showed up as ourselves."

"I don't know much about cosplay," said a boy from weight training. "But I've been into Marvel since I was a kid. Dressed up as Thor last Halloween. My girlfriend was Wonder Woman."

Ah, a refreshing, cross-universe relationship. I smiled as I wondered how often they fought about it.

"Cool," answered another distant voice. "My girlfriend and I cosplay as Sailor Uranus and Sailor Neptune."

A member from the Visual Arts Club chimed in. "I drew them on my Deviant Art once or twice. Or... more."

A girl in black ripped jeans and headphones around her neck quietly stepped forth. Her faux leather jacket barely covered her "*vegan from my head tomatoes*" shirt. "I've...er, watched all the Studio Ghibli movies." Her winged eyeliner crinkled. "You should see the plushies in my room."

"I know squat about anime, but I'm hooked on the TV show, Friends. Phoebe Buffay is my spirit animal."

"I wrote a letter asking David Tennant to the prom," Deanna admitted, turning pink.

"Nice. I'm a Whovian."

"And I'm a proud Janeite," announced a familiar voice.

No. No way in hail.

Slowly, I turned. My sister stood before me. She cradled a worn copy of Oscar Wilde's *The Picture of Dorian Gray* to her chest. "I thought you might like reading this, Alice. It's rife with epigrams and floriography." Hesitantly, her eyes met mine. "You know…the language of flowers."

Literati_Lady.

"Lori…*you*…?"

"Years ago, I wrote pastiches about Darcy and Elizabeth. About Dorian and Basil. I thought I was just writing homages to their relationships, but maybe it was something else as well…" My sister exchanged a meaningful look with me.

"I'd love to read your fanfiction, Lori."

A moment of understanding settled between us. Lori's pride toward fanfiction and my prejudice against her notions melted away. After reeling too long in the depths of her censure and severity, the cheeky grin on her face felt like a much-needed breath of fresh air.

Noticing the dozens of eyeballs staring at us, Lori cleared her throat. "By definition, a fandom is the fans of a particular person, band, team, fictional series, etc., regarded collectively as a community or subculture. Just a little PSA in case some of you wondered if you were part of a fandom—which, by the way, you probably are."

She caught Olivia's frostbitten eyes. "Whether you acknowledge it or not is a different matter."

"Never heard of a Janeite before," a boy near her murmured.

Lori lifted her chin with disdain. "A Janeite is one who belongs to the Jane Austen fandom." The boy gave her a blank stare. "You know, the author of Pride and Prejudice, that summer reading book you all choose to 'Spark Notes' instead of read." Squeezing the book tighter, she crinkled her nose and scuttled away.

Once Lori had disappeared from sight, Olivia whirled on the other students. Her sharp, angular features froze in a mask of disbelief. "Okay, so you guys are part of fandoms, but you're not obsessed with them the way Alice is." The Potterheads turned away.

"There are levels of socially acceptable weirdness," she pressed on, eyeing Deanna, "but Alice pushes *way* it too far. You guys don't." A group of Winterlanders gave her the cold shoulder.

Olivia wrung her hands and sprang on a lone Sherlockian. "You wouldn't actually get mad at the screenwriters if your favorite characters didn't end up together, right?" The Sherlockian cringed and backed away behind some Tributes.

She faced a Twihard. "I know you guys have your teams or whatever, but you don't actually get emotional about them, right?" When they didn't answer, her frantic eyes landed on two Thronies. "If your favorite characters died—"

"Give it up, Olivia," Claire whispered, putting a hand on her shoulder.

Olivia didn't listen. She spun around, addressing everyone now. "*You* don't sit by yourself at lunch with a stash of weaboo crap. You don't collect stuffed animals in your lockers like she does. You guys actually have lives outside of fandoms. *She* doesn't." Her voice shook. "That's what's weird. That's what's unacceptable. Sh-she can't be like that." Try as she did to regain control, the students near her started to inch away from the train wreck. I didn't blame them.

"You know what is unacceptable?" Deanna stuffed a hand into her satchel and thrust a piece of glittery paper into Olivia's hand. "Me accepting this thing. You can have it back. Have fun."

Olivia looked like she had been slapped in the face. She took the invite, crumpling it in her shaky grip. Her girl squad stayed by her side, but remained curiously silent.

I gazed at a Winterland poster on my locker door. That wish I had made on all those stars had actually come true.

I had shattered the status quo of Charles Dodgson High.

Grinning, I turned to Deanna. "Next mission: bring back cloaks."

She sighed. "Baby steps, Alice. Baby steps."

~~~~~~~~~~

The next day, I holed myself up in the library at lunch, replying to new comments on my fanfic—including a lengthy one from Winterpuff. I beamed. No longer an embarrassing secret or a subject of ridicule, my *Winterland* manga lay on the desk in plain sight instead of hiding behind a textbook. As I typed away, I glimpsed Olivia and her girl squad outside the hall.

"Sorry, we can't come Saturday night." Claire wore an apologetic expression. "We completely forgot, we have this huge Spanish project due on Monday. *Mucho grande.* We're like, super bummed about it, but I hope you understand."

"Of course. I understand perfectly." Olivia practically spat the words as she bolted through the library door, not glancing back at her friends. My brows drew together. I forced myself back to my fanfiction.

As the day went on, Olivia grew despondent over her lost following. I should have been happy. My finale was up. It had raving reviews. Andrew was no longer a closet fanboy. Fandoms were trending in Charles Dodgson High. And yet…a niggling feeling of guilt crept through me.

When the final bell rang, Andrew met me at my locker. "Hey."

I smiled and nervously smoothed my hair back. "What's up?"

"The sky." His eyes glowed with humor and flicked to his hand. A stub with a blue heart. "I was wondering if you'd, you know, maybe like to go with me…to the Winter-Con this weekend. Two guys from my swim team got tickets, but one of them can't come, so I have a spare now."

"You keep it."

His face faltered. "You don't want it?"

"No, I don't mean it like that. I mean, I *want to go* with you." My words tumbled out in a rush like a total fangirl, but Andrew didn't seem to mind. A faint smirk pulled at his lips.

"I just don't need the ticket, is all. Deanna already got ours. She's coming too…" I trailed off, distracted by a white envelope behind the Winter-Con ticket. "What is that?"

"This?" He separated the envelope from the ticket and shrugged. "Olivia's invite came in this. I told her I didn't need it, but she wanted me to keep it, just in case I changed my mind."

"Uh-huh." I swallowed hard, eyeing the initials, A.L., scrawled on the envelope. *There was no way.*

Andrew frowned. "Are you okay, Alice?"

"I'm fine," I lied. As if my mind had conjured her up, I caught a glimpse of Olivia in my locker mirror. I took in her smudged mascara and glassy eyes as she brushed past us. That look… I'd seen it before.

The Snow Queen's face sprang to mind. The blush of spring beneath her porcelain skin, the desperation in her angry eyes…that deliberating pause, and that look…the final look she had flashed me just before the Looking Glass imprisoned her. My stomach sank. Deep down, I knew that look had been one of pure remorse. I couldn't let the Snow Queen have an ambiguous ending.

I knew what I had to do.

"Actually, I think I will take it after all—thanks!" I plucked the spare ticket from Andrew's hand before he could reply and rushed to catch up with Olivia.

"Olivia, wait!"

She whirled around. "What do *you* want?"

I pointed to the convention ticket in hand. "I want to give you this." Olivia looked at me as though I had materialized from an alternative universe.

"Are you serious?"

I nervously brushed a strand of hair behind my ear. "The Winterland convention is still missing something."

Olivia glanced at my outstretched hand. Her winter blue eyes gleamed with distrust. "Don't insult my intelligence, Alice. I know this is a trick."

I shook my head. "What would Winterland be without the Snow Queen?" Olivia tilted her head, as if trying to decipher whether being called a Snow Queen was an insult or compliment. From her narrowing eyes, I surmised she took it as the former. Time to shift tactics.

I slung my backpack to the ground and withdrew my manga from it. I flipped to the page with the queen. "She looks like this."

"This?" Olivia stilled as she took in the image. A beautiful, diaphanous dress cloaked the queen. "Her outfit looks kind of…nice." The last part came out a ghost of a whisper. Olivia glanced up. Our eyes locked. We held our breaths. I never thought Olivia and I would ever stumble on the overlapping region of a Venn diagram. At least not again.

Her gaze drifted to the ticket in my hand, then to me. I could see the conflict in her eyes. The humiliation.

Okay, that's not how it's supposed to go.

I needed to help her shake this off.

"If you want, we can meet up before the con so Deanna and I could help you with your costume. I think you'd look pretty in a crown."

Olivia's nose turned pink. "I don't understand," she breathed. "Why...why would you even want me there?"

"I guess for the same reason as you," I said softly.

Olivia's face turned startled. "What?"

"I found this in the hallway the other day." I stuffed a hand in my overcoat and brandished a crumpled envelope. The cursive letters A.L. shimmered brightly. "I thought it stood for Andrew Lewis, but it doesn't, does it?" I stared her square in the eyes. "Andrew already has his."

Face frozen, Olivia took in the initials. My initials. The very ones she had hand written.

"I didn't mean," she started. "You weren't supposed to... I mean, a part of me felt bad after—"

"It's okay." She didn't need to explain. The fact that a tiny part of her had considered inviting me told me everything I needed to know.

"I know what it feels like to want to belong." I offered her a smile. "Maybe now we can all belong to something cool."

Olivia rubbed her pink-rimmed eyes and bit her lip. "You know...I still remember when we used to be friends in elementary school."

"Yeah?"

Were we really having this conversation now?

Olivia fiddled with a lock of hair. "I remember we'd role-play as cadets on the playground."

Her words struck me like a chord. For so long, I had repressed those bitter memories of our fallout. But now they were resurfacing, flooding me, vivid as ever.

My voice went thick. "We were a bunch of dreamy, nerdy kids, huh?"

"Yeah," she whispered. "It was kind of fun."

"Then why did Cadet Venus stop?"

At my words, she recoiled as though someone had drenched her with a bucket of ice water.

"Don't you remember that day? In the fifth grade..." Her voice trembled. "Those girls from junior high took pictures of us when we were role playing. They circulated them around school, stuffed them into lockers, even posted them online. Under that caption..." She didn't go on, but I remembered the caption clear as day.

Weaboos.

Olivia bit her lip. "We became the laughing stock of our grade for an entire week. I never felt so humiliated in my entire life."

"Me either," I said. "But I didn't do a 360 after that and stop hanging out with my friend. Or someone I thought was my friend." I couldn't hide the accusation in my tone.

"Well, I did." Her lips pressed together tightly. "I made a promise to myself that day. I'd become the girl everyone wanted to be. I distanced myself more and more from the stuff I used to do. Like that." She eyed the convention ticket. "I changed the way I dressed, the way I talked...the things I liked. When I looked into a mirror, I didn't recognize the girl staring back anymore."

Her unfocused eyes drifted to the ceiling. "One day those same girls invited me to hang out with them. I became part of their little clique. And then I felt...I don't know—*better* about myself. People who didn't acknowledge me before...they wanted to be my friends. I got invited to parties. Girls started copying my clothes." A wistful note tinged her voice. "I should've felt happy and thought I *was*, but every time I saw you nerding out, it just made me so angry. Like I couldn't do that. Be myself." Hesitantly, Olivia peered at me. "I guess deep down, something was...has been missing."

"Maybe you can find it now." I placed the Winter-Con ticket into her hand.

Olivia's face flickered through a series of expressions, unsure where to land. Remorse. Embarrassment. Gratitude. Relief. She looked down at the ticket in her hand, studying it like a cipher. Finally, she smiled.

"Thank you," she whispered. "And I'm sorry for hurting you while I was hurting. Really, I am."

Despite her smudged mascara, her face blossomed like a spring-time flower. I hadn't seen her with a genuine smile in so long. She had never looked prettier to me.

"I'll see you at Winter-con." Tucking the ticket into her Coach bag, Olivia darted off with a little wave.

A smile on my own face, I returned to my locker, grabbed my books, and met up with Andrew outside.

"I saw that back there." Andrew stuck his hands into his pockets and smirked. "*Cadet Venus?*"

My cheeks heated. "Olivia and I had history together." I paused. "I mean, have."

Andrew whistled. "Now there's a plot twist."

"More plot-twisty than that?" I pointed to his prefect badge, which he now wore in broad daylight.

"Maybe not." He gave me a lopsided smile. "You want to sit for a bit?"

"Okay."

Light flurries descended as we sat together on a bench. As we waited for the buses, we exchanged fanfic ideas, Winterland conspiracy theories and memes, anime recommendations, among other things of the geekdom nature. Andrew even showed me a cosplay skit —a reenactment of one of Winterpuff's crackfics—he and his friends had done. All too quickly, the whirring of an engine drowned out the claps and laughter in his YouTube video. My bus neared the curb.

"Looks like your ride's here," he said, putting his phone away.

"Aw man, just when it was getting to the good part."

"No worries. Winterpuff will PM it to SnowBaby23."

I clasped my hands together. "Grool."

"So," he said, running a hand through his mussed hair. "I'll see you this weekend at the convention then. Just look out for the Winter Prince."

"Oh, I think you'd make the purrfect Winter Prince." Grinning, I slung my backpack over my shoulder and curled my hands in a feline stance. "And you can look out for Shiroi Neko."

"Nice." Despite his smile, a tinge of disappointment colored his voice.

I blinked. "What's wrong?"

Andrew scratched his head. "My friend is cosplaying that character. Don't get me wrong, the convention is big enough for two Shirois. But more than that..." He met my eyes hesitantly and whispered, "I was hoping we could coordinate costumes."

A tingle ran through me. He couldn't mean...

"So I'd be...your Mirror Princess?"

"For hopefully more than just this convention." He dipped closer, his sea green eyes dancing at me. "What do you think?"

"I have only three words to that." Standing on my toes, I leaned against his ear. A Cheshire smile spread across my lips.

"*I ship it.*"

Alice's Dictionary

Anime - A style of animation originating in Japan that is characterized by artistically dynamic graphics, deep character development, and complex storylines.

AU - 'Alternate Universe'; term often used in fanfiction.

ASMR - Stands for Autonomous Sensory Meridian Response. Often triggered by ambient sounds, it is a physical sensation characterized by a pleasurable tingling that typically begins in the head and scalp.

Bawse - Coined by Lilly Singh, it describes one who exudes confidence in all they do.

Bishounen - A pretty boy in anime/manga. The female equivalent is 'bishoujo.'

Book hangover - The struggle to connect with reality after finishing a really amazing book.

Booktube - Community of booktubers who vlog about book challenges, reviews, bookshelf aesthetics, and quirky tag videos on YouTube.

Canon - Refers to the official storyline.

Chibi - Slang for 'shortie' in Japanese.

Con - Short for convention.

Cosplay - 'Costume-play'; the act of dressing up as a fictional character. Cosplayers often congregate at cosplay cons.

Crackfic - A fanfiction where the character interactions/plot is insane or implausible.

Dark Kermit - A captioned meme featuring a screenshot of the Muppet character, Kermit the Frog, conversing with a darker version of himself.

DDR - 'Dance Dance Revolution'; a popular dance game based on skills and timing.

Deus ex machina - An unexpected power or event saving a seemingly hopeless situation, especially as a contrived plot device.

Doujinshi - Fanmade comics of established manga. Many show what the original manga cannot, such as explicit relationships.

Drabble - A short, 'fluffy' piece of fanfiction.

Dubbed - The 'dub' of an anime is a version in which the Japanese dialogue has been voiced in English.

Fanart - Drawing of characters, objects, or situations from a piece of work the artist admires.

Fanfiction - Fiction written by fans of a particular fandom involving characters/settings/scenarios from said fandom. It's also referred to as fanfic or fic.

Fangirl - A female fan who loves sharing their enthusiasm of someone or something. The male counterpart is a fanboy.

Feels - A wave of emotions that cannot be adequately explained.

Fluff - A lighthearted fanfic or fanart that induces warm and fuzzy feelings.

Fujoshi - Female fans who read genres with BL/yaoi themes. The male counterpart is a fundanshi.

Harajuku - A district in Shibuya, Japan, it has become a hub of Japanese youth culture and fashion.

Headcanon - An idea or opinion, not specified in the original work, that is accepted by the reader or the fandom in general to be true. If the creator confirms it, it becomes canon.

Husbando - A male character you would claim as your husband if you could marry him. The female equivalent is a waifu.

Myers-Briggs Type Indicator (MBTI) - A questionnaire used to classify people into one of 16 personalities. MBTIs have even extended to pop culture characters.

Kawaii - Often used in anime, the word translates to 'cute' in Japanese.

Kemonomimi - Characters that look human except for added animal-like qualities.

Kpop - 'Korean pop'; a popular music genre from South Korea, often characterized by vibrant audiovisuals.

Lemon - Label found on fanfic or fanart that serves as a NSFW warning due to its racy content. 'Lime' contains further explicit content. All in all, be warned when coming across citrus fruits in fandoms.

Lolita - A fashion subculture originating in Japan (influenced by the Victorian era) that is characterized by intricately patterned dresses, ruffles, lace, and ribbons.

Manga - Japanese comics.

Mary Sue - A bland and seemingly perfect female character. The male equivalent is a Gary Stu or Marty Stu.

Meta - Short for meta analysis; a critical analysis of a topic (headcanons, plot theories, character analysis) usually in the form of an online essay.

Moe - Refers to feelings of strong affection mainly towards characters in anime, manga, and video games.

NaNoWriMo - 'National Novel Writing Month'; an annual Internet-based creative writing project where writers attempt to write a 50K word long novel in the month of November. The Viking Helmet is its symbol.

One Shot - A type of fanfiction that has only one chapter.

OC - 'Original Character'.

OOC - 'Out-Of-Character'.

Otome game - Or 'maiden game' is a story based video game targeted toward the female audience, where one of the goals is to develop a romantic relationship between the female player character and one of several males or occasionally female characters.

OTP - 'One True Pairing' (similar to the concept of One True Love).

Pocky - A popular Japanese snack, Pocky consists of chocolate coated biscuit sticks.

Plot bunny - A sudden idea for a story, the term is thought to be related to the John Steinbeck quote: "Ideas are like rabbits. You get a couple and learn how to handle them, and pretty soon you have a dozen."

Protip - Internet slang term to preface a piece of advice or suggestion.

Pwned - To thoroughly defeat an opponent or win by a big margin. The word originated from a game called Warcraft, where a designer misspelled 'owned.'

PWP - 'Plot? What Plot?' refers to a fanfiction which generally has no plot, other than lemon content.

Queerbaiting - When canon creators pander to queer fans by showing homoerotic tension between two fictional characters (without the intention of ever developing it into an actual relationship on screen).

Ravenclaw - One of the four Hogwarts houses, it is home to riddle solvers.

Reader Insert Fic - A type of fanfiction, usually written in 2nd person POV, where readers can insert themselves into the story and become the protagonist.

Reverse Harem - A genre in manga and anime where a female protagonist is surrounded by handsome boys/pretty girls who are all madly in love with her. The male version is called Harem.

Rickrolled - To be tricked into clicking a disguised hyperlink that leads to the music video, "Never Gonna Give You Up."

Rom-com - Romantic Comedy.

RPG - Role Playing Game.

Sailor Moon - A popular magical girl series with feministic themes that has become one of the most popular manga and anime series worldwide.

Self-insert fic - A fic where the author has written themselves into.

Seme - As opposed to the stereotypically submissive 'uke', the seme is the dominant character in yaoi.

Senpai - An upperclassman.

Shimatta - Equivalent of 'crap' or 'dang it' in Japanese.

Ship - Short for 'relationship', a ship consists of two characters who have an affinity for each other. Often, the two names are combined to form a single ship name.

Subbed - An anime voiced in Japanese but has English subtitles. Many fans consider dubs inferior to subs.

Teaboo - Similar to weaboo, it refers to one who fetishes British culture.

Troll - One who provokes others with inflammatory posts.

Wapanese - A combination of the words 'white' and 'Japanese' to describe a non-Asian who attempts to dress and act Japanese.

Weaboo - Similar to Wapanese, a derogatory term used to describe one who imitates aspects of Japanese culture in poor taste.

Yaoi - Pronounced 'ya-oh-ee', not 'yah-oy', the term refers to male pairings and is synonymous with slash. The female equivalent is yuri.

'Yuri!!! on Ice' - Crowned anime of the year in 2017, a popular ice skating series that reminds us all we were born to make history.

Acknowledgements

This novel wouldn't be what it is without some awesome human beings:

Thank you to Anna Peters and Shiela Tan for the beautiful cover art.

To the talented Mazumaro and Joe for the chapter illustrations. Mazumaro's artwork can be found at: mazumaro.deviantart.com

To Maduranga for the book cover design.

To Lia Rees for formatting.

To the Ravenclaw and NaNoWriMo writing group for their support, encouragement, and distracting memes.

To all the lovely beta-readers for their feedback: Carolyn T, Katie Topchishvili, Bryan Keys (who also wrote the first winterfic!), Zerphr, Roxy, Jes Nekuda, and Jenny Johansson.

To Lena Aelitha for the insightful edits. ^ ^

And last, but certainly not least, a shout out to all the fangirls and fanboys reading this. Whether it's creating fanfiction, podcasts, metas, covers, cosplay skits, or fanart —thank you for sharing your passion and imagination with the world.

You are inspiration.

Author's Notes

<u>Akihiko</u> - In Japanese, 'aki' translates to 'bright' and 'hiko' can be taken as a prince or leader of a clan.

<u>Bandersnatch</u> - A ferocious creature from Lewis Carroll's *Through the Looking-Glass* and poem "The Hunting of the Snark."

<u>Boushiya</u> - A hatmaker in Japanese.

<u>Chione</u> (also known as Khione) - According to Greek mythology, she is the goddess of snow. The daughter of the North wind, she attracted many Olympians with her icy beauty, including Poseidon (god of the sea) whom she had a short affair with.

<u>Fibonacci sequence</u> - A series of numbers where a number is found by adding up the two numbers before it. The sequence proceeds as 1, 1, 2, 3, 5, 8, 13, and so forth. The numbering system of the universe, this sequence can be found just about everywhere (flower petals, seashells, ocean waves, hurricanes, spiral galaxies, etc). Additionally,

two successive Fibonacci numbers have a ratio close to the Golden Ratio (1.62...), which many artists use to create aesthetically pleasing compositions.

<u>Language of flowers</u> (or Hanakotoba in Japan) - A means of cryptological communication through use of flowers. (In this story, pansies signify secret love, narcissus - egotism, winter cherry - deception, oleander - beware, gardenia - purity, honeysuckle - devoted love, holly - defense). The green carnation that Sanbou wears is an emblem of Oscar Wilde. Wilde frequently sported a green carnation—which the florist had to dye—in his buttonhole. Supposedly, only his followers and those in the know would understand the significance of the flower's synthetic color. Many claim that this was Wilde's way of thumbing his nose at a homophobic Victorian society.

<u>Metanoia</u> - Having Greek origins, the word describes a transformative change of heart or conversion.

<u>Ningyo</u> - Translates to 'human fish' in Japanese. Comparable to its Western counterpart of the mermaid, the Ningyo is believed to possess mystical abilities.

<u>Sangatsu</u> - 'Gatsu' is the Japanese word for month, and 'san' refers to the number three. Stringing them together,

you get the third month, or March, a fitting name for a March Hare.

Shiroi Neko - In Japanese, 'Shiroi' translates to 'white' whereas 'neko' refers to a cat.

Sprites - Entities of the fairy realm that are considered to be helpful or harmful to people.

Usagi - 'Rabbit' in Japanese.

Vorpal sword - The sword originates from Lewis Carroll's poem "Jabberwocky", where an unnamed hero slays the monstrous Jabberwock.

Yuki-onna - According to Japanese folklore, she is a beautiful snow spirit that preys on travelers lost in snowstorms.

About The Authors

D.K.S. Dhara is a writer, educator, and Professional Fangirl. She attended college on the East coast where she graduated with a B.A. in Mathematics. Her favorite fandoms include Sailor Moon, Harry Potter, Sherlock (and a slew of others). When she's not writing, you can find her lurking on the web, making puns, and taking shelfies on bookstagram. Connect with her on:

https://www.facebook.com/DharasBookNook
https://www.instagram.com/DharasBookNook

Taylor Tsuruye is a nomadic young writer and artist from the West coast. She has a B.A. in English Literature from Seattle Pacific University and teaches conversational English in Chiang Mai, Thailand. Taylor is a Potterhead, Sherlockian, Browncoat, and Janeite, but confesses her Tumblr page is angsty and outdated. Taylor wants to be a poet when she fails to grow up. Connect with her on:

https://twitter.com/aloeverasol
https://alysoninouye.wixsite.com/alysoninouye

Thanks for reading!